☎ 01603 580280

Ha
em
cul
Ma
inc
for
has
int

PUFFIN BOOKS

Where Were You, Robert?

Hans Magnus Enzensberger is one of Germany's most eminent authors. He is renowned as a poet, novelist and cultural critic, writing across a broad range of subjects. Many of his books have been translated into English, including The Sinking of the Titanic, Europe, Europe and, for children, The Number Devil. Where Were You, Robert? has been translated into thirteen languages and is an international best-seller.

UNIVERSITY
TECHNICAL
COLLEGE
NORFOLK

Donation 12/14

HANS MAGNUS ENZENSBERGER

Where were you, Robert?

Translated by Anthea Bell

PUFFIN BOOKS

PUFFIN BOOKS

Published by the Penguin Group
Penguin Books Ltd, 80 Strand, London WC2R ORL, England
Penguin Putnam Inc., 375 Hudson Street, New York, New York 10014, USA
Penguin Books Australia Ltd, Ringwood, Victoria, Australia
Penguin Books Canada Ltd, 10 Alcorn Avenue, Toronto, Ontario, Canada M4V 3B2
Penguin Books India (P) Ltd, 11 Community Centre, Panchsheel Park, New Delhi – 110 017, India
Penguin Books (NZ) Ltd, Cnr Rosedale and Airborne Roads, Albany, Auckland, New Zealand
Penguin Books (South Africa) (Pty) Ltd, 5 Watkins Street, Denver Ext 4, Johannesburg 2094, South Africa

On the World Wide Web at: www.penguin.com

Penguin Books Ltd, Registered Offices: 80 Strand, London WC2R ORL, England

First published in Germany as *Wo warst du, Robert?* 1998
Published in Great Britain by Hamish Hamilton Ltd 2000
Published in Puffin Books 2001

2

Copyright © Carl Hanser Verlag München Wien, 1998
Translation copyright © Anthea Bell, 2000
All rights reserved

The eye illustrations in this book have been taken from
Klinische Darstellungen der Krankheiten des menschlichen Auges,
published by Dr Friedrich August von Ammon, Berlin 1838

The moral right of the translator has been asserted

Printed in England by Clays Ltd, St Ives plc

British Library Cataloguing in Publication Data
A CIP catalogue record for this book is available from the British Library

ISBN 0–141–30680–7

To Katharina

PROLOGUE

It was a perfectly ordinary day when Robert disappeared, and the strangest thing about his disappearance was that nobody noticed it, not even his mother.

However, we are jumping ahead. Just now Robert is still sitting on the tall kitchen stool as usual. As usual except that it's such a bright summer evening. The sun casts dazzling white strips of light on the wall, on the kitchen cupboards, on Robert's mother's face. There are tiny holes in the Venetian blind over the door to the balcony, and the light paints a pattern of little curlicues everywhere. Robert has only to turn his head and the quivering specks of light tickle his face, dazzling him.

But everything else is the same as usual. Robert's father is probably somewhere on the motorway. He sometimes calls home around this time of day, but generally he's too tired, or he's in a meeting that will go on until late at night, or he has to have dinner with some important person. Before Robert's mother leaves – and she nearly always goes out somewhere in the evening: to her Italian class, or the opening of an exhibition, or the tennis club – before she leaves she gets his supper ready, cold meat and salad or a couple of pancakes, but as usual Robert isn't hungry, doesn't want any supper, is just lounging around. He leans over the kitchen counter, sitting there like a monkey, small and agile and always on the go. Robert is the kind of person who can't sit still.

There's something funny about his eyes, though: they're very pale in colour, and greenish. Where does he get that fixed stare, a glance no one can meet? He looks past his mother; he looks right through her.

'Robert, did you put your eyedrops in?'

I wish I knew what's the matter with that boy, thinks his mother. Goodness knows he has everything he could wish for! 'Oh, do stop rubbing your eyes! And please don't watch TV the whole time! I don't want you sitting in front of your computer games for hours on end the moment I'm out of the house either. You know all that flickering isn't good for you. You have to be careful.'

'Yes, sure,' says Robert.

'Everything's in order,' the eye specialist had said. Not an attractive character, the eye specialist: thick, bushy eyebrows and yellowish hair growing out of his nostrils. He'd stared at Robert as if he were a laboratory rat. 'What made you think there's something the matter with him? Has he been complaining of impaired vision?'

No fear! Robert hasn't the faintest intention of complaining, even though he does get that flickering in front of his eyes so often. Well, if it's not in front of his eyes then it's in his brain, but the flickering has nothing to do with watching TV, and it doesn't bother him. In fact he rather enjoys it. Robert doesn't know how it began, but it was a long time ago, further back than he can remember. He only has to close his eyes — before going to sleep, for instance — and the show starts.

First he just sees blurred patches, light and dark, moving slowly downwards, like something scrolling down a screen. This is the boring bit. Then come the purple and green stripes, quivering slightly, sometimes thick and sometimes thin, and before long he's seeing coloured snaky shapes, more and more of them, a fiery carnival of streamers. Now he only has to rub his eyes a little, very lightly, just passing his knuckles over his closed eyelids, and pictures emerge from the busy pattern of shapes: an orange sea with white breakers, whole squadrons of blue birds against a pale lilac sky, huge ferns, little ships moving quickly, their sails snapping in the wind. Finally the figures appear: shadowy people dancing in a cellar bar, or wrestlers rolling on the grass. At some point his enemy will turn up too, a gigantic figure, a chef in a white hat – any moment now he'll be shouting at Robert, but not a sound emerges from his wide open mouth . . .

Of course no one knows what Robert sees before he goes to sleep. Robert is no fool. He takes good care not to let on about his own private film show. He knows exactly what his father would say if he heard about it. You're crazy, he'd say.

No, Robert has learnt not to show any signs, particularly since he started finding himself switching into reception mode in the daytime, especially during biology at school. 'Absent-minded,' says Dr Korn the biology teacher. 'Sometimes I think your son isn't with us at all!' she told his mother.

And his mother often asks, 'What are you thinking about?'

'Nothing special,' says Robert.

Dr Korn may have no idea what he really sees, but she isn't entirely wrong. Robert always gets good marks, but the fact is that he's lazy. He can afford to be lazy because of his extraordinary memory. Not for what he hears, or the vocabulary he's supposed to learn by heart, but for what he sees. A page of his French textbook, a couple of equations on the blackboard – he only has to take one look and they're stored in his mind as if they were on film or saved to disk.

ix

Robert uses this trick in art lessons too. Art isn't on the regular syllabus, it's voluntary. Robert goes to art class every Thursday afternoon because he really likes the art teacher, Professor Winziger. A great giant of a man with an unruly mop of white hair – but when he starts to do a drawing he's as gentle as a hospital nurse.

Winziger is an old-fashioned kind of teacher. He makes his pupils draw and paint from life, and sometimes he brings an engraving or a drawing that he wants them to copy. He is amazed by the way Robert just has to look at the picture, and then he has it in his head and can draw it from memory.

Now and then the old man brings something valuable from his own collection to the art class. Not long ago, for instance, he was handing round an old sixteenth-century copperplate engraving. Robert remembers that picture very well – it showed the biblical story of the Prodigal Son. Before letting his treasures out of his own hands, Winziger looks round the room and says, 'Any half-wits with dirty paws can go home now, or play football. My originals are too good for you lot.'

By 'you lot' he mainly means Ratibor, who tends to sit at the back looking hopefully out of the window. Ratibor isn't interested in engravings. He is Robert's best friend. The two boys didn't like each other at all at first, which was hardly surprising: Ratibor plays hockey like a champion, Robert would rather read. Robert's parents are well off, Ratibor's have to struggle to make ends meet, and he has so many brothers and sisters that nobody, not even their mother, can remember all their names. Whereas Robert is an only child and doesn't know what it's like to scuffle with an elder brother. And so on and so forth.

One day each of the boys realized that he envied the other. Then they began admiring each other. And finally they realized that together they made an unbeatable team, and they've been inseparable ever since.

As for the visit to the eye specialist – well, Robert's mother needn't have bothered. It probably cost the earth, too, because the specialist's consulting rooms were spotlessly white. Even the carpets, the chairs and the pictures on the walls.

'I don't know what the matter is, but my son's always rubbing his eyes.'

'Well, we'll soon find out.'

It was a solemn ceremony, almost like being in church. The room was darkened. Robert had to sit on a high chair and wear a huge, heavy pair of glasses, not a telescope or a microscope but a combination of all kinds of lenses, shades and mirrors. Suddenly everything went dazzlingly bright, then dark again, and all the time he heard the doctor's voice, almost sending him to sleep: 'Is it clearer like that? Better? Blurred? Brighter? Darker?'

Robert tried to read the letters on the panel in front of him, but the words made no sense:

LAMRON
MAERD
NOITANICULLAH

Then a click, and a new set of lettering came up – goodness, it was hot and muggy in that white room. The last line said, in tiny letters swarming like ants:

EGARIM

But Robert wasn't so easily taken in. This was an obvious trick. You just had to read the words backwards. 'Mirage,' he said.

'Excellent,' said the eye specialist, raising his eyebrows. 'Right, now let's look at the retina!'

Robert saw a shining disc in the darkness, veined like a map. Tiny red rivers flowing into a white sea. 'That's your eye.' How can someone look at his own eye? Floating on the black background, it was like a moon shining in the night sky.

The specialist took the heavy glasses off Robert, the blinds were pulled up again, the sun was shining as usual. 'I can't find anything wrong,' the specialist said. 'There's no cause for concern.'

All the same, he prescribed Robert those eyedrops. They were clear like water, and slightly oily. When Robert put his head back and squeezed the little red rubber bulb of the dropper, they made his eyes burn slightly. Robert didn't like the feeling, and he hated the look of the green bottle. He wouldn't even touch the white note inside the packaging except with the very tips of his fingers, but since he read absolutely everything in print that he set eyes on he couldn't help studying it:

Ingredients: naphtazolin nitrate 2.5 mg, phenylephrin-HCl 12 mg, antazoline sulphate 20 mg.
Use: for dazzle, acute and chronic irritation of the lachrymal passages.
Side effects: possible systemic effects: irritation of the central nervous system, palpitations, rhythmic disturbances, headache.
Dose: 1–2 drops several times a day, applied to the conjunctival sac.
Keep away from children

'If you ask me,' Robert told his mother, 'you've paid an arm and a leg for nothing.'

He emptied the drops down the lavatory the very first day and filled the green bottle with plain water. Now, just to keep his mother happy, he puts his head back and bathes his eyes with a couple of drops of tap water several times a day. Tap water doesn't tingle. Robert has no palpitations, or headache, or irritation of the central nervous system. He smiles. His mother is happy.

She looks younger today, as she always does when she's going out. But it isn't her lipstick or her hair, or even the narrow, soft, high-heeled shoes she's wearing, it's just looking forward to her evening out that makes her beautiful. She's wearing a black dress made of a material that shows shimmering, snaky patterns when she moves – 'It's called moiré,' she explains – and she's pulling on a red silk glove that comes up to her elbow. She doesn't say where she's going.

Robert hears the door close, hears the click of her heels along the wooden floor of the landing, hears the hum of the lift.

'Will you be all right on your own?' his mother asks, as usual. Yes, Robert will certainly be all right on his own. He sits on his stool, pours himself a glass of iced tea and reaches abstractedly for his ham roll. He's sweating. Maybe a storm is about to break. Robert loves it when that first cold gust of wind sweeps through the trees, when windows and balcony doors slam shut, when the sky goes dark and then there's thunder, and icy lightning flashes through the sky above the city – the closer it comes the better he likes it – and rain beats against the window panes.

But the storm is taking its time. Robert puts down his ham roll. He isn't hungry. He wanders around the kitchen. There's a scarlet glove on the work surface by the stove; his mother has forgotten it. And she's usually so particular about the way she looks, thinks Robert in surprise. Then he switches on the TV set. Nothing but ads for cleaning products and cat food. He mutes the loud commercials with the remote control and begins searching around in his pockets.

He is wearing a khaki T-shirt under a thin blue linen jacket with at least six pockets in it. 'Why do you have to keep wearing that shapeless old thing?' says his mother. 'It's gone all baggy.' It's baggy because of all the stuff he carts about with him. A silly habit really. His friend Ratibor says Robert goes around nicking things. That isn't true; Robert is absent-minded, that's all. When he sees something lying about he just picks it up and puts it in his pocket. 'Talk about absent-minded . . . you're not with us at all, are you?' says Dr Korn when he's thinking of something entirely different during biology, and his mother says, 'Heaven knows where he gets it from. Not me, anyway.'

His pockets contain a lighter, a little calculator in a plastic case (it was a free gift advertising an airline), a piece of chewing gum, a wristwatch, a twenty-dollar bill from his first visit ever to America last year, a ballpoint pen, a few coins . . . what else? Oh yes, the Porsche, a little clockwork toy car . . . kid's stuff but fun all the same, with windows that go up and down and a bonnet you can open. Where on earth did he get that?

Ratibor does not like this habit of his friend's. He once even made Robert turn out his pockets before going home, and sure enough, Robert had somehow picked up a photo of his friend that was lying on the table, a Polaroid picture showing Ratibor in full hockey gear, helmet, kneepads, stick and everything, in front of a poster of Wild West cowboys. Ratibor looked good in that photo, fearless and defiant, with untidy red hair. Robert doggedly refused to give it back.

Well, that's Robert, and no one can break him of the habit.

Take away the tiny screwdriver he pocketed without thinking, and another time it will be a key-ring or an eraser that disappears. For instance, where on earth did he get this fire-wheel?

It's a child's toy, one of those metal things with a switch at the bottom. When Robert presses the spring down the little wheel turns, and two flints rub against a ring covered with emery paper and make the sparks fly. The little wheel has two windows, one red celluloid and one yellow celluloid. There are two black cats painted on the front, in the shape of a spiral that turns faster and faster the harder you press down on the spring. The cats' eyes glitter red and yellow, red and yellow, until the whole thing blurs into a circle of coloured light before his eyes.

Robert holds the toy up in front of the TV screen, which is showing a scene in some grey city. It's winter. Trucks are crawling along the broad, snow-covered streets. Women in headscarves are shovelling the snow into great heaps by the roadside. People in thick coats and tall fur caps hurry by.

Robert is about to slide off his stool and fall asleep. It's the heat of the room. He feels tired and slightly dizzy. He rubs his eyes. Two, three, four uniformed men in long leather coats appear on the screen, quite close up. Their boots are covered with dirt. There's an old woman standing next to them, looking straight at the camera. Beneath her long, white eye-brows her eyes are a watery blue, curiously expressionless. Is she blind? No, she's blinking. A procession is approaching along the street, a long line of silent people – maybe it's a demo? The old woman stands there, open-mouthed. A boy comes into the picture, moving fast, a nimble figure. He's visible only from behind: the nape of his neck, his blue jacket. He looks like Robert.

But where *is* Robert? Everything goes dark before his eyes.

He's going to slide off the stool – but no, Robert is supple, he's agile, you have to give him that.

Robert isn't in the kitchen any more. The TV set is still on, that's all, the ice in his glass of tea on the counter is slowly melting, and the kitchen clock says three minutes to nine, while the sky outside rapidly darkens and the first drops of the cloudburst patter against the window panes.

THE FIRST JOURNEY

The cold wasn't the worst of it. The wind was worse, sharp as a needle. On his bare skin it felt as if he were standing naked under an icy shower. Robert rubbed his eyes, but it made no difference. He was wide awake.

There he stood in the middle of winter, in a broad, straight street covered with snow, a street he'd never seen before. Or had he? Those women in headscarves shovelling the dirty snow, piling it high by the roadside, the grey buildings, all identical, the men in their long uniform overcoats – yes, he'd seen it all before! He was standing next to the old lady with watery eyes. The only new part of the scene was that man in the leather coat standing with his legs apart. He wore a flat-topped olive-green cap, and looked like an army officer. The coat reached his ankles, and he was holding a heavy black box in his arms, pointing it like some kind of weapon at the old woman, who was grumbling out loud to herself. Only when the man started turning a handle on the box and it began to whirr did Robert realize he was holding an old-fashioned cine-camera.

Farther off, a dense crowd of people was approaching, with men in shabby army coats at the front. You could hear women's voices in the background, chanting an incomprehensible slogan in chorus: *ram-tam-tam, ram-tam-tam* went the rhythm. Robert was shivering with cold. He had no idea how he had got to this place, but he felt that something violent was about to happen. He knew that from what he'd seen on the television screen. Whatever this agitated crowd was after – maybe these people were on strike, or hungry – anger was written all over their faces. Two olive-green trucks had now arrived from the opposite direction. They might have come straight out of some old war film, but they weren't American vehicles; they were too rickety and battered for that. The officer stopped filming and barked out an order. Soldiers jumped down from the trucks and formed a barricade across the street. They were carrying rifles, and they had wrapped woollen rags around their feet. Everything was perfectly still for a moment. The women in headscarves let their shovels drop. Then Robert heard a grinding noise in the distance. It must be tanks on the way.

Robert was frightened. He glanced around, ducked, and then ran for it. He slipped past two grinning soldiers, jumped over a pile of snow and stopped, breathless, outside the entrance to a building. He shook at the iron gate, but it was locked. To the left of the entrance a small flight of steps covered thickly with snow led down to the cellar. He stumbled, and felt snow slipping into his shoe. Angrily, he tried the handle of the cellar door. Luckily it wasn't locked. He looked around the bare, dark room. The smell of soap and cold steam told him it was a laundry room, although there wasn't a washing machine in sight. He stumbled over a pile of coal. A rusty stovepipe led to a stove with two large pots standing on it, but the stove was cold. Huge sheets were hanging from a line, and Robert took three of them down, checking that they were dry. He was frozen in his thin blue linen jacket. He wrapped himself in the sheets for warmth and sat down on a weathered wooden bench in the middle of the room.

The chorus of voices outside had stopped. Robert listened. The sudden silence seemed sinister. Then he heard a loud voice amplified by a megaphone, followed next moment by the first shots. I hope they're firing into the air, thought Robert. There were a few screams. He thought he caught the sound of people trampling and scuffling as they fled, then orders, the sound of engines, and the clatter of the tank tracks as they gradually moved away. And then all was quiet again.

Robert stretched out on the wooden bench, took off his shoes and socks, and began massaging his feet. They were blue with cold. He was gradually warming up inside his thick cocoon of sheets, and instead of trying to work out where he was and how he had got there he dropped off to sleep.

When he awoke he had no idea how much time had passed. It was pitch dark in the laundry. He found that his feet had gone numb, and hopped up and down on the cold cement floor until he felt all right again. He was hungry, too, and thought longingly of the ham roll he'd left at home. He couldn't stay here in this cold, damp room.

He put his shoes on, opened the cellar door a little way and peered out. The street was deserted. A few dim street lights rocked slightly in the wind here and there, their naked bulbs casting faint, quivering circles of light on the snow. Pulling himself together, he cautiously made his way up the cellar steps.

There was no sign of the afternoon's shooting. No clothes lying about, no blood, no corpses. Only the marks left in the snow by tank tracks showed that there had been a demonstration at all. Robert thought the street looked bleak. A smell of sulphur hung in the air. Drab buildings with crumbling

3

balconies lined the street in both directions as far as he could see. There wasn't a shop-window display or a neon advertisement anywhere, or a light burning in a flat. There didn't even seem to be a telephone kiosk in sight. He decided to follow the overhead wires above the street. A tram, perhaps. But there were no tramlines to be seen in the snow. Maybe the wires belonged to a trolley-bus service? There must be a city centre somewhere, with a hotel and a railway station!

Not a single car passed him as he walked along. The whole place seemed dead and deserted. Finally, at the fifth or sixth road junction, he saw a couple of lighted windows on the ground floor of a corner building. From a distance it looked like a shop, but the window was made of opaque glass, and there was no shop sign over it. He came closer, and saw translucent letters in the glass of the door, saying:

АПТЕКА

It was Russian! He was in a Russian city! The strange alphabet wasn't difficult to decipher, and Robert knew enough to guess that 'apteka' must mean pharmacy. He went closer to the frosted glass door, and looking through the translucent letters got a glimpse of what was inside. The room was all white, and looked more like an office or laboratory than a real pharmacy. There were no display cases or ads anywhere, no boxes of special offers displayed on the counter. It looked as if no one actually wanted to sell anything and all the medicines had been put away in drawers or wall cupboards.

The pharmacist was sitting on a shabby leather sofa. She wore a white cap which just revealed a chignon of blonde hair and a pair of nickel-framed glasses. Her head was tilted to one side, and Robert could see straight away that she was asleep.

There was no night bell for him to ring. He decided to tap on the window with his fingertips, quite gently at first, then harder and harder. The pharmacist woke with a start. 'Let me in!' he shouted. She shook her head, but rose to her feet, made her way over to the door and opened it a little way. At the sight of Robert she retreated and let out a small shriek. He pushed the door open, walked in and staggered straight over to the old leather sofa. His journey through the deserted streets had taken a lot out of him. As the woman stared at him in alarm, he sat down with a sigh.

There was a cracked full-length mirror going right down to the ground on the wall opposite, and Robert saw a ghost in it: a shapeless white figure with nothing but a pale face looking out of its wrappings. He couldn't help laughing. Without realizing it, he had walked through the sleeping city wrapped in those three sheets.

The pharmacy was well heated, with a cylindrical cast-iron stove roaring away in a corner. Robert began to unwind the sheets. The pharmacist watched, speechless, as the big sheets fell to the floor in a heap, gradually revealing a thin boy in a blue jacket. His teeth were chattering.

Robert knew he owed her an explanation, but unfortunately even he had no idea what had happened to him. Finally, just to say something, he gave his name – 'Robert' – and pointed at his chest. She shook her head, baffled. He looked round, found a notepad on the counter, took his ballpoint pen out of his pocket and wrote down: ROBERT. Then he handed her the pad, and she read the name aloud: 'Rovert'.

'No,' he told her. 'Not Rovert – Robert, Robert!' He went on until she could pronounce his name properly.

She took the ballpoint pen out of his hand and inspected it closely, as if she had never seen such a thing before. Tentatively, she drew a few squiggles on the paper, unscrewed the

5

ballpoint, reassembled it, pressed the end to make the tip disappear and then pop out again. Then she reluctantly handed the pen back. Robert made signs to indicate that if she liked it so much she could keep it. She understood that at once, picked up the pad and wrote, pointing at the front of her own blouse:

ОЛГА

Robert would have liked to oblige her, but he had no idea how to pronounce these peculiar letters. She helped him out by saying, 'Olga.'

'Olga,' he repeated, but she wasn't satisfied until he had learnt to pronounce the letter 'l' with a thick sound, almost down in his throat, as if he were trying to swallow his own tongue.

Olga seemed amused by this game; obviously it was a change from the boredom of being on night duty, at least. She was delighted with the ballpoint, and kept scribbling eagerly with it. So here was Robert in the middle of the night, taking his first Russian lesson in a pharmacy in the middle of nowhere. How could he explain to Olga where he came from? He tried drawing a few lines to suggest the map of Europe, with a fat arrow running from Germany to somewhere far in the east. But it wasn't a very good map. Poland looked like an egg, and there wasn't enough space left on the pad for Russia itself. Olga narrowed her eyes and examined the drawing. Obviously she could make nothing of it. Robert tore the sheet off the pad. He was feeling thirsty. Abandoning geography, he drew a picture of a round cup with a little cloud of steam rising from it. Olga nodded. She disappeared behind a screen and came back with a thermos flask, two glasses and some biscuits. 'Chai,' she said, pointing to the glasses, which were standing in small nickel holders. Then she placed a cube of sugar on Robert's tongue and showed him how to drink the bitter tea: to make it taste sweet you had to take small sips and let them run over the sugar cube. Robert thought he had never drunk anything so delicious in his life.

At last Olga looked at the white, loudly ticking clock that hung over the counter. It was ten past three in the morning. She folded her hands and laid her head on them, clearly saying it was time for bed. Robert wondered why the pharmacy closed at this time of night – weren't there any sick people in Russia after three a.m.? – but he couldn't ask Olga. She must be glad her night shift was over. She took a heavy, much-mended coat out of the cupboard and offered it to Robert. It was a winter coat to fit a giant; Robert's hands disappeared entirely inside its stiff sleeves. Glancing at himself in the mirror, he thought he looked like a character in a Charlie Chaplin film. Olga exchanged her cap for a fur hat, wrapped herself in a thick overcoat that looked like army surplus, and took a heavy bunch of keys out of her handbag.

It was bitterly cold outside, but the wind had died down. The pharmacist carefully locked the creaking shop door, and the two of them set out. There was still no one around in the wide streets. The skirts of Robert's coat dragged in the snow. Now and then they had to cross frozen, slippery puddles, and when Olga slipped Robert caught her under the arm. After that they went on arm in arm, an unlikely couple; a bystander might well have wondered where they came from and where they were going. Once they met two drunk militiamen who looked at them suspiciously, but they were not stopped.

Finally Olga stopped outside one of those industrial grey blocks of flats. The building looked unfinished, as if the construction workers had forgotten to fit the balconies or pave the entrance, which had a frozen puddle in front of it.

However, there were cracks in the walls and the plaster was crumbling, making it look like an old, neglected building. Olga took out her rattling bunch of keys and led Robert in through the entrance. There was a grey-haired woman sitting with her legs wide apart in a glass kiosk in the stairway, fast asleep. She was the caretaker, and looked like a dragon sitting there hunched over, with some knitting on her lap. Large flakes of paint had come away from the pea-green wall.

At least there was a lift. It was behind a heavy metal grating, and resembled a prison cell inside. The lift cabin started moving, with a groan, and stopped with a sudden jerk at the eighth floor. Outside the door of her flat, Olga put her forefinger to her lips. She unlocked the door soundlessly and tiptoed along a dark corridor smelling of vinegar. Robert followed her, groping his way. For some reason Olga didn't want to put the light on in her room, which seemed to be full of furniture. She gave him a gentle push, and he sat down on a kind of recliner or camp bed. But although he was tired to death he couldn't go to sleep. Once his eyes were used to the darkness he looked for the door. Where was the bathroom? He urgently needed the lavatory. Olga seemed to understand. She took his hand, and they made their way down the long corridor. The bathroom was full of soap-dishes and shaving brushes, and there were so many toothbrushes the place might have been a youth hostel. Coloured towels hung over the rusty tub from cords criss-crossing the room.

Back in Olga's room, Robert took off his wet shoes and lay down. He heard his hostess getting undressed and slipping into bed. Peace at last! He turned over, determined to go to sleep at once – but there was no wall beside the bed, only a curtain made of coarse sacking, and as soon as he closed his eyes he heard loud snoring on the other side of the curtain. Who could be there so close to Robert's head, asleep in Olga's room? He was too tired to think about it. He didn't want to see or hear anything else at all.

Next morning the sun was shining. Robert looked around him, blinking, and it was a moment or so before he remembered where he was – in some strange city, possibly in Siberia. Olga was already up and making her bed. When she saw that he was awake she sat down beside him, put her hand on his forehead, took a thermometer out of her breast pocket and lodged it under his armpit. '*Shar!*' she said, shaking her head disapprovingly. '*Temperatura!*' Well, it wasn't surprising if Robert had caught a cold from yesterday's icy wind, after his hours in the laundry and his long walk through the night. She conveyed that he was to stay in bed and left him alone.

When she came back she was carrying a glass of water and a bowl of porridge. He had to swallow two white tablets, and then she spoon-fed him like a small child. Robert didn't protest. He was very hungry. The porridge was reddish in colour and thick, with a salty taste. Funny kind of breakfast, he thought, but better than nothing! '*Kasha,*' Olga told him, putting the next spoonful in his mouth. That made another Russian word Robert knew.

He found it difficult to keep his eyes open. His face was burning. He didn't feel like wondering what was going to happen next. Half asleep, he gave himself up to the private film show unreeling behind his eyes, but soon he slipped into confused dreams. He had to pull a heavy sleigh uphill through the snow, and his school was at the very top of the slope. When he turned to see why the sleigh was so heavy he saw his mother sitting on Dr Korn's lap. Holding each other tight and laughing, they shouted at him, 'Absent-minded Robert! He isn't with us at all!'

Suddenly he was in the doorway of the kitchen at home. The coffee machine was gurgling. He saw the spice rack, his ham roll, the crumbs under the table. Even the TV set was still on, showing excited people running about in the snow on screen. But there were wet sheets and towels hanging from a low ceiling of cloud, and a hunchbacked old lady was sitting on his stool staring at him as her long yellow teeth bit into his roll.

He heard someone coughing next to his ear. The thick curtain dividing the room into two was pushed aside, and a middle-aged man in pyjamas came into view. He had side-whiskers and limped slightly. On seeing Robert he simply shook his head and disappeared into the corridor, humming. Was he a guest like Robert, or Olga's father, or her brother or her husband? It was hard to say, but all the same, I didn't much like him, thought Robert before he fell into a feverish half-sleep.

Towards evening he was feeling better. Olga had dis-appeared. He decided to explore the flat, got out of bed and dressed. Cautiously, he opened the door to the corridor, which now smelled of cabbage and fried potatoes instead of vinegar. He could hear loud voices at the far end. The whole corridor was crammed with shelves and huge cupboards, and any gaps between the furniture were filled with red mattresses and heavy bags of flour. Long rows of preserving jars full of pickled cucumbers stood on the shelves, along with old magazines and cardboard boxes.

Robert stopped at the open kitchen door. It was amazing how many people could fit into that small room. There were three women standing by the stove, grumbling to each other in an easy-going sort of way. The smell filling the kitchen rose from huge saucepans and frying pans. The men were sitting around the table, each with a glass of vodka in front of him, and they seemed to be deep in heated discussion. The bewhiskered man in pyjamas was waving his arms about. The scene reminded Robert of a play he had once seen, in which a couple of famous actors dressed as tramps spent the whole evening shouting insults at each other, and finally an angry woman killed one of them. Robert couldn't remember what she was so angry about. However, things didn't seem quite so violent in this communal kitchen. On the floor, three toddlers were fighting over a decrepit toy rabbit. The rabbit was pink, and the children were competing to pull long strips of stuffing out of its stomach. The women stirred the saucepans without taking any notice of this scuffling.

Robert stood there for some time before one of the men noticed him, a very tall, fair-haired man sitting in the corner. He stared at Robert open-mouthed, as if he'd never seen a boy in a blue jacket before.

'*Zdravstvuyte!*' said Robert. It was one of the few Russian words he knew; his grandfather, who'd fought in the Second World War, used to say it when he drank a toast with his friends. Everyone present immediately turned to look at Robert. The women put down their wooden spoons and even the children forgot their toy, crawled over to him and tugged at his trouser leg. Robert was surrounded by total strangers bombarding him with questions. He tried to explain that he didn't understand, but it was no use; they obviously couldn't imagine how anyone could fail to know Russian. Perhaps they'll decide I'm deaf or half-witted, he thought. It would never occur to the people in this kitchen that he was something much more unusual, in fact outright dangerous, a real live foreigner, and a foreigner from the West at that.

Gradually their initial amazement died down, and although the men kept casting suspicious glances at the stranger, hunger soon got the better of their curiosity and they sat down at the kitchen table again. One of the women – she was fat, with countless little laughter lines on her face – ladled out the soup.

She pointed to the saucepan with her ladle. Robert nodded. She gave him a plateful, and Robert squeezed in on the bench with the others. It was excellent soup, and they all fell silent for a while as they drank it. Then the fair-haired man pushed a glass of vodka over to Robert.

At this moment Olga came into the kitchen. She was beside Robert at once, snatching the glass from his hand, and began scolding the tall, fair man. They all started asking Olga questions, waving their spoons in the air. The women by the stove joined in too. Robert felt Olga's hand on his shoulder, and got the impression she was defending him. Everyone calmed down again and turned back to the fried potatoes, and the men topped up their vodka glasses. Only the man in pyjamas kept on talking. Perhaps he's jealous, thought Robert, or maybe he doesn't like having to share the room with me. Olga ignored him, and when they had finished their meal she took Robert's hand and they went back to their room.

Here Olga had another surprise for him. She produced a book from her handbag, a German–Russian dictionary not much bigger than a matchbox. Where on earth could she have found it?

Just before starting school, when he was six, Robert had once shoplifted a tiny dictionary like that from a department store. He remembered the incident now. When he took it, he'd thought that if you had a dictionary you would immediately know the foreign language inside out – all the words were in it, and you'd just have to pick and choose. It was a temptation he couldn't resist. He hid the tiny book under his pillow for weeks, taking it out and leafing through it before he went to sleep. But after a while he realized that there was more to it than that. He could recognize a few dozen English words all right – it was a German–English dictionary – but he couldn't form a sentence that meant anything. It had been a severe disappointment, although by now he could speak English reasonably well, having learnt it at school, from English-language films and on that visit to New York with his parents. He still had the little book he'd nicked. It was in the drawer of his bedside table at home, with his diary and his camera. At home and out of reach!

Robert wondered if he would ever sleep in his own bed again. Everything familiar was gone, had disappeared, vanished into thin air: his friend Ratibor, old Winziger's art lessons, the fridge in the kitchen. How was his mother taking his disappearance? Had she noticed he was missing yet? Had she gone to the police? Now he wasn't just 'absent-minded, not with us at all', as Dr Korn was always saying – he really *wasn't* with them, he was absent in mind and body alike.

Seeing that he was upset, Olga tried to comfort him. She felt his forehead, looked in the little dictionary and managed to say, in German, 'Fever gone now! Robert better!' He couldn't help laughing, although he felt more like crying. The dictionary passed back and forth between them, and Olga clapped her hands with pleasure as she laughed at Robert's comical attempts to speak Russian. Once she looked grave, though, when he told her what country he came from. '*Nyemez*,' he said, pointing to himself. 'German.' Perhaps she'd never seen a German before. Or then again, perhaps she had? Robert thought of the war films he'd seen. How long ago was the war? How old was Olga? Could she possibly remember the Second World War and the invading German tanks? Perhaps her own father had been killed in battle or in a prison camp?

But then she smiled again, and tried teaching him the Russian words for 'bed', 'hand' and 'window'. Robert was surprised she was so lively and cheerful. She had slept for five hours at the most, and she'd soon have to go back for the night shift at the pharmacy.

When she left for work, Robert looked around her room. It was small and shabby, but there were traces of past splendours: a chest of drawers with little gilded pillars, a Chinese vase, and a photograph on the wall showing a couple dressed in white standing outside a garden summerhouse with two greyhounds at their feet. He looked at Olga's bookshelf, and managed to decipher some of the words on the spines of the books: Tolstoy, Chekhov, Far-ma-zew-ti-ka, Gete. Gete? Only when he took the book out of the shelf and leafed through it did he realize that it was Goethe's *Faust*, and the Russians insisted on spelling the great poet's name as 'Gete' instead.

However, his greatest shock was still to come. Olga had brought a newspaper with her as well as the dictionary. It was on the little table jammed between the bed and the chest of drawers. The title looked familiar to Robert. It said *Pravda*. He looked the word up at once, and saw that it meant 'truth'. *Truth* was a very thin newspaper, only six pages, all print and no pictures except for postage-stamp-sized photos of four men at the top of the front page. Two of them had big beards, one had a small pointed beard, and the fourth just had a bushy white moustache. And then Robert's eye fell on the date. It said, printed in black and white: *12 dekabr 1956*.

1956! That's impossible, thought Robert. He hadn't even been born in 1956! But it wasn't an old newspaper he was holding. It smelled of fresh printer's ink. Just to make sure, he looked up the word in the dictionary. No doubt about it, *dekabr* meant December, and he certainly knew from last night that it was winter. But what about the year? Could it be a printer's error? Robert had no idea what to think. Then he saw a pocket diary on the chest of drawers – and yes, the date 1956 was embossed on the binding!

So he hadn't just landed in darkest Russia, he'd fallen through a deep hole in time. All the while he'd had a feeling that something was very wrong. Everything he had seen in the last couple of days was so strange: the camera that was worked by a handle, the rickety lorries, the laundry, the pharmacy – even in colour, it looked like an old black and white film. He remembered how Olga had marvelled at the ballpoint pen. Were there ballpoint pens in 1956? In America, maybe, but what about Russia? He'd heard about the Soviet Union at school, and Stalin and Communism, all kinds of gruesome stories about penal camps where people starved to death – but that was ages ago! He got gooseflesh just thinking of it. And now all of a sudden here he was in the middle of Soviet Russia, and he didn't know anyone he could tell. Or did he? Could he talk to Olga? Perhaps he could trust her, but with only twenty words or so of Russian he couldn't possibly explain that he must have travelled in a time machine. She didn't seem to mind having him to stay for a while, that was one good thing! He would probably have frozen to death in the street if she hadn't let him in when he knocked on the pharmacy door.

Next day she brought him a pair of green rubber boots and gave him a rabbit-fur jacket. When he put it on he realized that it buttoned on the wrong side. It must be from Olga's own wardrobe, and she didn't have many clothes to wear herself! This wouldn't do. If he went on being a burden on her – and what choice did he have? – then he'd have to make himself useful. But how?

He decided to start by exploring his immediate surroundings. He could safely venture out into the street in Olga's winter clothes, and it seemed rather livelier outside now. Schoolchildren were throwing snowballs at each other, men with battered briefcases and women with brightly coloured net shopping bags were hurrying past. There was even a crowded trolley-bus stopping at the corner, painted the same pea-green as the walls in Olga's building. The Russians obviously had a liking for this unattractive colour.

After the crowd of people and the shooting, and then his first night in the laundry, the city struck him as almost normal this morning, except that there were far fewer cars and far more uniforms than he would have expected, and it was difficult to find a proper supermarket. The few shops he passed were pathetic. People were queuing up in a bakery for a loaf of bread and just three kinds of canned foods on offer. He'd have liked to take Olga a present, maybe a nice cake or a bottle of toilet water, but apart from the fact that he couldn't see a cake shop or a perfumery anywhere he realized that he had no money to buy anything at all. Roubles, he thought, that's the Russian currency. He had never seen a rouble note. He searched his pockets and found a few small German coins, but they'd be no use here. Anyway, maybe a cake wouldn't be the right sort of present. The food in the communal kitchen had tasted good, but why was there no meat?

In the end he squeezed himself into one of the crowded buses and rode into the city, not bothering about his lack of a ticket. After all, his whole life had turned into a journey for which he hadn't bought a ticket. The bus drove slowly down straight streets that all looked the same. But why were they so wide when there were hardly any cars about? Once again, Robert wondered if this city had a centre at all. The smell of coke and sulphur was getting stronger. A huge factory with tall chimneys and boilers came into view behind the blocks of buildings. Then the bus route passed a barracks and some sooty black warehouses, the road curved round in a loop, and the last passengers got out. This was the end of the line. Robert had taken the bus going the wrong way. The driver gave him a surly look, and although he would have liked to stay put Robert had to get out too.

He was in a rather unwelcoming area full of sheds and all kinds of storage depots. A few old timber-built houses with brightly painted decorations still stood here and there. None of the snow had been cleared, and Robert was glad he was wearing rubber boots. He passed a fence of boards, and out of curiosity peered through a knothole at two men making their way surreptitiously towards a lorry and opening the tarpaulin that lay over it. One of them climbed up and threw a couple of heavy crates down to the other. They forced one of the crates open. Robert couldn't see what they took out. Then they stowed their loot in two sacks and made off through an iron-barred gate.

If they can do that, thought Robert, so can I. He looked for a gap in the fence, squeezed through it and found himself in the yard. There wasn't a soul in sight. He examined the open crate. It was half empty, but he discovered what the two thieves had been after under a layer of newspaper. Frozen chickens! He took three of them out of the crate, wrapped them up well and hid them under his fur jacket. He was quite surprised to find that he didn't feel afraid of being caught. He left the yard through the rusty iron gate, strolled over to the bus stop and got into the bus. Nobody took any notice of him, even though he now looked remarkably fat. The chickens were cold and heavy against his chest, but he felt nervous only about getting out at the right stop, since all the blocks of flats lining the long street looked the same. He was glad when he recognized the run-down bakery.

He made his way past the caretaker and her knitting without being spotted, and took the stairs rather than waiting for the lift. By the time he reached the eighth floor he was out of breath. He was in luck: Olga was at home and let him in.

The chickens were a sensation. Olga was delighted, which was the main thing, even if she couldn't imagine where he had found them. That evening the mood in the kitchen was almost exuberant. Robert realized he had risen in the estimation of the other occupants of the flat. Even the man in pyjamas, who obviously never went to the trouble of putting on anything but these shabby green garments, enjoyed the meal.

Gradually Robert became used to the routine of everyday life in Russia and the strange habits of his companions. It wasn't that he was resigned to his fate: he brooded about his situation every evening before he went to sleep, and he could see no way out. But he liked Olga and Olga liked him. Their conversations were getting more animated; when they were lost for words they made do with a kind of sign language, or they scribbled little drawings on pieces of paper. On these occasions the ballpoint pen featured prominently. One day Robert wrote down the year in which he had been living until quite recently, but Olga could make nothing of it. She just shook her head, as if saying: Who knows if we'll still be alive then?

But this domestic peace was not to last long. One night the bell rang, and fists hammered against the door. Robert sat up in bed. Olga put the light on and began dressing at once. Out in the corridor, someone was shouting orders. Robert got his clothes on too, still feeling drowsy. The door was flung open, and he saw two broad-shouldered men in the doorway. They watched without a word as Olga quickly packed her things: toothbrush, sponge-bag, night-dress, papers. The elder of the two men began searching the room. He pulled the drawers out of the chest and tipped their contents on the floor. Then he opened the wardrobe and searched through Olga's clothes. He seemed interested in anything on paper. He swept entire rows of books off the shelves, and stuffed any notes he found into his briefcase.

By now the whole flat had been roused. The others were in the corridor, whispering to each other. Even the small children had been taken out of bed and were crying. Olga's room looked as if a madman had been rampaging in it. Only now did light dawn on Robert. He'd seen scenes like this in any number of films about secret agents, hadn't he? The words *secret police* came into his mind. Olga's calm surprised him. She handed him his fur jacket and rubber boots, and even salvaged a pair of gloves for him from the chaos on the floor, as if such an invasion in the small hours was the most natural thing in the world.

The man who slept next to Robert now emerged from behind the curtain. He surveyed the devastation created by the policemen with a grin. Robert thought the man was probably hoping to be rid of him for good. Maybe he didn't like Olga either. Of course – that must be the explanation! The pyjama-clad man was a spy. He wanted Olga's room to himself. Robert was ready to believe him capable of anything.

At a sign from the older of the two officers, they left the flat. It was snowing again outside. A shabby black car stood outside the building with its engine running. Olga had to sit in the back between their two guards, and Robert sat beside the driver, who didn't condescend to give him a glance, but stared straight ahead at the street.

Robert was sweating. On the long drive he kept trying to work out what it was all about. He remembered the frozen chicken incident. Could it be his fault they'd arrested Olga? But he was sure no one had seen him among the warehouses in the yard, and anyway, he guessed that the Soviet secret police had better – or worse – things to do than bother about a couple of stolen chickens.

The car finally stopped outside a large, gloomy brick building. A heavily armed guard opened the iron gate, which was fortified with barbed wire, and their journey ended in a neglected back yard. Olga and Robert were taken into the guardroom, where a fat man behind a heavy black desk was speaking into a heavy black telephone. He hit the telephone rest several times and shouted into the receiver at the top of his voice, as if he didn't trust the connection to carry it far enough. Then he pushed some papers over to the two police officers for them to sign, took the older man's briefcase, and called over two of his subordinates, uniformed men with shaven heads who stood to attention in front of him. 'Empty your pockets!' he bellowed, and when Robert didn't immediately understand his meaning he signed to one of the soldiers, who searched Robert with his huge paws. Before long all his possessions were lying on the desk: a few coins, chewing gum, his watch, the dictionary, the fire-wheel, his calculator, the toy Porsche, the crumpled twenty-dollar note, the lighter and the photograph of red-headed Ratibor proudly showing off his hockey gear. Nothing was missing but the ballpoint pen which he had given to Olga. She stood there saying nothing, and resisted only when one of the soldiers took her arm to lead her away. She hugged Robert hard, and he saw she was crying. Then they were torn apart, and Olga disappeared down the corridor, never to be seen again by Robert.

The black telephone rang. The man on duty picked up the receiver, said, 'Da . . . da . . . da . . . ' several times and hung up again. Then he looked Robert curiously up and down, as if inspecting a particularly unusual specimen of humanity. He barked out another order, and Robert was led out by two police guards. They seemed to think he was a dangerous jail-breaker, since they frog-marched him away, one on each side of him. Robert was taken through a maze of passages to a flight of steps and then propelled down them. A long, dimly lit corridor led past a series of iron doors with gratings over the peepholes in them. One of these doors was opened, and Robert found himself all alone in a bleak prison cell.

It contained no furnishings except for a plank bed with a grubby blanket, and a tin bucket. There was one tiny window, but high up and out of reach, and the pane was so dirty that hardly a glimmer of light could make its way into the cell.

By now Robert was thoroughly fed up with his involuntary adventure. Why did this sort of thing have to happen to *me*? he thought. I mean, I might quite have liked to go to Russia some day. Why not? But I never booked *this* trip.

The calendar business wasn't playing fair either. What was he doing here in 1956? Everything was so dirty and unattractive. If this was the past, then he could do without it. Not to mention these unwashed characters shoving him around. What did they *want* from him?

They left him kicking his heels in that cell for some days. Now and then a warder looked through the peephole, and food arrived twice a day: lukewarm tea and a piece of bread for breakfast, and in the evening a bowl of disgusting soup made of cabbage and disintegrating potatoes, which tasted like dishwater. On the second day an old man in convict's clothing came and emptied the bucket, and that was all.

At first, whenever Robert saw the warder's eye at the peephole – a cold blue eye, distorted and magnified to giant size by the convex glass – he began shouting and protesting. 'Let me out of here! I want to go home! You bastards! Terrorists! Criminals!' Nobody paid any attention, the flap over the peephole fell back into place, and after a while he realized it was no use getting steamed up.

Robert had made up his mind about one thing: he did not intend to go mad. He started singing. The latest hits, operatic arias, advertising jingles from the radio, anything that came into his head. He tried deciphering the graffiti scratched on the walls of his cell, but he couldn't make much of his predecessors' Russian curses and appeals for help.

Finally, on the fourth day, they came to fetch him. This time the party included a real officer in a real uniform, a man of about thirty with bushy eyebrows. His manner was rather stiff, maybe, but he wasn't a gorilla. Robert tried out a couple of sentences he had carefully composed in Russian, but he got no answer. They took him up the stairs and through the winding passageways to the guardroom he'd seen already, and once again there were all kinds of documents and papers to be signed. The officer took a briefcase and a cardboard box tied up with string from the man behind the desk, opened them and carefully examined the contents. They contained the things from Robert's pockets. He was surprised to see how thoroughly the Russians studied these perfectly ordinary items, as if they were valuable finds.

Out in the yard, the battered black car in which he had arrived was already waiting. Well, that was a good sign! They must be going to take him back to Olga. The whole thing had to have been a simple misunderstanding! But the streets along which they drove did not look familiar. The buildings were grander than anything he had seen in Russia so far. Once Robert even spotted a skyscraper, incredibly ornate, almost like a cathedral, with weird little turrets round the top. Quite imposing really, thought Robert. So this city did have a centre after all.

The driver stopped outside a long building with white pillars in front of it. Robert guessed that this was the railway station. The officer strode ahead and he trotted along behind, flanked by two soldiers. Whole families were camping out on the floor of the big booking hall with their cases, bundles and boxes. A large notice hung over the exit, with lettering in black and white. It said:

НОВОСИБИРСК

At last Robert knew where he was: in Novosibirsk. He knew the name of the city from his school atlas. It was far beyond the Urals, a place on the map full of little blue lines, in the marshes of Siberia! That was all he was ever going to see of Novosibirsk, since there was a long train already waiting at the platform. The electric locomotive looked brand new and had a red star on the front. The carriages were painted dark green, and bore a brightly coloured crest showing the hammer and sickle in front of the globe. For the first time Robert felt a kind of nervous eagerness; he was anxious to be off. It was no wrench to say goodbye to this place, although he was worried about Olga.

After his experiences of the last few days the train compartment seemed positively luxurious. The moss-green upholstered seats smelled slightly of mothballs, but they were very comfortable, and so broad that you could stretch right out on them. They had the whole compartment to themselves – the two military guards with pistols at their belts, Robert and the officer, who had bolted the door behind them as soon as they were all inside.

When the train started Robert breathed a sigh of relief. Maybe this was the beginning of his journey home, he thought. In fact he even felt slightly proud of his escort. No one had ever before put on such a performance just for him, Robert from Class Nine at school. Even the officer seemed to be enjoying the journey.

After a while Robert ventured to ask a question. '*Kuda?*' Where to? He knew the words by now, it was just his grammar that wasn't very good yet. 'Moscow?'

The officer, who had just lit his pipe, simply nodded, pulled out a little folding table from under the window and began setting out cards for a game of patience. The train had left the city and was moving through a bleak, marshy plain. Frozen pools glittered in the slanting evening sunlight between stunted birch trees. Robert had hung up his fur jacket, because it was very hot in the compartment. The smell of the jacket reminded him of Olga. Was she free again? Was she quarrelling with her unpleasant flatmate, the man in pyjamas? Perhaps she was back working on the night shift at the pharmacy by now?

Someone rattled the door handle. One of the soldiers opened the door, and a plump woman in a white apron brought them tea and hot sausages. Robert ate and drank voraciously; after the horrible soup in prison every morsel tasted delicious. When it got dark outside the soldiers folded the beds down. Beds with clean sheets! Robert was determined not to think of anything: not home, not the extraordinary behaviour of the calendar, not even his friend Ratibor or Olga. He slept like a log all night.

The journey lasted days. The officer smoked pipe after pipe and bent over his playing cards, and Robert watched him. He understood a little about the game, because his grandmother was always playing patience in her residential home, and when he saw a way to bring it to a successful conclusion he couldn't resist picking up the correct card and playing it. The patience came out. The officer looked at him in surprise, laughed, shuffled the cards and dealt them out again. He was suggesting a different game, one for two people. Robert turned out his pockets to show that he couldn't play for money, and even pointed to the cardboard box containing his possessions up in the netting of the baggage rack. The officer just shook his head and put down the ten of hearts.

Sometimes the train stopped in the middle of nowhere. The landscape was so monotonous that Robert lost all sense of time. The travellers could get tea any time they liked at the far end of the carriage, where the woman in the white apron sat dozing gently over a metal urn. You woke her up, gave her a kopek, and got a glass of hot tea and a sugar cube. Robert had never drunk so much tea in his life. Small, deserted stations slipped past, all exactly like each other. You might have thought the train was going round in circles. It was only after several days that one of the soldiers pulled up the roller blind over the window in the morning, and Robert saw a dazzlingly white mountain range in the distance. Soon the first roads and farms came into sight. He was glad to see any sign of life, a snow plough, a level-crossing keeper's hut, a horse and cart. The officer had gradually become more friendly, but he couldn't be induced to say a word on the subject that interested Robert most keenly. When he shaved carefully one morning, shook out his uniform jacket and adjusted his cap in front of the mirror, Robert knew they must be approaching the end of their journey.

Moscow! The station was enormous and looked like a refugee camp, full of Mongolians carrying heavy bundles, moustached southerners, farmers with chickens in cages, military recruits, policemen, women carrying babies on their backs, all swarming around as if half Russia and half Asia too had set off on a journey of migration. Robert didn't get the chance for more than a brief look at the huge station hall, since he and his companions were expected. The officer saluted a white-haired man with gold brain on the coat of his grey uniform. They went to a side entrance away from the caravanserai of the main station, where a black limousine was waiting outside. It certainly made a change from the rickety police car in Novosibirsk! The long, heavy vehicle was like a Cadillac out of a motoring museum. A uniformed driver opened the doors. Robert didn't know what to make of this reception; the man in the grey coat must be at least a colonel, if not a general. When he thought of those frozen chickens, Robert nearly laughed out loud. As his old French teacher used to say, *Tant de bruit pour une omelette!* So much fuss just for a couple of chickens!

The two soldiers weren't allowed in the car. They probably had to take the underground, or perhaps they were going straight back to Siberia by the next train. The limousine had white lace curtains over the back and side windows, just like his grandmother's curtains before she went into the residential home. He pulled them back and looked out at Moscow. The city was bathed in bright winter sunlight; there was snow lying everywhere, and when they drove past a park he saw children skating on a frozen pond. No point in worrying, thought Robert. He had slept well, and was wondering what the colonel or general – he could make nothing of Russian uniforms – intended to do with him. The man had taken his coat off, to show a whole galaxy of orders gleaming on his chest.

This time Robert wasn't taken into a back yard; they drove up to a magnificent building painted red and white. A guard opened the heavy bronze doors, and they entered a large wood-panelled hall. A lift took them up to the second floor, where Robert was led into a big room with curtained windows. Nine men were sitting around a gigantic oval table, some in uniform and some in civilian clothes. The civilians looked like professors out of some kind of costume film, and wore pince-nez or gold-framed glasses. The officer who had escorted him on the train solemnly put the briefcase and the cardboard box containing Robert's possessions down on the table. Robert himself was seated next to the colonel at the end of the table, while a beefy army officer with even more gold braid on his epaulettes and even more medals on his chest took the chair of this meeting.

A long discussion began. Robert understood hardly any of it. His companion of the journey across Siberia opened the box, and the items from Robert's pockets were handed round. The professors weren't interested in the fire-wheel and the lighter, and put them aside. However, they turned the little Porsche this way and that, inspected the Polaroid photo from both sides, looking very grave, and played reverently with the pocket calculator. One of them put the watch to his ear, shook it, and then pushed all the knobs on it one by one, while another triumphantly held up the twenty-dollar bill. It was hard to say who was most surprised, the bigwigs around the table or Robert, who couldn't make out why they should be so interested in these ordinary things. Finally the chairman spoke, and the professors had to give Robert's things back. When the beefy officer had finished they all rose to their feet, the guard was summoned, and Robert was led out.

This time he was not taken to a dungeon cell, but escorted to a small office bursting with bundles of files and card index boxes, and left alone there. After a while one of the professors from the big room came in and sat down, sighing, in a deep club armchair covered with greasy leather. It was the bald-headed one with the pince-nez. He leaned back and looked Robert up and down.

'Well,' he said, 'it's about time we began investigating your case.' Robert was stunned. The man spoke perfect German with a slight Viennese accent. His tone was soothing. Robert had an uncle who was a lawyer and always spoke just like that, as if he had to pacify someone running amok.

Attack is the best form of defence: Robert had often heard his father repeat that saying. He didn't actually believe it, but it might be worth a try.

'I don't know what there is to investigate,' he said firmly. 'Your people arrested my friend Olga, dragged me out of bed and left me kicking my heels in a cell for three days and three nights. I still don't know what I'm supposed to have done. It's a very suspicious business – *that's* what you ought to be investigating.'

The professor looked at him ironically, and sighed. Or was he really a professor? When the police want to get something out of a suspect they always set two detectives on him. One of them is brutal and acts violently, then the other one turns up, nicely mannered and very understanding, and in sheer relief their prisoner begins to talk. Robert knew all about that; he'd watched at least two hundred thrillers on TV while his mother was out in the evening.

'Patience, patience,' said the professor. As he hadn't introduced himself, that was how Robert went on thinking of him. 'We can come back to all that. Now, tell me your real name. That can't be too difficult.'

'Robert,' said Robert.

'And where are your papers and your passport?'

'I don't have them with me.'

'Then can you tell me how you got into the Soviet Union?'

Robert did not reply.

'Our border troops are famous for never letting anyone into the country without a passport and a valid visa.'

Robert could hardly argue with that. But how was he to explain the way he became involved in the whole business? Just tell the truth? No, he couldn't possibly. The man would simply laugh at him.

'How did I get in? I wish I knew,' he said. It didn't sound

very convincing. The professor shrugged his shoulders.

'Well, we have plenty of time,' he said. 'But you ought to be aware of one thing: espionage is no game for boys. It's a dangerous business. Deadly dangerous, in my opinion.' With these words he suddenly produced the cardboard box from under the desk like a conjuror, fished out the twenty-dollar bill and held it under Robert's nose.

'Why won't you tell me who sent you? Was it the Americans or the Germans?'

By now Robert was feeling uneasy. They actually thought he was a spy! If only his friend Ratibor knew – wouldn't he be impressed! However, now he knew why they were taking so much trouble over him. The search of Olga's flat, the police station, the limousine, the solemn meeting in that big room – it wasn't all about a couple of frozen chickens. This was serious. The professor was right. Robert was definitely not cut out for espionage!

'You think I'm a spy? Oh, really, I ask you! I mean, look at me. If my friend the pharmacist hadn't taken me in I'd have frozen to death in the street. And your colleagues must have found out by now that there's nothing suspicious in her flat.'

'Very well,' said the professor. 'Just as you like. Let's talk about your equipment, then.'

'My equipment?'

'I have a very interesting instrument here, and it was in your possession. It looks like a watch, but instead of clockwork it has a tiny electric motor. Our experts tell me it's operated by means of a quartz crystal. To tell you the truth, we don't fully understand the circuits yet, but as far as we can tell the instrument will function as both a stop-watch and a range-finder. And then there's this other machine, which is a calculator, a sophisticated and extremely expensive instrument.'

'Oh, come on!' said Robert. 'It's only an advertising gimmick. They give you one of those for free if you fly their line.'

'We have already made enquiries,' replied the professor, not turning a hair. 'No such airline company as this exists.'

Robert felt like giving up. He was sick and tired of the whole interrogation. 'Why are you making such a mountain out of a molehill?' he cried. 'If you absolutely must have my things, well, you can keep them, but just leave me alone, will you?'

'As you like, Robert. That's enough for today. I'll make sure you're well treated while you're with us. Oh yes, my dear boy, I consider you a very useful and valuable find!'

With this compliment, which struck Robert as distinctly ambiguous, the professor dismissed him, and the guard took him to a cell which was almost inviting compared to the police cell in Siberia. It even had a proper bed and a proper lavatory.

He sat there twiddling his thumbs for three days. No sign of the professor, only a wardress who brought his food on a white tea trolley like something out of a hospital. All the same, Robert felt by no means 'very useful and valuable', just rather miserable. When he felt miserable he usually reached for a piece of chewing gum, so he automatically searched his trouser pockets. What he found there was not one of his own possessions – they'd all been taken away from him – but a round, wooden object, and he had no idea how it had got into his pocket. It was a small stamp, and he tried to decipher the red mirror writing on it:

Robert knew that three of those letters said: KGB. Then he suddenly remembered: while he was sitting in the professor's office, left alone there for a few minutes by the guard, he had explored the crowded desk out of sheer boredom, and he must have put the stamp in his pocket. Dr Korn was right, sometimes he really *was* absent-minded. This was a really stupid habit of his! If they found the thing on him of course they'd suspect him more than ever. In a way it was flattering to be taken for a dangerous spy, but that didn't mean he wanted to languish in a Russian prison! He wondered if he could hide the stamp somewhere in his cell, but he was afraid of the sharp-eyed wardress, so in the end he stowed the wretched thing away in the lining of his fur jacket.

A couple of boring days passed, and nothing at all happened. Finally he heard the heavy boots of the guard out in the corridor, and the muted voices of people speaking Russian. The door was opened, but it wasn't the professor who came into the cell but the officer who had met him at the station, followed by a grumpy looking little man in a grey three-piece suit and a silver-grey tie who bowed slightly, offered his hand, and said all in one breath, 'Allow me to introduce myself, von Gabler, Acting Embassy Councillor, German Embassy Moscow.'

Robert, who wasn't expecting such politeness, was about to offer the man his own stool, but his visitor waved the offer aside and simply said, 'You can get your things on.'

Robert did so with alacrity. He put on his rubber boots, took his jacket and trotted along after the military officer – who hadn't said a word – the embassy councillor and the guard. A Mercedes with the German flag on one wing stood outside the magnificent entrance. The military officer gave a perfunctory salute; Robert got in, the diplomat climbed in beside him, and the chauffeur drove off. As simple as that!

Robert could hardly believe it. He liked this old-fashioned car. Chrome trim everywhere, and a plastic vase with two small flowers in it beside the driver in front. Von Gabler stared straight ahead. He was holding the precious cardboard box on his lap, clutching it like a treasure. All he said during the whole drive was, 'That's the Kremlin over there.'

The German Embassy was in an old villa painted bottle-green. A Russian policeman stood guard in a kind of sentry-box outside. The villa was surrounded by a garden covered deep in snow, and there was another, wooden building beside it. The embassy councillor and his guest were bound for this building.

A Christmas tree with a few meagre decorations stood in the corridor. Robert had quite forgotten such things existed. 'I'm really very sorry about this,' muttered Gabler. 'Just before the Christmas holiday too . . .'

They were expected in the office. A giant of a man stood in the doorway, snapping his fingers impatiently. He took Robert's arm and looked keenly into his eyes.

'Extraordinary,' he remarked. 'Not at all how I expected the fellow to look. Where's the material?'

The embassy councillor indicated the cardboard box – rather reluctantly, it seemed to Robert. He had the feeling that these two men didn't like each other.

'Please sit down,' said Gabler, using the polite form of the pronoun 'you'. It was ages since Robert had been addressed like that, and he had to admit there was something to be said for the diplomat's old-fashioned courtesy. The other man obviously had no intention of introducing himself. What was more, he looked as if he'd just come in from the beach, with a wonderful tan in the middle of the Moscow winter – where on earth did he get that?

'Well, come on, let's hear about you!' he snapped at Robert.

'Name, date of birth, address, names of parents.' This was information that Robert could hardly refuse to provide. He remembered only just in time that he hadn't even been born in 1956, but he mustn't admit that, so he pretended to have been born back in the 1940s. He answered all the other questions truthfully, and the man noted it all down.

'Very well,' he said. 'So now kindly explain how you got to Novosibirsk, and what you were doing there.'

'I've no idea,' said Robert, and that was the plain truth, too, although by now he knew very well that the plain truth was not what anyone wanted to hear.

'You're lying!' the giant shouted.

The whole scene seemed to strike the embassy councillor as embarrassing. 'If I may make a suggestion,' he said, 'why don't we let our guest get some rest? After all he's been through –'

'If you like,' said the other man. 'Very well. Meanwhile I'll get back to head office and check his details. But I can tell you one thing, there's something fishy here. Very fishy, in fact. I have a nose for such things.'

He was about to leave the room with these words, but in the doorway he almost collided with a stout man on his way in, holding a cigar. The tall man stepped back, saying, 'Sorry, Ambassador.'

'Well, Gabler, what do you make of this business?' asked the ambassador, taking no notice of the giant, who hurried out. The embassy councillor had jumped up, and now approached his boss with the air of a conspirator.

'Ambassador, if I may say so, we must proceed with the utmost circumspection.' He whispered, 'It's a miracle! Such a thing has never happened before!' Robert had some difficulty in understanding his low-voiced remarks. 'The Foreign Ministry actually apologized!'

The ambassador seemed disinclined to go along with all this secrecy.

'Yes, well, Gabler,' he boomed. 'Very likely the state visit's behind it. I expect this is some new trick on the part of our KGB friends. At the most they sacrifice some peasant, and we have to pay up again as usual.'

'But it's incredible. They even gave back the material.'

'Material? What kind of material?'

'Apparently there are some technologically very interesting items involved.'

'Really? And what does our man from the Firm say about that?'

'He was very excited. He's already been in radio contact.'

'Well, well!'

'And I hear there have already been disagreements on the other side in this case. The order must have come from the very highest authority, and it's obviously caused bad feeling.'

'Glad to hear it. So what about the boy?'

'He won't talk. He says he knew nothing about anything.'

'Ah.' The ambassador let himself drop into von Gabler's chair with a sigh, and looked more closely at Robert. 'We can wait, my boy,' he said at last. 'We'll get to the bottom of this somehow.'

'Look, I'm sick and tired of all these interrogations!' Robert protested.

'I'm not surprised. That's what comes of getting involved with the Russians. I can think of a cushier posting than Moscow myself.'

At this moment, 'our man from the Firm', the gigantic and bad-mannered man, strode into the room, red in the face.

'All lies!' he announced. 'The boy's trying to fool us. Look at this – a radio message from head office! The address he gave us doesn't exist. There's no trace of his alleged parents.

The site is just rubble, and the registry office couldn't come up with anything.'

'Then you'll simply have to work out what to do next, my dear fellow. Enjoy yourself! I have to see about that reception for the British. Good evening to you.' The ambassador waved his cigar in the general direction of von Gabler and disappeared.

'If he goes on pretending not to know we'll have to try a different approach,' said the man from 'the Firm'.

'You'll need authorization from your head office for that. Can't be done without special permission. And I shall be obliged to inform Bonn,' objected the embassy councillor. Robert was impressed by the way the little man didn't let this Rambo character terrorize him.

'If you say so,' muttered the giant, and went out of the room.

There was a pause. Then Robert said, 'What does he mean about a different approach?'

The embassy councillar cleared his throat. 'Well, if you ask me he wants to squeeze you until, as they say, the pips squeak.'

'But that's behaving even worse than the Russians!'

'And then they'll put you on a plane, and if you still insist you don't know anything they'll send you to a hospital for examination.'

Robert could hardly believe his ears. Hospital? What sort of hospital? I'm not ill, he thought. Then he realized what the embassy councillor meant.

'You want to put me in a mental hospital!' he cried.

Von Gabler jumped. He hadn't meant to make his meaning so clear. Robert was beside himself with fury. He looked around, and his glance fell on a heavy bundle of files. Without stopping to think, he picked it up and hit the astonished embassy councillor on the head with it. Von Gabler collapsed in the chair where he was sitting. Robert looked desperately for a rope, but all he could see was a long, white silk scarf hanging from a hook. He used it to tie von Gabler to the chair as tightly as he could. 'Look, I'm really sorry about this,' he whispered into his prisoner's ear. 'Specially now, just before Christmas.' Then he picked up his cardboard box and fled.

He was in luck. It was already dark outside, and there was thick fog over the city. He stole towards the gates. The guard had retreated into his sentry-box and seemed to be dozing quietly. Ducking down, Robert flitted past the soldier unseen and was out in the street, where he forced himself to walk slowly so as not to attract attention, and mingled with the passers-by.

He wondered how long it would be before von Gabler freed himself from his silk scarf and raised the alarm in the embassy. He felt sorry for the embassy councillor, and wished he hadn't had to do that to him of all people, when he'd been so polite. It was going to be awkward for the diplomat to have to admit to his colleagues that a boy of fourteen had knocked him out with a bundle of files.

But Robert couldn't afford to let such thoughts delay him. He knew he had only a few minutes' start on pursuers from the embassy. He walked on until he saw the brightly lit 'M' for Metro of an underground station ahead. There was no ticket office. Robert put his hand in his pocket, but then remembered that he had no money at all. He looked around to see if there was an attendant about, and saw only an old woman by the turnstiles in front of the escalator. Quickly, he jumped the barrier. A man with a wooden leg shouted something after him, but he was already on his way down an endless escalator. He boarded the first train that came in, travelled three or four stops, and got out again at a station where the platform was particularly crowded. There was no barrier and no ticket collector at the exit.

The city looked unreal in the fog. Everything was white: the car headlights, the snow, even the air. It was cold. Robert had no idea where to go, where to hide, where to spend the night. He walked on at random, saw the illuminated towers of the Kremlin in the distance and crossed a bridge. A neon sign penetrated the fog on the far bank. Coming closer, he read:

КИНО

A cinema! That meant safety! He could sit and get warm in the dark, at least for a few hours, and no one would notice him. Once again, he remembered that he had no money, which was a definite drawback. He'd never stopped to think much about Communism before, but one thing he did know: Communists wanted to do away with money altogether, but you still seemed to have to pay for everything in Moscow, just like you did at home. And just like you did at home, if you hadn't any money you must cheat: dodge paying fares, steal, get by somehow.

The cinema foyer was magnificent: wood-panelled walls, heavy red curtains, fat usherettes wearing little white aprons; only the lavatory Robert prudently visited was dilapidated. It stank, and of course there was no paper. Outside the auditorium, Robert waited until a large group of people were showing their tickets, and slipped into the darkened cinema after them. Only now did he discover that he was still clutching his cardboard box. It was much too large for the few things rattling about inside it, and he wondered why he was carting all this junk around anyway. On the other hand, it was all he had in the world. He stuffed the contents of the box into his pockets and put the empty box itself down on the floor.

That scene in the embassy, his one-sided fight with poor Gabler, his flight through the foggy city of Moscow – now that he was sitting in an overheated cinema it all seemed to him unreal, like part of some bewildering film in which he, Robert, had to play the part of James Bond. And now that he was safe for the time being, despair caught up with him. There was no escape. He didn't know a soul in this vast city. What was he going to do when the lights came up again and the cinema closed? To comfort himself, he put his last piece of chewing gum in his mouth.

He had been paying no attention at all to the screen, but now, to his surprise, he heard voices he could understand. The actors were speaking English. He looked up. It was a colour film in English, with Russian subtitles.

The camera roamed over a seaside scene. The sea was inky blue, the weather sunny. A rocky peninsula came into view, and you could see small figures clambering around among exotic shrubs. The camera zoomed in. The figures were children, dozens of children in brightly coloured clothes, and they appeared to be searching for something. Easter eggs? A lost dog? Or were they just playing hide and seek? They seemed to be having a good time, anyway.

Robert felt a wave of self-pity wash over him. It was all right for some! Here was he in the middle of the Russian winter, pursued by some kind of secret service agents, no bed to sleep in, no money, no friends, and this lot were enjoying a happy summer holiday! He heard them laughing and shouting, and tears rose to his eyes.

Suddenly one of the bigger boys on the screen shouted excitedly, 'Found it! Found it!' Everyone else came running up and surrounded him. He bent down, and another boy

38

helped him to lift a chest. The camera zoomed in on their find; the chest was heavy, bound with rusty iron. The children were shouting with glee.

Robert was near crying. He rubbed his eyes. Indistinctly, through his tears, he saw a boy of about his own age, wearing a blue jacket and standing with his back to the camera. Then it all blacked out. Robert had no idea where he was, and everything went dark before his eyes.

THE SECOND JOURNEY

'Stop! Stop!'

Robert opened his eyes. The voice was shouting so loud that it almost cracked.

'Are you crazy? Where did that lad in the fur jacket spring from? Miss Gresham! Never around when we need her. Wardrobe! Freddie, get that boy out of the picture, and fast!'

Robert felt someone grabbing his fur jacket from behind. Turning round, he saw a young man in a bush shirt, who snapped, 'Give me that! And take your jacket off, too! For heaven's sake, this isn't Siberia, you know!'

Robert was so surprised that he put up no resistance. The man was right, too. The sun blazed down on the cliff, and he realized that his forehead was running with sweat. The man took Robert's things and marched away.

Slowly, Robert came out of his bemused state and looked around him. A number of children were standing around among the shrubs and rocks. No one moved. Some of them were staring at him as if he'd done something wrong. Robert saw wooden scaffolding a little way off, trucks with rounded wings that glinted in the sun, and an old-fashioned crane on rails. On a platform at the very top of this crane two men were bending over a huge camera with large spools of film. It looked a real museum piece.

All the people had gathered into small groups and seemed to be waiting for something. Robert was particularly struck by the sight of a bald man in a light-coloured baseball cap, sitting on a folding chair and gesticulating wildly. He was surrounded by assistants talking to him and trying to calm him down. At last he clapped his hands. One of the assistants handed him a black megaphone, and the director shouted into it. 'Okay, we start all over again. Everyone into position! Quiet! Take two, please. No sound! Action!'

The crane with the camera started moving at once, and the children began running around on the rocks again. Robert wondered what they were looking for. He made his own way to the top of the rocks through the tangled undergrowth, and almost stumbled over an ant-hill just as he heard the big boy shout, 'Found it! Found it!' Robert was faster than the others who came racing up, laughing and shouting, so he was next to the lucky finder when the boy bent down to pick up the rusty chest lying in a hollow at their feet. 'Give us a hand,' hissed the boy, and amidst the jubilation of the other children surrounding them the two of them hoisted the heavy chest up.

Robert felt as if he were sleep-walking in broad daylight. It was a very odd sensation to see this scene for the second time, only not from the outside now, not sitting in a dark cinema in the middle of Moscow, tormented by anxiety, but right in the middle of the action itself, in a film being made heaven knew where, in some kind of fairy-tale seaside setting.

'Cut!' called the director in the white linen suit, rising from his chair. He looked quite small. 'That's it for today. The second take was okay. You can pack up now.'

The production team immediately got moving. The children

watched the crane being brought in and the heavy camera taken down. The team members were swarming everywhere. Cars drove up, and the director was the first to leave the location. The children scrambled down the slope, giggling. There was a yellow bus waiting for them at the foot of the cliff: an old-fashioned, tall vehicle with rounded mudguards. A blonde woman was standing beside it with a list in her hand, calling out names: 'Linda Greenaway . . . Jack Brouwer . . . Hella Kowalski . . . George Lindhardt . . .' Once they answered to their names they were ticked off the list and got into the bus. Gradually, the ranks of children thinned out.

Robert guessed that his own name would not be on the list. He turned away, and looked among the assistant cameramen for the one who had taken his rabbit fur and blue jacket away from him. 'Hey!' he called. 'My things!' The man laughed and said, 'No worries!' He took Robert's clothes out of the boot of his car. 'Not quite right for this time of year!' he added, chucking the clothes over.

When Robert turned round again, all he could see was the tail lights of the yellow bus taking the children away. But two of them had stayed behind: the tall boy who had found the treasure chest and a slender, pretty, green-eyed girl. They were still standing there and seemed to be waiting for something.

'So where did *you* come from?' the boy asked him. The place was gradually emptying as the truck took everyone away, throwing up large clouds of dust as it drove off. 'Was it your first time here?'

'Yes,' said Robert.

'This is my sister Caroline. My name's Michael.'

'And I'm Robert. What are you waiting for? Why didn't you go in the bus?'

'Why didn't *you*?'

'I wasn't on the list.'

'Typical,' remarked Michael. 'These film people are loopy. Hopelessly disorganized, and acting like they're so important.'

Robert was glad to find he could understand every word Michael said. It was a funny kind of English people spoke here, but at least he could communicate without any difficulty. I've probably landed somewhere in America, he thought, and was surprised to discover that he no longer felt any real surprise. After what he'd been through in Russia, this was paradise.

'Did they leave you behind too?' he asked.

'No, of course not,' said Michael's sister, giving him a teasing glance from her green eyes. 'We're being fetched. Would you like a lift? Where do you want to go?'

Robert had no idea. 'Well, away from here, anyway,' he stammered.

'Here they come!' called Michael. Sure enough, a long white limousine with its hood back was driving towards them. Another of those old vintage cars! Chrome trim all over the place, snow-white hub caps. It was the kind of American model Robert had never seen except in old movies, an old-fashioned Buick. There was a chauffeur in a white peaked cap sitting behind the wheel; when the car stopped beside them he got out and opened the door. A woman in a thin white dress, who was sitting in the back seat of the car, waved to the children.

'Michael! Caroline!' she called. 'How did it go? Was the great man pleased with you? Come on, what are you waiting for? Hop in!'

What a shame, thought Robert. Now they'll go home with their mother, leaving me here – not that I know where *here* is.

'Who's that with you?' asked the woman.

'They forgot him,' Michael explained. 'Left him behind.'

'His name's Robert,' said Caroline. 'I think we ought to take him with us. Okay, Mum?' She added, rather more quietly, 'I like him.'

'Well, why not? Sit in front with Twicky, would you, Robert?'

Twicky was obviously the chauffeur. Robert didn't wait for a second invitation but got in. Michael and Caroline joined their mother in the back, and they drove off. It was a wonderful feeling! Robert leaned back as the car glided almost silently along the road. They were skirting a wild, rocky coastline. Now and then you could see empty beaches of white sand down below by the sea, and once Robert spotted a colony of dignified-looking birds, all in black and white, standing side by side as if they were at a business conference. Penguins! He could hardly believe his eyes. This wasn't a zoo, either. These were penguins in the wild!

He dared not ask where he was. It would have sounded too peculiar. A person without any idea where he was had to be either crazy or some kind of suspicious character. In his mind he ran through the places where penguins lived. The South Pole! No, you didn't get trees growing at the South Pole, and it wasn't hot like here but very cold. Could he really have landed in America? Maybe California, where the sun always shone?

Then the road turned away from the coastline, and they followed a winding route leading through hills. Everything in this landscape looked so different. Even the trees struck Robert as strange and fantastic, as if they came from another planet. Somehow it was as if they'd run wild, or were mutations of their original species. Then a couple of animals suddenly ran across the road, so close to the car that the chauffeur had to stand on the brakes. They were light brown, larger than rabbits but smaller than deer, and they ran on two legs, taking great leaps. Kangaroos, no doubt about it. Smaller than the kangaroos he'd seen in the zoo, but unmistakably kangaroos.

Aha! thought Robert. Australia! Thank goodness he hadn't asked. This must be the fastest journey ever from Moscow to Australia – faster than the swiftest jet in the world could do it! No ticket, no money, no safety belt. The ideal way to travel, really.

'You're very quiet, Robert. What's the matter? Are you hungry?' A husky voice from the back seat broke into his private thoughts. It was Michael and Caroline's beautiful mother asking how he was. Hard to say . . . no, he wasn't hungry, he was feeling fine, just rather overwhelmed by this new world where he'd suddenly been cast ashore. So he shook his head and said, 'No. No, I'm not hungry, thanks.' The most sensible course would be to say as little as possible.

After driving for an hour or more they came to a slightly more built-up area. Farms, market towns, small factories. At first sight everything looked perfectly ordinary, but at the same time it was all strange and artificial, like a film set: the petrol station guarded by two white plaster lions, where you couldn't buy anything but the petrol itself, which an old man pumped into the tank of the car from a kind of red pillar; the ironmonger's with a façade that looked as if it were made of pink icing; the villas with their little cast-iron pillars and shady verandas, hidden behind hedges bearing mauve flowers.

They came to the outskirts of a large town with dusty parks and tennis courts, where you could hear the sound of the balls bouncing. There were buildings like nineteenth-century palaces along the main roads. A grand hotel? The main post office? A parliament building? A railway station? Robert couldn't tell one from the other. Was this the capital of Australia? Robert didn't think it could be, because there wasn't much going on. The shops had tiny display windows, and there weren't even any traffic lights at most of the street junctions. The whole place had a rather sleepy atmosphere about it. Perhaps all the people were away at the beach?

'Well, where shall we drop you?' asked Caroline's mother. Once again, Robert had no idea what to say, so he said nothing. Although it was not very polite, it was the simplest thing to do.

'You know what I think, my dear? I believe you've run away from home.'

She doesn't know how right she is, thought Robert. Although she hadn't got it quite correct, because if he'd run away it was by mistake.

'Well, Robert – that's your name, isn't it? I'm Mrs Sutton, by the way – I think you'd better come home to the farm with us, and we'll call your parents tomorrow morning. They must be really worried about you.'

This idea had not really occurred to Robert before. Yes, his parents could have no idea what had happened to him. He imagined his mother getting home late, perhaps not till the small hours of the morning. She'd have noticed his disappearance by breakfast time at the latest. Had she been very upset? And what about his father, who had probably stayed in a hotel somewhere overnight? 'I expect Robert went over to spend the night with his friend Ratibor. Wouldn't be the first time . . .' That, or something like it, was what they'd have told each other. His parents weren't the sort to go chasing straight off to the police in a panic. Were they missing him much at all?

He didn't want to waste time wondering about that. He was quite enjoying this visit to Australia; no need to let unnecessary anxieties spoil it. It wasn't like being in jail in Siberia – this was something else! By now they had left the city behind. The air smelled of eucalyptus, and the wind ruffled Robert's hair. There were vineyards here, and date palms, and trees with what looked like dense bunches of grass instead of leaves. Brightly coloured birds perched in the tree-tops, screeching.

Then the landscape became wilder again. Did you call it steppe, or bush, or savannah? He remembered such words from his illustrated atlas, but he didn't know which was right for Australia. The earth was brick-red for miles around, and there were sheep everywhere, thousands of sheep.

They went down a long avenue lined with plane trees and reached a handsome old house. Was this what Mrs Sutton called a farm? The property looked like no kind of farm he'd ever seen. You couldn't exactly describe it as a castle, but it was obvious that Michael and Caroline's family were well off from the entrance with its tall iron-barred gate, and the carefully clipped hedges. Old white wicker chairs stood on a wide terrace under colourful sun umbrellas. The whole place looked very grand to Robert.

'Welcome to Annaby,' said Mrs Sutton. 'Don't you have any luggage?'

'He can borrow some of my things if he wants to change,' said Michael, and Caroline took Robert's hand.

It was pleasantly cool inside the house. They went through a wood-panelled hall and up a large staircase to the first floor. 'This is your room,' said Caroline. Robert looked around him in amazement. A four-poster bed, a tall old oak wardrobe, a chest of drawers with old silver-framed photographs on it, an embroidered sampler with pictures of flowers and angels on the wall – he'd never have imagined a farm at the other end of the world looking like this. It was more like an English country house, he thought.

'Wonderful,' he said. 'You know what this reminds me of, Caroline? *Alice in Wonderland*!'

Caroline laughed. 'Yes, well, this is one of the oldest houses in the area. I expect you know that here in Australia we think anything built in Victorian times is absolutely ancient. Even the bath –' she opened a door, and Robert saw a huge bath-tub on feet like a lion's paws – 'even the bath is at least fifty years old. My father's really keen on old stuff like this, you see.'

She left him alone. When Robert looked out of the window into the garden he saw a large swimming pool. It too had old wicker furniture beside it, and the pool itself looked like some kind of antique. But before Robert could start wondering which year he had landed in this time, there was a knock at the door, and a maid brought him a freshly ironed light-coloured suit, a clean shirt, two towels and some washing things. 'Dinner is at seven-thirty,' she said. 'I hope you'll be comfortable here.'

She could say that again!

As Robert changed, something fell out of his jacket. Those baggy pockets, and all the unnecessary stuff he carted around! But he couldn't bring himself to throw the things away. He couldn't help laughing when he remembered how earnestly the top brass of the Soviet secret police had studied their find, as if they'd discovered extraordinary treasures in the pockets of his jacket. He shrugged his shoulders, swept up his little pile of possessions and put them away in the chest of drawers.

What had actually been in that treasure chest he and Michael found among the rocks on the coast? Perhaps it was empty, just a stage prop? And what happened next in the film? He remembered a book he'd once read, called *Treasure Island*. The author was British, though Robert couldn't remember his name. But that one was a story about pirates and sailors and mutineers, not just a few children finding a chest. Had he found himself in the closing scene of the film? Indeed, had he,

Robert, ever been in it at all? After all, that Moscow cinema was showing a film that must have been made long *before* he came to Australia. Or did he mean *after* he came to Australia? If he thought about the subject much more he'd go off his head, that was for sure, so he'd better leave it alone! Now he had to wash his hands, comb his hair, and look relaxed. He was a guest in this house, and they'd be waiting for him.

When Robert came down to the sitting room he saw a decorated Christmas tree. Christmas, he thought, Christmas in midsummer! There was a calendar on the wall above a small desk. It said:

1 9 4 6
Saturday
22
December

Of course! He'd quite forgotten that the seasons were all the other way around in Australia. When it was winter at home it was summer here, and vice versa. Celebrating Christmas in this heat must be very odd, but at least he now knew not just where he was but *when* he was. He hadn't simply jumped from one place to another but from one time to another as well. Somehow he seemed to keep moving *backwards* – or rather, backwards and forwards *at the same time*. He'd have to try to work that one out, but not now! The thing now was to behave properly and make sure he didn't drop any bricks.

'Is Mr Sutton away?' he asked. 'Or will he be coming home later?'

'Oh, Geoffrey!' said the mistress of the house, smiling. 'Yes, he's away again!'

'Well, I just hope he gets back for Christmas,' said Caroline. 'I'll be simply furious if he doesn't.'

'He'll be here if he makes it, but I don't imagine he will,' Michael put in.

'He's made it every time so far,' said his mother, and turning to Robert she explained. 'You see, my husband Geoffrey has some unusual hobbies. One is that he's taken it into his head that he has to cross the whole continent by car once a year, driving along the most impossible roads – if you can call those bush tracks roads at all.'

'Come on, Mother, admit it: he's off his head!'

This was from Michael, but Mrs Sutton just shook her head.

'Let's eat in the kitchen this evening,' she suggested. 'Anyone object?'

It was an old-fashioned and very comfortable kitchen. Copper pots and pans hung on the walls, the drawers in the dresser were porcelain-fronted, there was even a genuine coal-burning stove with a chimney hood and an enormous fridge with a bulging front from which Mrs Sutton produced all kinds of delicious things as if by magic. A slender young man with curly black hair and a small moustache appeared. 'Robert, this is Michael and Caroline's tutor, Mr Arbuthnot,' said the children's beautiful mother. They all sat down at the long, dark, polished kitchen table.

'Where do the others eat?' asked Robert.

'What others?'

'I mean Twicky the chauffeur, and the maid.'

'Oh, in the building next door, of course,' Michael explained. 'With the cook and the gardener and the rest of the staff, not forgetting old Crombie. He's what you might call our factotum. He used to be a blacksmith, but now he just does odd jobs about the place. You wouldn't believe how many people it takes to run a farm like this!' He went on: 'There's the two stable boys, and all the farmhands . . .'

'How big is your farm?' Robert asked.

'Well, I don't know. A few hundred square miles, I suppose. You can ride around here for days and still be on our land.'

Robert was greatly impressed. 'So how many sheep do you have? I didn't see any sheds for them.'

'The sheep live out of doors all the year round, you idiot! I guess we have about ten or twelve thousand. We don't count them till the sheep-shearing in autumn. That's quite something. We need twelve shearers, and they're a pretty rough bunch. But when they aren't drunk they can shear two hundred sheep a day each. Sixteen pounds of best merino wool from each animal. Anyone can see you're a town boy, Robert. You've no idea about anything, have you?'

Caroline immediately sprang to Robert's defence. 'No need to act as if you were God's own answer to sheep-farming! You don't bother with the farm at all – if it was up to you we'd do nothing but play croquet all day. It's lucky we have Mr Arbuthnot here or you wouldn't even be able to read and write.'

But Michael did not rise to the bait, and simply said, 'She's got a point.'

Mr Arbuthnot took no notice of Robert, but spent the whole time talking to Mrs Sutton. The meal went on rather too long, and when it was cleared away Robert was glad to go upstairs and get between the clean sheets of his wonderfully comfortable bed.

This is too good to be true, he thought just before dropping off to sleep. The questions will start again tomorrow morning.

'Now, we must call your parents. Just write your phone number down, and I'll explain it all to them.'

But nothing of the kind happened. Mrs Sutton asked no questions, and Robert sat at the breakfast table looking as much at his ease as if he were one of the family. Perhaps she saw through him? Perhaps she guessed he didn't have a home at all – or anyway, not in Australia. Robert had a feeling that Mrs Sutton liked him, and he was very grateful to her.

Life at Annaby certainly wasn't dull. Caroline showed him the stables, the glasshouses and the garage where the jalopy was kept. 'And that's where old Crombie spends his time,' she added, as they passed a shed overgrown with ivy. Robert could hear the sound of hammering from inside.

'Want to take a look? Don't let it alarm you – his workshop's like a scrap-heap.' They went in, and standing among a number of lathes and rusty engines Robert saw a heavy-set, white-haired man bending over a piece of metal and swearing as he turned it this way and that.

'Crombie, this is Robert. He's staying with us for a while.'

'Oh yes?' growled the old man. 'Another idler going to sit about all day doing nothing?'

Caroline laughed. 'He's always on at us! It's just his way – he doesn't mean it.'

Old Crombie looked keenly at Robert. 'Well, I don't know, he might make good if he learnt something useful. Know how to handle that?' He picked up a heavy tool shaped like a cylinder. Robert looked at it blankly. 'Never seen one before? It's a welding iron. I'll show you how to use it if you like.'

'I don't think Robert wants to learn metal-working,' objected Caroline. But Robert, who had taken a liking to the old man, took a closer look around the workshop. All kinds of tools were hanging from the walls, along with a number of worn saddles and rusty horseshoes. The wreck of a car

53

stood in the middle of the big workshop, and right at the back, in a corner, he saw an unmade bed on an iron bedstead, with a few beer bottles on the floor beside it. The whole place smelled of engine oil. Robert sniffed, registering a very faint odour of hay, leather and horse manure.

'Do you live here?' he asked.

''Course I do. Where else? Drop in and see me some time if you like, but you two can leave me alone for now.'

'He likes mending things,' Caroline said when they had left. 'Mad about it. He salvages everything we throw away – Dad's old car, the tractor that doesn't go, the mowing machine we were going to throw out years ago, our rusty old pumps and the sheep-shearing machine we don't use any more.'

'Why does he live in that dirty old workshop?'

'He likes it. He hasn't been in our house for years. He thinks we're too posh.'

'Posh?'

'That's the word he uses. Books everywhere. Silver cutlery! Mother playing the piano. And a tutor too. He can't stand Mr Arbuthnot, and he doesn't want to eat with the others either. He usually cooks himself something on his oil stove in the shed there. He's one of the old sort, you see. I mean, the first settlers here were either convicts or people who didn't feel at ease in England. You'll find odd characters like that on any big farm. Want a swim?'

They spent all morning beside the pool. Robert had borrowed a pair of swimming trunks from Michael; they were far too long, and came down to his knees. Caroline was wearing a one-piece bathing suit with blue and white stripes, more the kind of thing you'd expect an old lady to wear, but Robert still thought she looked terrific. In the afternoon the three of them played croquet. It took Robert some time to grasp the rules of the game, but he was almost winning the second round when Twicky the chauffeur came running out of the house, shouting, 'He's coming home! He's on his way. They telephoned from Peterborough. He should be here in ten minutes.'

The whole house was in uproar. Everyone gathered in the drive, including the gardener, the maid, and the cook in her apron and cap. The only person missing was old Crombie. Mrs Sutton was looking nervously at her watch. They were all very excited.

'What's all the fuss about?' asked Robert.

'You don't know what it means, driving almost five thousand kilometres through the bush in just a few days. Suppose you come off the road out there and break down? No water, no human beings for miles except the savages.' This was Michael speaking, and he sounded rather annoyed.

'Savages?' asked Robert. 'What savages?'

'Coal-black savages, I can tell you! They live there in the outback, nobody knows just how. They don't have proper houses; they go hunting with spears and boomerangs. You sometimes see a few of them around here, too. I have to say they seem rather spooky.'

'We're really glad every time Daddy comes home safe,' said Caroline. 'I wish I knew why he has to do that dangerous drive every year all alone, but he just can't seem to give it up.'

A loud rattling and the noise of an engine were heard in the distance. Michael was looking through a pair of binoculars. A great cloud of reddish dust rose above the road. The roar of the engine grew louder, and Robert saw a bright red sports car approaching. Its roof was open but it wasn't really a cabriolet, since the side windows were closed. However, the engine was turning over very fast. Those snaky silver pipes along its sides were the superchargers. It was a post-war English roadster – or could it actually be a racing car? No,

Robert guessed it was an Aston Martin or a Lotus. Were there Lotuses around then? Ratibor would have known at once; he could even have pinpointed the year it was made. But anyway the car went like a bomb. Now Robert could see a man in a leather cap at the wheel, wearing a large pair of dark glasses to keep the dust out. Brakes squealed; the engine was switched off. The driver removed his cap and glasses, opened the car door, which was really just a small window of yellowish celluloid, and got out.

'Daddy!' the children shouted. He hugged them and kissed his wife. Robert saw that he was going grey at the temples. His face might have been made of fine, thin leather. It was very sunburnt, and he had two deep red scars, one on his forehead and one on his chin.

'This is my friend Robert,' Caroline told him. 'He's been here for a day or so. We put him in the green room. He can stay, can't he, please, Daddy?'

'Why not? I've no objection!' said the master of the house, looking more closely at Robert. 'So where did you two pick Robert up, then?'

'Oh, he was in our film too, and then they forgot to come and collect him.'

'Why, yes, your film! How did it all go? Was the director – what's his name? – anyway, was he pleased with you?'

'It's all in the can,' said Michael proudly. 'And we earned fifty pounds each.'

Robert felt a slight pang. *He* hadn't been paid anything, although he could have done with some money of his own. But admittedly no one had engaged him to be an extra either.

Now he had to keep his cool, make sure he didn't seem odd in any way, and act as if being a guest at Annaby was the most normal thing in the world.

'Thanks, sir,' he said. Geoffrey shook hands and assured him that he was welcome.

Christmas came – a Christmas without any snow, a mid-summer Christmas. Robert was worried because he had no presents for anyone. He searched his chest of drawers, but he couldn't find anything of his own suitable to give the Suttons. Maybe the fire-wheel? He hesitated. It wasn't much. Would Caroline like it, or would she think it was childish? He decided to ask her mother.

When he knocked at Mrs Sutton door, she was just doing her face and hair.

'Mrs Sutton,' he began, shyly.

'Come on in, it's all right. And do call me Lea if you like.'

He came closer. She was sitting in front of the mirror putting on a beautiful string of pearls, and Robert saw a jewel case open on the dressing table. An emerald necklace nestled inside on its blue velvet lining.

'What beautiful things you have,' Robert breathed.

'My father gave them to me. They were all I brought when I came to Australia. You can look at them.'

Inside the case Robert read, in gold lettering:

Salomon Hirschberg
Royal Court Jeweller

'Lea,' he said, 'Lea, I feel really bad – you see, I don't know what to give Caroline for Christmas.' But he took the fire-wheel out of his pocket and showed it to Lea.

'Why, that's amazing!' she said, smiling. 'I've never seen anything like it. How it sparkles! Brighter than my necklace here. I promise you, Caroline will love it!'

She was right. When it came to present-giving time in

the big sitting room, Caroline was delighted with the little fire-wheel and kept playing with it, ignoring her new bicycle, her French scarf and even her elegant jodhpurs. The pile of presents included a pair of stout walking shoes for Robert. He'd have been glad of those in Russia. That reminded him of Olga: what had become of her? It seemed years since he'd been sitting in her pharmacy. It *was* years, too . . . he did a quick sum. Exactly ten years, from 1956 to 1946. He felt quite dizzy when he thought of it. He'd gone four days forward and *at the same time* ten years back in time, as it were. Enough to drive anyone round the bend!

Then the cook banged the gong for dinner: roast beef and Christmas pudding. Robert had some difficulty swallowing the rich brown pudding that tasted of suet, cinnamon and raisins. It struck him as a revolting combination, but the others appeared to think it a delicacy.

In the candlelight, the scars on Geoffrey's face looked bright red. Robert quietly asked Caroline if her father had been in a car accident.

'No, it happened in the war, when Daddy was in New Guinea fighting the Japanese. A fragmentation bomb got him. He was wounded all over – it must have been awful. He won't admit it, but he's never been the same since. Once upon a time, when I was little, he used to take me everywhere with him, and now he hardly speaks to us.'

After dinner Lea sat down at the piano. Mr Arbuthnot the tutor stood beside her and sang. Robert was surprised to find that he had a good baritone voice. He might be a curly-haired wimp, but you had to admit he could sing! Robert couldn't have said just why he disliked the man, for after all, the tutor had never done him any harm, but whenever he set eyes on Mr Arbuthnot he felt annoyance rise in him.

Apart from that, however, he was happier than ever before.

He took each day as it came, and he didn't intend to think too hard. He decided he'd rather be stupid and happy than clever and worried to death, the way he was in Siberia. In the New Year Caroline began teaching him to ride. At first he was so clumsy that he was almost thrown, but Caroline was a patient teacher and his horse an obliging animal. Soon they were spending whole afternoons riding around the area, and didn't get back until dusk.

Once they rode past a settlement of corrugated iron huts. Half-naked children were playing in the road, and men with beer bottles in their hands were shouting after them.

'What a slum!' said Robert. 'I didn't know you had such places here.'

'That's just the itinerant labourers,' Caroline explained. 'They don't have anything to do now that it's summer, so they spend all day drinking and then beat their wives in the evening.'

Robert looked at her in astonishment. She didn't seem at all disturbed.

'Well, you know what Australians are like!'

As a matter of fact he didn't.

'All they think about is sport, cars and beer. They think we're silly because we read books. I can't even talk to the neighbours' children.'

'Why not?'

'They're so boring!'

'I can't understand you, Caroline. I really like it here.'

'Yes, well, we're quite comfortably off, and Annaby's a nice place. But in the long run . . . You know, I'd really like to get away from here, somewhere a long way off! I want to see the world, travel, have adventures of my own.'

She sounds like a blind person describing colours, thought Robert. He really couldn't wish *her* to end up in some chilly underground cell in a foreign country, under suspicion of spying. Looking at her, he felt he had to protect her.

'If I were you I'd stay here,' he said at last. 'You won't find such horses anywhere else, or a cook making you that Christmas pudding you like!'

They rode on in silence for a while, and it was not until they were unsaddling their horses outside the stable that Caroline said, 'You think I'm just a spoilt brat, don't you? Maybe I am. Everyone says I'm a Daddy's girl, even though he's taken so little notice of me recently.'

'The main thing is, you're well off here,' said Robert, trying to pacify her, but she lost her temper and cried, 'Oh, you don't understand! Do you think I want to spend my whole life on this stupid farm?'

At that he just put his arms round her and held her until her anger had evaporated.

In the morning, when Michael and Caroline had lessons with Mr Arbuthnot – in the cool hall because of the heat – Robert usually hung around the stables, the glasshouses or the other outhouses. He had gently but firmly declined to attend the lessons in which the tutor tried to teach his pupils trigonometry or English history. As far as Robert could see the man was a dead loss.

However, he liked old Crombie. He hung around the workshop and spied through the window until one day the old man came out and growled, 'What are you staring at, then? Got nothing better to do? You'd better come in if you want to, not lurk around outside there!'

The shed smelled of lubricating oil and burnt rubber. 'Finished it yesterday evening. Want to look?' asked Crombie, pointing to the wrecked car Robert had noticed on his first visit. It was an old Bentley with curving mudguards, wide running-boards and a spare wheel on top of the boot. The carriagework was no longer jacked up as he remembered it; the old man had mounted it on the chassis again.

'Got her back on the road,' said the smith. Robert looked incredulously at the car. The paint was peeling everywhere, the exhaust was rusty, and the windscreen looked as if a stone had hit it.

'You're never going to drive that old thing?' asked Robert.

'You bet I am! Built in 1934, it was; that's still good, solid work. They don't make 'em like that no more. You don't believe me? You can come along if you like.'

'Where to?'

'Just a little drive over to see my cobber in Cowper's Winch – test her out. Hop in!'

Well, why not? Robert felt that an outing would be fun. Crombie threw another can of petrol and a tank of water on the back seat, and then drove off.

First they passed through a few dusty and apparently deserted little settlements. Soon there were no fields and no fences any more. Nothing but tangled trees and coarse grass grew on the vast, dry plains. Once they passed a huge lake as white as snow.

'Salt, just salt,' Crombie explained. 'You can't see the water, it's under that thick crust. Two metres thick. No fish, they can't stand it.'

When they had been driving for four hours Robert began to feel uneasy. 'Look, Crombie,' he began, 'where are we actually going?'

'You'll soon see.'

'The thing is, I have to be back at Annaby for supper, or Lea – I mean Mrs Sutton – may worry.'

'Ah, the lovely Lea! First name terms, is it? Well, good for you!'

'You don't like her, do you? You don't like any of the Suttons.'

'So? I'd rather be with my mates. I'm the only one who stayed on in Annaby, seeing I'm too old for the bush. You know something? Those Suttons, they're not real Australians. They think they're special just because they have a lot of money and act like they was home in England.' He snorted, scornfully. 'So how about you? You one of that sort too?'

'Well,' said Robert, 'well, I'm not really from around here at all. But I have to say they've all been very kind to me.'

'Then it's time you saw something different.' And Crombie would say no more. The landscape was so monotonous that it almost sent Robert to sleep. Once the old man nudged him, and Robert saw a herd of camels coming towards them, at least two dozen animals trotting along the road at their ease. Robert thought he must be dreaming. *Were* there camels in Australia? But Crombie didn't seem surprised, and just steered his beloved Bentley, an even odder sight than before in these deserted surroundings, through the gaping herd. 'Right pests, they are,' he said. 'Destroying the vegetation, breeding like rabbits. Thousands of 'em we've shot, but it don't make no difference.'

Twilight was already coming on when Robert saw a chain of hills in the distance. They were white. It couldn't be snow – salt again, maybe?

'Soon be there,' said Crombie. 'That's Cowper's Winch ahead of us. See the dump, that heap of earth over there? You'll find one everywhere the diggers is working. What – you don't know what a digger is? Call yourself Australian?'

Gradually Robert got the basic facts out of the old man. Once upon a time over a thousand people had lived here; now there were only a few tin shacks left. 'Diggers' were the prospectors who had come from all over the world to excavate the ground for jewels.

'Opals,' said the old man. 'Finest opals in the world! If you're lucky, if you find a black one or a harlequin, you can get a good few hundred pounds for it. Has to have a deep shine, though, brilliant play of colour, no milky patches, see? My old cobber Bill Mulligan's been digging here these twenty years. He knows all about it, he does!'

Huge hillocks of light sand were now visible in the middle of this desert of scree, and here and there the openings of abandoned mine shafts and galleries. There was not a human soul in sight.

'Where are the diggers, then?' enquired Robert. He'd resigned himself to spending the night in this wilderness, but even in this bleak spot, he thought, there must be beds somewhere, an inn, something to eat . . .

'You'll soon see.' That was all Crombie would say, and a little further on they met the first opal hunters. They looked ragged and unwashed, but very strong. The whites of their eyes gleamed in their muddy faces, and there was dust in their hair. Robert had a feeling that it would be better not to cross them. Crombie steered his old car right into the sand and suddenly stopped.

'Here we are,' he said. 'You can get out.'

Robert looked around him. There was no sign of life anywhere.

'Here,' said the old man. He had stopped in front of a hole in the ground. 'Bill!' he yelled. 'Come on out!'

A hollow voice answered, and there was a glimmer of something inside the hole. By the light of a dark lantern, Robert saw a neatly cut flight of steps leading down. A sturdy man, naked to the waist, came up from below, welcomed Crombie, clapped him on the shoulder and hugged him, swearing and laughing at the same time. The two of them danced for joy like a couple of bears. Robert was forgotten.

'Come on in,' said the digger.

'Brought this lad along. Parked himself on the Suttons – know who I mean? But I reckon he's not so bad.'

Robert stumbled down the steep steps behind the two of them and into a deep shaft. It was pleasantly cool there. Bill had made himself a kind of cave dwelling three or four metres underground, with a camp bed, a spirit stove, a water tank and a locker, and further back, in a corner, there were picks and spades, a sieve, a chisel and a heavy, mud-encrusted hammer drill. That was the entire furniture of the place.

The digger immediately produced bread, smoked meat, knives and glasses, and most important of all a crate of beer. Robert ate and drank with the men, but he was exhausted, and after a while Bill unrolled a sleeping bag for him. It smelled of paraffin. He heard the two of them talking, swearing, singing and bawling for some time yet, but although their voices were very loud he finally dropped off to sleep.

When they came up to the surface next morning, light was blazing down on the treeless plain. There was much activity among the big dumps already. The diggers were scraping, hoeing and drilling everywhere in their galleries and passages. Many claims were being excavated as professionally as regular mines, and their owners had blocks and tackles, heavy drilling machines mounted on iron rails, shapeless vacuum suckers. Others were toiling away with picks and spades.

'Can anyone have a go?' asked Robert.

'Want to dig, do you? Better let it be! You wouldn't last more'n three days!' said the old man grimly.

'Oh, let him try,' Bill said. 'We all started out in a small way. Listen, son, you can get a permit here for next to nothing. And once you've got it you can stake a claim. Of course all the good places were snapped up way back, so your chances are round about nil. But only what's underground belongs to the digger. The stuff he's looked through and thrown on the scrapheap don't belong to no one, so you can root around in it all you like. Them poor bastards, they're just noodlers. That's what we call 'em, fellows without a claim of their own. You could feel quite sorry for them. Still, every now and then someone finds something.'

'Nonsense,' muttered old Crombie. 'All nonsense. I don't believe a word of them noodler stories. Let's get a beer before I leave. Elly's place still open, is it? I'll buy you both a drink.'

But Robert didn't feel like a couple of beers so early in the morning. 'I think I would like to have a go if you'll lend me a spade,' he told Bill. The two men laughed at him. Crombie tapped his forehead, but his kindlier friend said, 'Well, even a blind chicken sometimes finds a grain of corn.' So they left him alone, spade in hand, in the desert where thousands of human moles were digging underground passages.

Robert hardly knew where to begin. He began digging at random in the nearest heap of sand, but as the sun rose higher his enthusiasm rapidly waned. There wasn't a patch of shade in sight. The longer he prodded the debris of the dump with his spade, the more dust he raised. He was already regretting not going with the others. He imagined Crombie and his cobber Bill sitting in a shady tent, and the idea of a cold beer made his mouth feel dry.

'Might as well give it up!' A hoarse voice from behind made him jump. He turned and saw a small, dark-skinned, bearded man with a broad nose, bushy eyebrows, and shaggy hair that showed under his broad-brimmed hat. This must be one of the aborigines, the black people Caroline found so scary. But the man looked quite normal with his sunglasses and his beige trousers, the colour of the sand.

'Where'd you spring from, then? You'll get sunstroke if you carry on that way, young fellow, without a hat and gloves.'

'I'm not from around here,' said Robert, letting the spade drop. He didn't know why, but the little man made him feel shy.

'None of you are from around here. I guess I'm the only one who is. Want some gum?'

It was a long time since Robert last had a piece of chewing gum – back in the Russian cinema. The taste of peppermint was exactly what he needed at this moment. It was even better than a beer.

'Thanks. Thank you very much,' said Robert. 'But how come you're the only one from around here?'

'Why, the others are just riff-raff from all over the world.'

'Not real Australians, you mean?'

'There's no real Australians, son. The whites think this is their home, but nobody asked them to come. It was pure chance they landed here.'

Exactly like me, thought Robert.

'What do they want here, anyway?' cried the man. He seemed to have forgotten about Robert. His eyes were glittering, and his voice almost cracked as he went on. 'It's our land,' he said hoarsely. 'We've been here for ever.'

'I – I can't help that,' stammered Robert.

'No, right, so you can't. So what are you doing here?'

'Looking for gemstones. My friend said anyone can dig here.'

'Oh, you can dig for ever with your silly little spade, young man. Seven years I've been here and what do I get for it? Not so much as a pair of new shoes. Those opals just bring bad luck, damn them! Don't you know that, or are you just pretending?'

The man obviously didn't feel like working any more than Robert did, so the two of them talked about diggers and noodlers, and Robert learned a good deal that was entirely outside the experience of the Sutton family of Annaby.

When old Crombie reappeared in his rusty Bentley the sun was already high in the sky. He gave the little aborigine a nasty look and gestured to Robert to get in. Robert bent down and put a few bits of stone in his pocket as a memento – it was that silly habit of his, the one he couldn't break. He said goodbye politely to his shaggy-haired friend, who watched them go with an inscrutable expression, he thanked Bill for the loan of the spade, and they set off for home.

'Better make sure that fellow didn't pinch nothing off of you,' Crombie told Robert. 'You want to watch out with that lot.'

'I don't have anything *for* him to steal,' said Robert, emptying his trouser pockets to prove it. 'Just a bit of dirt. That's all I found.'

'So what did I tell you?'

They didn't talk much on the long drive back. Once they ran out of petrol, and Robert had to fill the tank from the reserve can.

'Careful!' cried the old man as a black snake slid across the track. Robert leaped aside. 'That's what comes of going into the bush with such daft shoes,' grumbled Crombie. 'You was in luck, you was. S'posing it had got you, you'd be done for. Them creatures, they're deadly, they are.'

Crombie was an old grouch, but Robert liked him, and even if he hadn't found any opals he'd enjoyed the adventure at Cowper's Winch. All the same, he was glad when they saw the lights of Annaby ahead of them late in the evening. Perhaps all of them are right, thought Robert: old Crombie, Bill the digger, that Aborigine, the savage who wasn't really savage at all. Perhaps he, Robert, was just as spoiled as his friend Caroline. But when Lea scolded him for going off for two days without telling anyone, and put a glass of iced tea and a couple of sandwiches in front of him, he felt pleased and relieved.

It was a week after his expedition with Crombie that Robert happened to be passing the stables and heard someone sobbing in one of the boxes. Going in, he found Caroline crouching on the floor in tears. She had her hands over her ears and was rocking back and forth in desperation.

'What's the matter? What's up?'

She just shook her head and wouldn't say. He began stroking her, but she pushed him away. He felt helpless.

'It's all right, you can tell me,' he said.

'I want to get away from here!' she said. 'I just have to get away!'

He gently held her head in his lap and waited to hear more.

'It's Mother,' she said at last. 'She has a lover.'

'Oh, come on, you're imagining it, Caroline.'

'No, I'm not!' she positively shouted at him. 'I'm not!'

'But how can you know? And who do you think it is?'

She looked at him with tears in her eyes. Then she made up her mind to speak.

'Okay then, so I had to get up in the night yesterday – Daddy had gone into town to the wool exchange; he has to watch the prices, you see – and I saw Mr Arbuthnot coming out of Mother's bedroom.'

'You mean your tutor? That creep of a schoolmaster?'

'He was kind of *slinking* out. So then I knew what was up. You see, things haven't been too good between Mummy and Daddy for quite a while. Well, not since he was wounded. And now it's all over. I want to get away from here – but oh, if only I knew how!'

Robert could bear her grief no longer.

'Imagine you could go anywhere you like,' he whispered. 'Just like that!' And he snapped his fingers. 'Where *would* you go?'

'To England, of course.'

'All alone? That might not be much fun.'

'With you,' she said quietly.

At that he could no longer restrain himself. 'Listen, I'm going to tell you a secret. Only you mustn't tell anyone, not even your mother.'

Caroline nodded.

'How do you think I got here?'

'Well, in our Buick, of course.'

'Silly, I mean how do you think I got to Australia?'

'By sea, probably. From Germany.'

'How do you know I'm from Germany?'

'You think we didn't notice? I mean, anyone can hear you're from Germany! Michael said all along you were a Hun.'

'What do you mean, a Hun?'

'Well, that's what we've called the Germans ever since the First World War. But Mother said he wasn't to talk like that. She thinks your parents must have escaped from the Nazis. That's right, isn't it?'

Robert gulped. He wasn't prepared for this, and he didn't want to tell her a lie. He plucked up all his courage.

'Look, do you remember how I suddenly turned up on that cliff where you were all filming the treasure hunt story?' he asked. 'You'd been acting in the film before, hadn't you? Did you see me before that day? No? You see, there I was all of a sudden, just like that. And I can disappear again just as easily. So can you.'

'You're making all this up,' she cried.

'I can prove it if you don't believe me. It won't take a minute.'

She demurred, but then followed him to his room. Once there, he pulled the whole top drawer out of the chest and emptied its contents on the table. Baffled, Caroline looked at the jumbled objects.

'Here,' said Robert, holding his Russian dictionary in front of her. 'Look, I brought this back from Siberia. And I got this in Moscow.'

She took the stamp, and he told her what it said. ' "KGB – Secret". I picked it up from the political police. They put me in jail for a couple of days there.'

'You're crazy,' said Caroline. But there was no stopping him now.

'And the fire-wheel I gave you is from Germany. So's the money.' He pressed his modern Deutschmark coins into her hand.

Caroline sat down on the bed and looked at him in amazement.

'I can't help it,' he tried again, after a while. 'It's something to do with my eyes. You know how it is when you rub your eyes before you drop off to sleep at night – the things you see then? Sort of colour effects, that's all. Only all kinds of other things happen to me, too. Suppose I'm watching something in the cinema or on television, without thinking much about it, of course, then I sometimes get into this state, whatever you like to call it. Well, look, one of my teachers at school always says I'm absent-minded and somewhere else entirely. And when this happens I just have to rub my eyes and I *am* somewhere else. I'm there.'

It didn't sound too convincing. Caroline frowned.

'Television? What do you mean?' she asked. 'Like a telescope or something?'

He could have kicked himself. The situation was complicated enough anyway, and now he'd gone and forgotten the
time problem. Back then, or rather back *now*, there probably
wasn't any TV to speak of in the Australian outback.

'Well, never mind,' he said hastily. 'I mean, suppose I see
something in a film and I rub my eyes, then I'm there.'

'Where?'

'Wherever the film's being made. That's how I got to
Russia, and the second time it happened I landed up here in
Australia.'

'Robert, I don't believe a word you're saying.'

'Okay, don't. I know it sounds weird. That's why I didn't
tell anyone before. Only you. I thought you'd understand.'

Caroline thought for a moment. Then she gave herself
a small shake and said, with a smile that was still rather
doubtful, 'Well, if it's so easy, why not show me how you do
it?'

'You bet I will! Straight away if you like. We'll try it out
first and then go off on our travels. You wanted to go to
England, right?'

'Yes, but there's no cinema here. The nearest is in Elizabeth,
fifty miles away.'

Robert thought about it. 'Maybe it'll work with a photo,'
he said hesitantly. 'Do you have a book about England somewhere? A book with pictures in it?'

'Sure. Wait a minute, I'll get one from the library.'

When she came back she was carrying an illustrated book
called *Great English Country Houses*. They leafed through
it, looking for the one they liked best. At first they couldn't
agree, but then they found just the right house. It was white,
with green shutters, standing in rather wild grounds, and it
was neither too large nor too small.

'So what do we do when we get there?' asked Caroline. 'I

mean, we don't know anybody in England. They probably won't even let us into that house. Or they'll ask who we are and where we come from. And what do we say then?'

Robert laughed. 'I can deal with that,' he murmured. 'You remember how I was left standing there when the director said that was it for today, and the bus came to pick up the other children? Well, I didn't even know where I was. I'd probably still be standing there if you two hadn't taken me with you. I mean, there's bound to be *some* risk. But I've found out how to cope.'

She was still looking doubtfully at him, but the temptation was too great. 'All right,' she said, 'though I still don't believe it.'

He picked up the book and warned her, 'Don't think of anything at all. Just look at the picture! Your head must be entirely empty, understand? And then rub your eyes. I'll count to three. One, two, three.'

They sat side by side on the bed, rubbing and rubbing their eyes until Caroline began to feel silly. Angrily, she drummed her fists on Robert's chest.

'I knew it!' she cried. 'You just invented all that stuff to fool me. And I fell for it! Oh, go away! Leave me alone! I hate you!'

She flung herself on the bed and began crying again. Robert was ashamed of himself. In fact he felt so miserable that tears came to his own eyes. Very carefully, he put his arms round Caroline, and she did not resist. 'I'm sorry,' he whispered. 'I only wanted to help you. Because you're not happy here any more. I wasn't telling lies.'

She sighed slightly and said no more.

They lay on the bed in one another's arms. Forgetting her anger, Caroline let Robert comfort her, and soon she stopped thinking about their failed journey. At last the two of them fell asleep from sheer happiness – yes, it is possible for happiness to send you to sleep.

Towards evening they were abruptly woken. The door was flung open, and someone shouted, 'What on earth are you two doing? Are you crazy?'

It was Michael's voice. They sat up with a start, and Caroline's brother advanced on Robert with his fists up. He was beside himself with anger. Grabbing Robert by the arm, he shouted, 'You just leave my sister alone, you bastard, or . . . or I'll murder you!'

'He hasn't done anything to me,' said Caroline firmly. 'At least, not what you're thinking. Anyway it's nothing to do with you. Go away, Michael! Get out!'

Michael withdrew, looking sullen. Robert was about to stand up, but Caroline held him back. 'He always thinks he has to keep an eye on me,' she said crossly. 'And he's only my half-brother too! I bet he's going to tell Daddy about us.'

'He'd better not,' said Robert, trying to calm her. 'He'll be sorry if he does.'

However, he had miscalculated. A few days passed, and both and he and Caroline thought everything was all right, except that creepy Mr Arbuthnot kept winking at Caroline as if he knew something. Lea showed no awareness of anything, and Michael avoided them and kept quiet. But then one evening, after supper, Geoffrey tapped on the table for silence, and to everyone's surprise made a little speech.

'You've always wanted to study in England, Caroline, haven't you?' he began. 'Well, and so you shall! Sounds like a good idea to me. But if you really want to go to Oxford, then what little you can learn from Mr Arbuthnot –' here he cast a cold glance at the tutor – 'what little you can learn from Mr Arbuthnot won't by any means be sufficient. I've been making enquiries about a good boarding-school, and you can leave next week. Your passage is booked. Your mother will help you pack. I think that's the best solution for us all.'

There was a deathly hush. Robert saw Michael looking fixedly past Caroline. It was his doing! He'd given his sister away. What a schemer! Lea, resigned, raised her hands as if to show there was no appeal against her husband's decision.

'And kindly don't look so miserable!' added Geoffrey. 'This is what you've always wanted, Caroline.'

Most of the rest of the evening was spent in silence.

Over the next few days the atmosphere at Annaby was unhappy. Even the weather seemed to feel it. There were several violent storms, and the family stayed in their own rooms. Lea and Caroline were busy preparing for Caroline's journey. Robert felt lethargic, as if he had flu. Just once he arranged to meet Caroline at the stables, and they went out riding. After a long time, she said bitterly, 'So you were right. Snap your fingers and the fairies will grant your wish! I never should have rubbed my eyes!'

'I didn't mean *this* to happen, Caroline. You know I didn't. It's Michael's fault. Him and his stupid jealousy! I could strangle him.'

'So could I – except I don't know how to. Anyway it wouldn't be any use.'

The one person who noticed nothing was the cook, who was merely surprised by Caroline's poor appetite. 'She always wanted to go to England, and now suddenly she's changed her mind!'

On the morning of Caroline's departure everyone assembled outside the house again. Even old Crombie had turned up this time. The only person missing was that slimy charmer Mr Arbuthnot, who had left the evening before, and no one seemed to miss him, not even Lea. Geoffrey watched, his face

74

impassive, as Twicky the chauffeur put Caroline's big trunk in the car. Lea dabbed at her eyes with her handkerchief, smearing her mascara. Then they all embraced Caroline, who had pulled herself together, although there were tears in her eyes. Robert kissed her goodbye too, looking defiantly at Michael as he did so, as if saying: Even you can't do anything about that.

When the white Buick had disappeared in a cloud of dust, Robert went indoors. He wasn't going to stay at Annaby a day longer. I'd rather try my luck in Adelaide or Sydney, he thought.

This time he didn't intend to leave anything to chance. He put on his best clothes, the ones he'd borrowed from Michael. Let Caroline's treacherous brother go around in his old blue jacket with the baggy pockets and missing button!

Robert shook off these vengeful thoughts. He took his few possessions out of the top drawer and put them in his pockets. After all, they might come in useful.

There was a knock at the door, and when he opened it he saw Lea.

'What are you doing, Robert?' she asked. 'Are you going to leave us too?'

He hardly knew what to say.

'Come along, let's make ourselves comfortable. I really need a cup of tea after all this.' And she led him to a small sitting room which she had never invited him to enter before.

'Believe me, I know how you feel, Robert. Things aren't too good here at Annaby, but I've known worse times than this.'

'Me too,' said Robert. 'Tell me, how did you come to Australia? Or were you born here?'

'No,' she said, smiling. 'I came here more or less by accident – much as I think you did. Am I right?'

Now Robert was close to tears again. How annoying, when he'd made up his mind to be perfectly calm and collected! But then he thought about home, the father he saw so seldom, his mother, his friend Ratibor, even his grandmother in her residential home and his painting lessons with old Winziger, and much to his surprise he felt an unfamiliar sensation. Probably what they called homesickness.

'Shall I show you something?' asked Lea, looking at him with sympathy, as if she guessed what was going on inside him. She picked up a photograph album lying on the tea table and handed it to Robert.

He opened the leather-bound volume and leafed through it. The photos were all old, some of them already slightly faded. They showed men in tail-coats, with orders hanging from ribbons around their necks, they showed ladies in wedding dresses and grandmothers with white-clad baby grandchildren on their laps. He turned the page again, and saw a picture that stopped his breath. It was a photo of a girl in a black bathing suit. A slim man had his arm around her shoulders, and they were both smiling at the camera, but that wasn't what had taken him by surprise. It was the swimming pool, the changing rooms, the church tower in the background, the iron railings overgrown with wild vines behind the man and the girl in the photo.

He recognized it all, down to the very last detail. It was the open-air swimming pool at home, the pool where he spent every spare minute in hot summer weather. *His* swimming pool, but out of reach, far away on the other side of the world! The photo blurred before his eyes. Perhaps he was going to cry after all. He took out his handkerchief and rubbed his eyes.

Lea was holding the teapot, pouring herself another cup of tea. When she looked up, Robert had vanished. She let out a cry, and dropped the teapot. Mechanically, she mopped the hot splashes of tea off her dress. 'I'll have to send it to the laundry.' That was all she was able to think.

THE THIRD JOURNEY

This time it was easier. This time Robert knew exactly where he was. The grass where people lay sunbathing, the fence, the white-painted changing rooms – it was all the same as ever. And the light-coloured linen suit he was wearing was just right for the time of year, which he guessed was August. Only the bike he was sitting on wasn't familiar. In fact he was just getting off it, so it obviously belonged to him. That was a good sign.

On the grass in front of him – which as usual on hot days was populated by dozing sunbathers and children running around shouting – a man and a girl were leaning against the railings while another man looked in the viewfinder of his camera. He was about to take a photo. 'This is your last chance,' he said. 'My film's running out. You're supposed to look at me, you fool, not Lea!'

Robert left his bike where it was, vaulted the railings and ran towards the photographer.

Lea? Could this really be Lea? No, impossible. It was just hearing the name that had sent him running forward impulsively – *absent-mindedly*, so to speak, but anyway without thinking. He stared at the girl. For a moment he felt he could be looking at Caroline, but this young woman had a fuller face, black eyes, and dark hair showing under a white bathing cap. She couldn't be twenty. She might have been Caroline's elder sister – but Caroline had no elder sister, and anyway . . . anyway, this was all nonsense. She looked enchanting in her close-fitting one-piece black bathing suit. The man beside her was holding her tight as if he would never let her go and kissing the nape of her neck. She pulled away, laughing, and Robert heard her protest, 'Stop it, Albert! Come on, you two – I must go home, or Papa will be cross!'

Yes, that was Lea's voice. But only a few minutes ago she'd been offering him a cup of tea! 'I came here more or less by accident – much as I think you did.' Those had been her last words to him.

Robert was about to call 'Lea!' but the name remained unspoken. What could he say? That he'd seen the snapshot the man had just taken in a photo album on the other side of the world? That he'd been near tears – only *near* tears – because he'd been parted from his best friend, her daughter Caroline, who by now was fast asleep in a ship's cabin on her way to an English boarding-school? No, impossible. Robert stood there, completely at a loss.

She looked at him in surprise. For a split second he thought she recognized him. But then she turned away, sweeping both men off with her, and the three of them disappeared past the pool attendant's hut into the changing rooms, which were not at all as he remembered them. They were made of plain wood with a little heart shape cut in each door, like the lavatory door of a farmhouse in the mountains where Robert had once stayed the night on holiday.

He followed Lea and her friends, feeling as if he hadn't arrived properly yet. He leaned against the wall and closed his eyes. The smell of wet clothes on the wooden floor rose to his nostrils, and he remembered how he and his friend

Ratibor once stood behind one of these doors to look through a hole in the partition. After that he even dreamed once or twice about the two women they saw in the next-door cubicle, drying each other from top to toe, and when they were dry they began playing with one another . . . how long ago *was* that? A few months, or an eternity?

He shook off the memory; he didn't like it. Only now did he really look around him. The swimming pool looked as if it had only just been opened, not tatty the way he remembered it. Everything except the changing cubicles was freshly painted, and only the big diving platform was missing. There was just a wooden plank instead. He looked in vain for the ice-cream kiosk by the exit too.

But the little wooden hut where the pool attendant sat was exactly the same. I know my way around here, thought Robert, I'm practically at home here, nothing can really happen to me here. It's not like Siberia or the Australian bush.

It was clear as day *where* he had ended up this time. But *when*? That was the question. This wasn't his first experience of being pushed around in time. Maybe he didn't know how it happened, or why it affected him of all people, but he had to accept that it *did*, and the best he could do was try to make sure that it didn't happen too often. First, he realized it was risky to shed tears, and second, he mustn't rub his eyes or he might start the whole thing off again, which he didn't want.

He walked the few steps to the pool attendant's hut and peered into the dark room. The attendant's small chair was empty, but an advertising calendar hung on the wall behind it, showing a scantily clad blonde with bobbed hair sitting astride an inflatable dinghy. The wording underneath said: 'Paddle Your Klepper Boat Away To Summer'. The numbers on the calendar were too small for him to make them out, but above the coloured picture it said, quite clearly:

AUGUST 1930

Unimaginable! Over half a century before his birth! Robert turned resolutely towards the changing cubicles. The photographer was the first to reappear, followed by his friend the amorous Albert, now wearing a ridiculous pair of check plus-fours. Finally Lea came out too, looking pretty in a flowing white dress. Talking animatedly, the three of them made for the exit. Robert jumped the railings and got on his bike.

Outside, the trio had stopped beside a small, open two-seater, a stylish old BMW in two colours, blue and beige. The photographer got behind the wheel, Lea squeezed herself in beside him, and finally her boyfriend in his plus-fours got in too. Robert pedalled along behind them, but however hard he tried he had no chance of keeping up with the open car, and he soon lost sight of Lea's hair blowing in the wind.

Now what? Robert looked around him. In the heat of the chase he had taken very little notice of his surroundings, and he didn't recognize the road junction where he had stopped. The buildings looked old and black with soot. A tram rattled past, squealing as it went round the corner. There was an open platform at the back, and the passengers inside were sitting on a wooden bench. It looked tiny, almost like a toy! Everything seemed small, drab and colourless: the entrances and façades of the buildings, even the people. It was the same town he knew, and yet not the same. Instead of traffic lights, a policeman in a white helmet was directing the traffic. The few cars looked like black boxes and hooted excitedly, even though the streets were almost empty. A horse-drawn cart carrying sacks rumbled comfortably along through the city; the carter stopped at the crossing and spoke to the policeman, perhaps asking him the way. And the passers-by were so shabbily dressed!

The shops were quite different too. Robert had stopped outside a ladies' and gentlemen's outfitters with funny little display windows. The prices were on handwritten notices. You could buy a suit for only thirty-two marks. There were tall black mirrors to left and right of the entrance, with gold lettering on them saying:

Successors to Goldschmid Brothers
Founded 1872
Fine Fashions for Ladies and Gentlemen
Knitwear and Hosiery
Everything For
Young and Old!

The policeman waved his white glove imperiously, showing that Robert had right of way, and he cycled on. He was thirsty, and he stopped when he saw a little dairy a few streets further on – it was just a small stall near the tram stop, with the word

MILK

on it in fat white letters. A black slate said: 'Large Glass Full-Cream Milk With Chocolate Waffle 10 pfennigs'. How cheap everything was here! Robert asked for a waffle. It tasted really good.

He hadn't stopped to think how he would pay, but now he put his hand in his pocket to find some change. When he handed the woman in the white cap a ten-pfennig piece she stared in surprise, held the coin up to the light and then began yelling at him in a surprisingly deep voice, like the cannibal

83

in the puppet play. 'Toy money, is it, then? Fake money! You young rascal! What's the idea, you limb of Satan? You don't fool me, oh no, you don't fool me!'

Horrified, Robert looked at the rest of the change in his hand. Of course! These coins had been minted fifty or sixty years in the future, in a country the fat woman in her little dairy booth would never know, though she was holding the proof of its existence in her clenched fist as she leaned out of her little window and shouted for the police at the top of her voice.

Robert knew it would be useless to explain his mistake. He jumped on his bike and rode off as fast as he could without a backward glance. He could still hear the shouts of the woman he had cheated two streets away.

Gradually he began to get his bearings in his own home town, strangely different as it was. He had automatically set out for home, as he always did after spending the afternoon at the open-air pool. Not only did everything look much smaller than usual, as if seen through a pair of opera glasses held the wrong way round, it smelt different too – of soot and coal instead of petrol. And long before he had reached *his* part of town and *his* street, the houses ran out. Ahead of him, the yellow-painted iron tramcar drove round a loop in the tracks and stopped. This was the end of the line!

He cycled on, past wooden sheds and heaps of scrap metal, and came to some allotments with the odd name 'German Africa' on a notice outside. He was beginning to think he had lost his way when he saw the old gasworks behind the allotment gardens, and the water tower over to the left. But the street he went down every day wasn't where it should have been, or the telephone kiosk at the corner, or the super-market, and the building where his parents lived had gone. Or rather, it wasn't built yet. Stupid of him! He should have thought of that before. 'Nineteen thirty!' he said out loud. 'Nineteen thirty! Get that into your head, you idiot!'

An old man standing at the entrance to 'German Africa' with a big basket looked at him in surprise. Perhaps it was as well his home hadn't been built yet. He wouldn't have found his mother there anyway. When was she born? Some time after the war, 1950 or 1951 – he always forgot her birthday, and her feelings were always hurt. Well, it would be a waste of time looking for his parents. He'd have to think of something else.

It was already beginning to get dark. Robert wondered if he could spend the night in a hut on one of the allotments, but a glance over the fence told him that this was not a good idea. There were lights in most of the garden sheds, and dogs were barking all over the place. Some of the allotment gardeners actually seemed to live out here.

There was nothing he could do but go back into town. A hotel room, however cheap, was out of the question. He couldn't buy anything here with late twentieth-century Deutschmarks. The inner city was badly lit, with small gas flames, yellow and tinged with blue, flickering in the street lights. There were no neon ads anywhere, and if the buildings hadn't been so old and crooked his home town might have reminded him of Russia. Even the railway station wasn't the same. Instead of being all steel and glass, it looked like an outsized villa painted in yellow ochre. Robert got off his bike and went into the booking hall. There wasn't much going on this evening. Late travellers were on their way to the platforms. An old man in a ragged jacket was lying on a bench, but an official in a blue cap immediately appeared and shooed him off. Without a word the old man picked up his bundle and slunk away.

'Where's the Travellers' Aid?' Robert asked the official, thinking of the modern organization for helping rail passengers in difficulties.

The man looked at him suspiciously. 'Travellers' Aid? Never heard of it. If you mean the Salvation Army it's over there, other side of the square, third street on the left.'

The Salvation Army! Robert would never have thought of it, but perhaps he could spend the night there? He took his bike and rode off. The tunnel-shaped room was crowded and stuffy. It contained a long table with a number of men sitting at it, many of them in blue overalls but most in shabby, much-mended suits. The old man from the station was there too. They all stared at Robert as if he were very much out of place here. Looking down at himself, he understood what they were thinking. His freshly ironed linen suit stood out like a sore thumb in these surroundings. To look at him, no one would have thought that he didn't have a penny in his pocket – or not a penny he could spend *here*, anyway.

A woman at the end of the table rose to her feet. She had a brisk manner, and two boys in smart red and blue caps stood beside her. They all wore Salvation Army uniform. Someone fetched a music stand, and they started singing a cheerful marching song about the goodness of God and happiness in the future. Some of the older men sang along with them, out of tune. Then there were prayers. A talkative bald-headed man, standing next to Robert and telling a stream of jokes, received a reproachful look from the lieutenant – that was the rank of the woman in charge of the prayer meeting. She concluded with a short speech about unemployment and the housing shortage, saying that these evils were a severe trial, but those who faced them bravely would find that God was with them.

Now a hatch was opened at the back of the room, and everyone immediately clustered around the little window. Two uniformed women ladled out hot soup. Robert stood at the very back of the queue. He didn't feel good about this.

Would there be a room with a bed for him here? He dared not ask.

After the soup the woman lieutenant, who was obviously used to being in charge and had a small moustache on her upper lip, clattered her bunch of keys and gave instructions.

'You know the house rules. Absolute quiet overnight, please! You'll be woken at six. Everyone makes his bed and folds the blankets, and I want you all out of here by six-thirty. Good night.'

The men obediently shuffled after her. Their dormitory was a long room with its walls painted brown. There were iron bedsteads in a straight line, each with three bunks like a sleeping compartment in a train. An argument about the best beds began at once. Were they the upper or lower bunks, or the beds by the window? Robert had no idea, and just took what was left over. A musty smell rose from the bedclothes, and soon the first sleepers began snoring, but Robert was too tired to let that disturb him, and slept well.

When the alarm went off at six in the morning he was still bemused with exhaustion, and he was just about to rub his eyes when he remembered that it might get him into deep trouble. The stink took his breath away. A night in the Salvation Army hostel wasn't such a pleasant prospect as a night at Annaby with Caroline just two doors away, but if he got caught in the whirlpool of time again, where would he fetch up next? He cautiously dabbed the sleep from his eyes with the corner of a towel in the bathroom where the men stood at a long zinc tub, having a brief wash. Those who had little mirrors shaved, or parted their hair. They were the optimists who still believed the future held something for them.

In the dining room they were each given a tin cup and a piece of bread. The hot drink tasted horrible. It was the first time Robert had drunk coffee made from malt. The woman lieutenant rattled her bunch of keys, and then he was out in the street again.

'My bike! Where's my bike?'

The others just laughed. He hadn't even padlocked it. No wonder some poor soul went off with it, thought Robert, and strictly speaking it wasn't mine anyway. I just found myself on the saddle when I arrived from Australia, goodness knows how.

He searched his pockets distractedly, but there was no more chewing gum in them. Of course, he'd finished his last piece in that cinema – where was it? Oh yes, in Russia. Instead, he brought a crumpled piece of green paper out of his pocket. His twenty-dollar bill! He'd entirely forgotten it. Perhaps it would still be worth something. There'd always been dollars, surely? Most American films featured them. *In God we trust!* Dollar bills always looked the same.

He went along a few more streets until he reached the city centre, where he had a pleasant surprise. He recognized the handsome old bank building next to the opera house, and not much else had changed in the square either. He wandered around until the bank opened at nine. Inside, there was a glass dome over the main hall, with stained glass pictures like something in a church or a museum. Hesitantly, he handed the cashier his twenty-dollar bill. The man glanced at it, held it up to the light, and without more ado gave him a few banknotes and coins. 'Exchange rate of four-twenty to the dollar, less one mark commission, that makes exactly eighty-three marks. There you are, sir.'

Outside on a bench Robert took a closer look at the money. The brown notes said 'Reichsmark', not 'Deutschmark', and the coins were real silver.

Well, he was solvent again for the moment. At least, he

worked out that he could have bought two and a half gentlemen's suits from Goldschmid Brothers for eighty-three marks, so this must be enough money to last him a few days at least.

Robert decided his priority was a proper breakfast. He went into the Opera Café and ordered real coffee and two scrambled eggs with ham. The café did not look at all shabby; in fact it was rather grand. The elderly ladies sitting drinking hot chocolate with cream wore large hats trimmed with flowers and black or white veils, and white lace gloves. Eighty-three Reichsmarks made all the difference between the Opera Café and the Salvation Army hostel for the homeless!

When he had finished eating, Robert made a plan. If he couldn't visit his own parents, and he certainly didn't have parents here, then what about his grandparents? He'd always been good at mental arithmetic. He didn't know much about their lives, but although his maternal grandfather had died ages ago his grandmother had celebrated her seventy-fifth birthday only a few years back, before moving into the residential home. So she'd be a child of nine or ten now. Incredible! But absurd as the idea might be, he began to relish it. Robert the private detective! He liked the idea, and surely he could find out where she lived. With her own parents, presumably. With Robert's own *great*-grandparents. What a weird thought! He also remembered that his grandmother's maiden name was Scherz.

He called the waiter. 'Do you have a city address book here?' he asked, very much the professional detective.

'Yes, of course, sir!' You certainly couldn't complain of the service, for the waiter helpfully brought the fat volume over. There were four different Scherzes listed. One was described as Senior Regional Court Councillor, Retd., so Robert could forget about him. Then there was a woman stage designer and a furniture factory. Neither of them sounded very probable.

In fact the only likely candidate was Police Sergeant Friedrich Scherz who lived on the second floor of the back building at 22 Möbius Street. There was no phone number, but even if there had been, how could Robert have introduced himself? 'This is your great-grandson Robert speaking!' No, impossible.

The address was not difficult to find, but when Robert made his way to the drab block of rented flats he wasn't sure what to do next. Keep watch on the place? Easily said, but very boring after a bit. Find out more? Yes, but where from? There wasn't a soul in sight on the quiet street, only a woman with a careworn face and elbows propped on a red cushion in a window in the building opposite, watching closely as he walked undecidedly up and down. He supposed he was the only novelty around here; the woman would know everything else by heart – the pub called the Green Oak on the corner (although there was no oak in sight anywhere), the advertising pillar in front of it, the small, sleepy-looking laundry ('Hot Mangle Available – Use Our Service!'), with a dachshund lying in the sun in its doorway.

Robert took cover behind the advertising pillar and read the ads on it:

The German People Unite To Reject
Lies About the War Debt!

Sensational Success!
The Blue Angel
WITH MARLENE DIETRICH AND EMIL JANNINGS
A Unique Sound Motion Picture Experience!

And beneath this hung a bright yellow poster with large lettering. Robert read it:

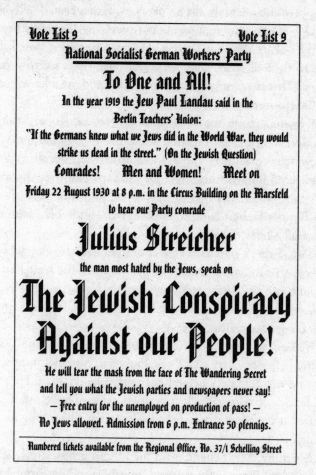

Vote List 9   **Vote List 9**

National Socialist German Workers' Party

To One and All!

In the year 1919 the Jew Paul Landau said in the
Berlin Teachers' Union:
"If the Germans knew what we Jews did in the World War, they would
strike us dead in the street." (On the Jewish Question)

Comrades!   **Men and Women!**   **Meet on**

Friday 22 August 1930 at 8 p.m. in the Circus Building on the Marsfeld
to hear our Party comrade

Julius Streicher

the man most hated by the Jews, speak on

The Jewish Conspiracy Against our People!

He will tear the mask from the face of The Wandering Secret
and tell you what the Jewish parties and newspapers never say!
— Free entry for the unemployed on production of pass! —
No Jews allowed. Admission from 6 p.m. Entrance 50 pfennigs.

Numbered tickets available from the Regional Office, No. 37/1 Schelling Street

What daft ideas they had about the Jews then, thought Robert! Totally weird! His father kept going on about it, and they'd been shown pictures of the gas chambers in history lessons at school. He felt sick at the sight of those piles of corpses. But his history teacher was really keen on everything Jewish, and if someone on television was a Jew they always made a big point of saying so. How did they know, anyway? Jewish people looked exactly the same as everyone else. The whole thing was a mystery to him, but here was this disgusting poster on the corner of a quiet street. He tried to tear it down, but it was so well stuck that he could only rip a narrow strip away. There was stickiness left on his hand, and he wiped it on his trousers.

A woman came out of the door of No. 22. Robert was on the alert at once. She must be about forty years old, possibly a few years younger, but it was hard to tell because of the embittered look on her face. Or perhaps embittered wasn't the right word: anxious or careworn, as if life here wasn't much fun. Robert would have agreed with her. She was carrying a heavy basket.

It was her – it had to be! He couldn't have said exactly why he was so sure, since she certainly wasn't in the least like his elegant mother. But something about her, maybe the way she walked or raised her head, made him certain that this woman was his great-grandmother.

Without stopping to think, he hurried up to her and said, 'Can I help you carry that?' She looked at him in amazement, as if no one had ever helped her with a heavy load. He took the laundry basket, which contained a pile of bedclothes, and carried it the short distance to the laundry advertising its hot mangle.

'Morning, Mrs Scherz,' said the plump proprietress. So he was right! There were ironing boards standing around the steamy room, and at the back he saw a machine with black rollers. 'How're you doing, then?'

'Thanks very much,' said Mrs Scherz to Robert. Great-grandmother – suddenly the word sounded childish, like something out of a fairy-tale. It certainly didn't seem right for someone who, he now saw, was thirty at the most. He began thinking of her simply as Mrs Scherz. He stood by the open door, listening to the two women talking. That was what he was here for, after all. Private detectives have to snoop or they don't get anywhere.

'Oh, only so-so, you know how it is, Mrs Novak. I'm afraid you'll have to put this on tick again. We're always short at the end of the month, and now our lodger's moved out. Couldn't afford the rent any more.'

'Well, your husband's in the police. You can think yourself lucky. Mine's not so well off. If you knew what . . .'

'I'll bring you the money on the first of the month, don't worry. Can I fetch the things tomorrow?'

'After three, Mrs Scherz. Goodbye, then.'

When Mrs Scherz left the laundry, Robert followed, and spoke to her just as she reached the door of her building.

'Excuse me, but I couldn't help hearing you have a room to let. I've been looking for something suitable for a day or so.'

She looked closely at him, but he seemed to pass her scrutiny. 'Well, it's only a small room,' she said. 'And we can't let it for less than a month. Do you want to see it?'

The flat was on the second floor at the back of the building, and was tidy if rather bare. Obviously the Scherzes weren't very well off. Robert got a glimpse of the kitchen. There was a little room beyond it, not much bigger than a broom cupboard, with a child's bed and a doll enthroned on it. This must be his granny's room. She was probably at school now. The lodger's room was tiny too, with just one window, giving a view of a wall to prevent the spread of fire and a straggly maple tree in the back yard. It contained a bed, a bedside table, a chair, a wardrobe, a small kitchen table – and that was all.

Robert was perfectly happy with it. 'What do you charge?' he asked.

'Well, the gentleman we had here before paid thirteen marks,' said Mrs Scherz.

'I'll give you fifteen,' said Robert, without a second thought. He saw how delighted she was, and felt sad. Just for two marks more! These people must be having a really tough time. He vaguely remembered the words *world-wide economic crisis*, and now he began to grasp what they actually meant. The Salvation Army hostel, no money for the laundry, a scratched kitchen table for a lodger who couldn't afford the rent any more. Robert guessed that the screaming headlines on the posters he'd seen were all connected with it too.

'You can move in tomorrow, Mr . . . ?'

'Just call me Robert, Mrs Scherz.'

'Very well. I'll have to turn the room out and put clean sheets on the bed. Breakfast's included, of course.'

'I'll give you the first month's rent in advance,' said Robert, and once again he felt quite sad to see how pleased she was.

He spent the rest of the day wandering around the town centre, and ate some braised beef in a smoke-filled restaurant with dark tiles. When he came out, he saw that the sky had become overcast, and a violent thunderstorm soon broke. He took refuge in a department store, where he bought a raincoat. When evening came he found a cheap guesthouse. The proprietor looked at him suspiciously because of his lack of luggage, but seemed satisfied when he paid in advance for a night's lodging.

The room was very uncomfortable. No sooner had Robert thrown himself on the bed to rest than he heard music in the room next door. It was so loud that he could make out the words:

'It's a dance with fire, it's a dance with passion,
and it costs you nothing, so it's sure in fashion.
Even now the times are hard
The tango's a dance we can all afford.'

The song had a slushy, sentimental tune, and sounded scratchy. The man in the room next to Robert's had a gramophone, one of those old things with a big black horn, and the record must be the kind that turned very fast and finished playing in a few minutes. Robert had seen something like that in the Museum of Technology. The man must be besotted with his gramophone, because he kept playing the same record over and over again.

Finally he stopped, and Robert planned his next step. He couldn't move in with the Scherz family without a few basic necessities. How long would he be there – months? Years, even? A depressing thought. Well, at least he must have a toothbrush, a comb, soap and toothpaste. His good linen suit was looking rather the worse for wear too. Socks, a couple of shirts, a second pair of shoes – that would be the minimum. He counted his money. He had only thirty-eight marks and a few pfennigs left, but if he was careful that should last a week. He'd have to earn some more – but how? There were crowds of unemployed around already.

Once again he turned out all his pockets and lined up his possessions on the bedspread. Perhaps some of them might be worth money? His watch, for instance. He knew there was a pawnbroker's in every town of any size, where you could pledge your valuables when you needed money – not that you'd want to. And I don't know if the watch is worth anything, he thought.

Then his glance fell on a piece of sandstone that he must have picked up somewhere or other. A reddish, irregularly shaped lump of rock, not much bigger than a matchbox. Oh yes, that was all he'd brought back from his long expedition in the bush with old Crombie. What a fiasco! He turned the stone back and forth, and saw a deep crack running through it. He held it under the dim yellow glass shade of the ceiling light, which was so weak that he couldn't make anything out. He tried his lighter. When he held the flickering little flame very close to the crack, he saw something shimmering inside the stone, a thin stratum changing from blue to green. Held at a certain angle, it even had a fiery red glow. He peered incredulously at the narrow crack until the lighter was too hot to hold. Could he possibly have picked up something after all when he was digging at random in the dumps at Cowper's Winch? What was it kind old Bill had said? 'Even a blind chicken sometimes finds a grain of corn.'

If there really was an opal inside this chunk of sandstone, then he'd be all right for the time being. Robert fell asleep torn between doubt and hope.

Early in the morning the yowling of the gramophone woke him again.

> 'She bought a little pussy cat
> in Angora for a song
> and she showed it, showed it, showed it,
> showed it to me all night long.'

Fed up with listening to this kind of thing, Robert got out of bed, splashed his face with cold water from the enamel basin – there was no tap – picked up his raincoat and his other things and left the Excelsior guesthouse.

He couldn't take his find to the pawnshop. They'd simply laugh at him if he put a lump of rock on the counter, and he wasn't sure if it was worth anything. What did he know about gemstones? Perhaps it was just fool's gold he was carrying around in his pocket.

He rather liked the clattering tram, and took it to the city centre. The first thing he bought was a travelling bag. His cash began to shrink alarmingly as he gradually filled it with the bare necessities – shirts, socks, toilet things.

Out in the market place, he looked for the big department store on the corner, but in vain. Of course, that ten-storey concrete block wouldn't look right here. It wasn't due to be built until after the war, on the site at present occupied by stalls selling toys and pottery.

There it was again – that sense of confusion. It made his head ache when he really stopped to think about it. The past was a distant country. Robert's father often talked about what the city looked like after the Second World War. The whole of the Old Town must have been a vast heap of rubble after the fierce air raids. As a boy of five, said Robert's father, he used to play among the ruins before they were cleared to make room for new buildings.

Beyond the fruit market stood a handsome nineteenth-century building, its yellow walls ornamented with huge, muscular statues supporting the weight of the balconies and bay windows on the first floor. The ground floor arcade contained some very stylish-looking shops. Elegant gold lettering above one of them said

SALOMON HIRSCHBERG

and below it, in smaller lettering, were the words

ROYAL COURT JEWELLER

Robert knew that name. The blue velvet lining of Lea's jewel case! Her emerald necklace! It must be more than coincidence. He spent some time standing in front of the display window, which contained some very expensive items arranged against a black background. Then, plucking up all his courage, he went in.

A small, thin man, who stooped slightly as he sat behind a small glass-topped table, rose, offered Robert a chair, and asked how he could help him. Could this be Mr Hirschberg in person? He had a slight tic around his eyes, a nervous twitch, but he spoke courteously.

'Look,' said Robert, producing his lump of sandstone. 'I wanted to show you this. I thought maybe as an expert you could tell me if it's worth anything.'

The jeweller took the stone in his hand and held it up to the light. Then he wedged a black magnifying glass into his left eye, turned the piece of stone this way and that, clicked his tongue, and put it down on a black velvet cushion in front of him.

'Interesting,' he said. 'May I ask where you got this stone?'

Robert hesitated. It was no good; he'd have to tell another lie.

'A seagoing friend of mine brought it back from Australia for me.'

'Indeed – and I presume you have brought it to me because you think there may be more to it than one would think at first glance. You could be right, too. But I can hardly tell with the naked eye. I can examine your stone in my laboratory, if you like.'

'I'd be very grateful, Mr Hirschberg.' Robert was guessing that this was Mr Hirschberg himself, and he had obviously guessed right, since the jeweller only said, 'Then will you come back tomorrow morning, please? Goodbye.'

Robert was sweating with excitement, not just at the idea that he might have been successful as a noodler, but because he was on Lea's trail too. Who could have given her the emerald necklace made by Salomon Hirschberg? Her friend Albert from the open-air swimming pool, who acted as if he had some kind of claim on her? Or Geoffrey? But no, how could Geoffrey have been here in Robert's home town? And didn't Lea say her father had given her the necklace? This was another puzzle he decided he must solve.

But first he must see about his lodgings. He spent what was left of his money on a teddy bear for his grandmother.

They were expecting him already in Möbius Street. 'This is my Magda,' said Mrs Scherz. Grandmother was about ten years old and very shy, but when she saw the cuddly toy it broke the ice. 'Say thank you,' her mother reminded her, like mothers everywhere. The child didn't want to; she just did a little bob and looked in wonder at Robert with her bright blue eyes. He knew that penetrating blue gaze. Magda still had it, even in old age. Whenever he visited her in the residential home her eyes shone like that, although she usually couldn't remember his name these days.

'My name's Robert,' he told the little girl. 'I'm going to live here for a while, so I thought I'd bring you a present. I hope we'll be friends.'

Mrs Scherz took him into the living room, where a heavy sideboard had pride of place. A brown wooden box stood on it, flanked by two flower vases. Robert realized that it was a radio. The grandfather clock in the corner struck five times, with a muted sound.

'Can I offer you a coffee?' Robert shuddered at the thought

of the malt coffee he'd drunk in the Salvation Army hostel, and politely declined. He felt slightly ashamed, since his hostess undoubtedly meant well, but that malty brew had made him feel quite sick.

'Robert's our new lodger,' Mrs Scherz told his little grandmother. 'That reminds me – you never told me your surname.'

'Oh, never mind that. Just call me Robert. I mean, I'm not the usual sort of lodger. I'm only fifteen, and still at school, so do please use my first name.'

For some reason Robert didn't want to tell her his surname, and he was beginning to feel awkward about calling her Mrs Scherz all the time. After all, they were related, even if she couldn't know it.

'Just as you like, Robert. When does your school term start? Magda went back to school a week ago.'

He hadn't thought of that. 'Oh, in a couple of days' time,' he said, since nothing better occurred to him. But then what? He could see she'd make sure he set off for school at seven-thirty on the dot, missed no lessons and did his homework. That was what came of taking lodgings with his own family!

Magda was playing with her teddy bear, oblivious to all else, and Robert went to his room to unpack. He heard the door of the flat open and shut. Then there were heavy footsteps in the corridor. Robert listened.

'Robert,' called his great-grandmother, 'could you come here a moment? My husband would like to meet you.'

Sergeant Scherz was standing in full uniform in the middle of the room. He wore a funny kind of police helmet with his green uniform. As he took off his belt, his pistol and finally this helmet, sighing, he looked at Robert and Robert looked at him. One thing was immediately obvious: they had not taken a liking to each other.

'So you're the new lodger,' said the sergeant. There was a pause. To think the man was called Scherz, meaning 'joke' in German! There could hardly have been a less suitable name for this dour character.

'Where did you get that?' he asked little Magda, who looked at him in alarm and clutched her bear tight.

'Robert gave it to her. It was very nice of him, Friedrich.'

'You'll spoil the child,' growled her father. 'Presents are for Christmas. Off to bed you go, Magda.'

Robert thought it best to go out, and they gave him a key. As he left the flat he could still hear Mrs Scherz trying to pacify her husband. 'He paid a whole month's rent in advance,' she was saying. Clearly the policeman had no reply to this argument.

Robert had to admit that his generosity had been a mistake, since now he was broke again. He simply wasn't any good with money. He wandered around town until late in the evening, his stomach grumbling because he couldn't go to a restaurant. Next morning he was glad of his bread and margarine for breakfast, and the milk he asked for instead of that horrible malt coffee. The master of the house hadn't put in an appearance yet. He'd probably be resting after a long shift of duty.

Robert couldn't even afford a tram ticket, and it was nine o'clock by the time he reached Mr Hirschberg's jeweller's shop. A boy was just pulling up the grille in front of the display window. Robert walked nervously up and down the arcade. He felt like tossing a coin or casting dice to find out how the opal story would end. He imagined his embarrassment if Mr Hirschberg just laughed at him. 'My dear young friend, who's been pulling your leg? The inclusion in the stone here is just an ordinary bit of mica.' What a fiasco that would be!

But that was not the kind of way Salomon Hirschberg spoke to his customers. He was smiling as he asked Robert to sit down.

'I must say I'm surprised, sir,' he began. 'To be honest, I've never come across anything like this before. Here's your rock sample.' He unwrapped the piece of stone from a small silk cloth and set it in front of Robert. 'I had to split your find, naturally. Look, this is the matrix, and here's the black opal. You can only see a very small part of it, of course. We'll get a better look at it once we've freed it from its prison, but it gave up its secrets under fluorescent light. I can already tell it has a deep base tone, a brilliant play of colour, hardly any inclusions, excellent transparency. With luck it will yield a fifteen-carat stone, maybe even seventeen carats, depending how it's cut.'

Robert could hardly contain his excitement. He felt like jumping up and dancing for joy, but that was not the way to behave in Mr Hirschberg's shop. He mustn't show any emotion.

'And its value, Mr Hirschberg? What would you say it's worth? I mean, I have no use for it myself, and you could certainly make it into a very beautiful piece of jewellery.'

He was surprised to hear how calmly he brought out these words, just like a man of the world with experience in such matters.

But before the jeweller could answer, a woman came through a padded door behind the display cases, saying, 'Sorry, Papa, I just wanted to say goodbye! We're off! Albert's put all the luggage in the car.'

It was Lea, the beautiful Mrs Sutton! Robert bit back the words on the tip of his tongue – 'Don't you recognize me, Lea?' She'd put a round case made of white morocco leather down on the little table and was kissing her father, who had hurried over to her. The case was a hatbox – Robert had never seen one except in movies.

'Look at this, Lea. Most interesting! An Australian opal, still inside the matrix. A very fine stone indeed. This gentleman brought it in.'

Lea cast Robert an unfathomable glance. Was she remembering the scene at the open-air swimming pool? Or could some presentiment have flashed through her mind? For a moment she closed her eyes. Perhaps, thought Robert, perhaps she was seeing a dim picture, like a Polaroid photo not yet fully developed, of herself sitting in a room on the other side of the world, drinking tea with him while he admired her necklace of emeralds lying on their bed of blue velvet in a box inscribed 'Salomon Hirschberg, Royal Court Jeweller'.

But the moment passed. She nodded politely at him, whispered something in her father's ear, picked up the hatbox and hurried out, full of pleasurable anticipation. Robert watched her leave. The little BMW with its open hood was waiting for her outside. She waved to her father once more, got into the car, Albert started it, and she disappeared.

'Do forgive me,' said Hirschberg. 'You were asking what your stone is worth. Hard to say . . . somewhere between six hundred and eight hundred marks, I'd think. Of course I'm interested in the stone, but . . .'

'If I leave it with you, could you give me a deposit?' asked Robert quickly. 'I'd trust your judgement.'

'Would you be happy with an advance of three hundred marks for the time being?'

Robert agreed at once, although the sum struck him as ridiculously small. Three hundred marks! Why, he had that much in his savings account at home. But then, just in time, he remembered that the same sum was a fortune here, where no one seemed to have any money and you could buy a raincoat for only a few marks. As he stood outside the shop with the crisp new notes in his pocket, his feelings were strangely mixed. Yes, he'd been lucky, he was rich. But at the same time he was sad because he knew he would never see Lea again.

Life in Möbius Street fell into a routine. Mrs Scherz woke him every morning at six-thirty so that he wouldn't be late for school, and what could he do but go along with the pretence? He fell into the habit of spending his mornings in the municipal library. Whether he liked it or not, he had to get used to the past that was his present now, and the news-papers and leaflets in the library were a help. 1930 – what a turbulent time it was! He couldn't make out why these people were so angry with each other. Even in the quiet reading room you got an idea of all the denunciation and agitation going on, the kind of thing suggested by the poster he'd seen outside the Green Oak. Sergeant Scherz adopted the same unpleasant tone when he came home. He was always ordering his wife and daughter about. Robert avoided the flat at this time of day; he went out walking, and ate in the evening at a small restaurant where he was soon welcomed as a regular.

In the afternoon he often talked to little Magda, who had overcome her shyness and trusted him. He got on well with Mrs Scherz too, and they soon reached the stage where she asked him to call her just Wanda. Her solicitude was rather a nuisance, but he couldn't stay in his bleak little room all the time. He needed her company and she needed his, because she was afraid of her husband, and when the sergeant was there she felt lonelier than ever.

One day, looking for a shoe that had slipped under the bed, Robert found a box there, painted black and locked. Had the last lodger left it by mistake? He asked Wanda, who seemed embarrassed. 'It's for your own good, Robert,' she said at last. 'There's one under my bed too. It's because of the earth rays, you see. They're very strong around here. They make you sleep poorly, and they're bad for your health if you don't do anything about them.'

Robert had never heard of earth rays, but he gradually discovered that Wanda held a whole series of peculiar beliefs. She lent him a magazine she took. 'You have to protect yourself against these mysterious forces and make sure the good spirits are on your side,' she assured him.

The magazine was called *The White Flag*, and Robert clutched his head as he read it. The articles were about the art of divining the future with a swinging pendulum, and clairvoyance, and all kinds of conspiracies. An advertisement described the danger of earth rays and offered the apparatus under his bed for 'only 32 Reichsmarks, cash on delivery, or if preferred ten convenient instalments of 3.50 RM, money back if not completely satisfied'.

Obviously his great-grandmother was very superstitious. When she was out shopping Robert found a screwdriver and opened the box. It held nothing but a few wires, a capacitor, a coil with copper winding and an old-fashioned radio antenna. The parts were wired together in a circuit that made no sense at all. And poor Wanda had been swindled into paying 32 marks for this rubbish!

Robert screwed up the box again and decided not to say anything about it. The money was gone, and there was no point in undeceiving her. Who knows, perhaps she really did sleep better with this ridiculous thing under her bed? Maybe it helped her to forget her troubles, at least by night, and that was worth something, after all.

One day, when little Magda wasn't at home, he had a talk with her mother. 'Look, I happen to have some spare money, Wanda,' he told her. 'You're welcome to it. I mean, I know you're short of housekeeping money.' For by now Mr Hirschberg had given him another four hundred marks, and the black opal was already shining in his window, set in a white gold ring.

Wanda stared in astonishment at the three 100-mark notes on the table in front of her.

'I did a couple of good deals,' Robert reassured her. 'Only you mustn't tell your husband. You know how suspicious he is.'

'For heaven's sake!' she cried. 'I can't possibly take it! God knows what sort of deals you mean! I don't want anything to do with them!'

He saw how upset she was, and had an idea.

'Shall I tell you a secret? Promise not to tell anyone else? Not even your best friend.'

She stared at him, wide-eyed.

'I solemnly promise,' she whispered.

'It's quite simple – I have the second sight,' announced Robert. 'Well, not always, just sometimes, before I fall asleep.'

Strictly speaking this was not entirely a lie, since he really did know the future, or at least a few scraps of it.

'Think what that means!' he went on. 'If you know in advance what questions the teacher is going to ask you don't have to worry about exams. You're always sure to get good marks. And it's the same with money. You know in advance if shares will rise or fall, so you can always make a profit.' In fact he knew nothing whatsoever about the stock market, but there was no need to say so.

Wanda Scherz believed him implicitly. Robert was too pleased with the idea that had occurred to him to notice how she was staring at him, hanging on his every word. He wasn't just a helpless victim tossed around from place to place like a parcel after all. Wherever he landed he'd know more than anyone else; he knew what was going to happen in the future, and the power that gave him was both alarming and exciting. His great-grandmother asked, anxiously, whether he didn't find such a gift a great burden. Robert thought for a while. 'Yes,' he said. 'Sometimes I have horrible presentiments. I see flames coming out of the buildings, and this whole city burning. There'll be a lot of dead people. Don't *you* feel something's going to happen? All this fuss in the newspapers, and posters everywhere! It can't end well. You must be prepared for anything to happen, Wanda. I'm telling you this in confidence: there'll be a war, and you'll have to take good care of little Magda. I'd rather not say anything about your husband.'

Perhaps he should have spared himself that last remark; he had never heard his grandmother mention her father. Why not? Had he joined the SS? Did he have some kind of shady record? Robert didn't know what to think, and was slightly ashamed of himself for being ready to believe the worst of the police sergeant just because he didn't like him.

Wanda was scared to death, but fascinated too. He went to some pains to soothe her fears. 'Listen, you must hide the money somewhere safe, and spend it in secret when you really need it. I know you *will* be needing it some time.'

Luckily Magda came home just then, otherwise he wouldn't have known how to bring this conversation to an end. From now on his great-grandmother regarded him as a powerful magician, and he had to put up with both her awe and her admiration. At least she no longer ventured to ask him about his school homework, which was a relief.

The monotonous life Robert was leading began to bore him. What was he doing here, anyway? He went to the cinema, the museum, the library. Once he even visited a dance-hall, where black musicians were playing the latest hits. There was a loud saxophone, and a woman in a tight dress glittering with sequins sang:

> 'She bought a little pussy cat
> in Angora for a song
> and she showed it, showed it, showed it . . .'

He knew that song already. A thin girl asked him to dance, and he let her lead him on to the dance floor, which was lit from below. After the first dance she said she'd like to drink a bottle of sparkling wine with him, and called him 'sweetie-pie'. Robert drank one glass of wine and left the place in a hurry.

He spent whole afternoons in the open-air swimming pool. When he was lying in the sun, eyes closed, listening to the children squealing under the cold shower and the shouts of the water polo players, he felt at home. He almost thought he sensed Ratibor's shadow as his friend leaned over to tickle him with a blade of grass, but of course that was nonsense. He wouldn't even see Lea again, although she had been here only a couple of weeks ago. The man called Albert had taken her away as if they were married. Perhaps they were on their honeymoon. Something about Albert reminded Robert of Michael – a touch of arrogance, and those big ears! Or was he just imagining things? Michael was a year older than his half-sister. So he must have been born – Robert did a quick sum in his head – he must have been born in 1931. It certainly seemed that Geoffrey wasn't his father.

He did not pursue the idea. Why try to ferret out Lea's family secrets? She'd been so kind and welcoming from the first, when he was standing on that film set like a piece of lost luggage. In his mind's eye he pictured the kitchen at Annaby where they always had breakfast, old Crombie's forge, the stables – he saw them all with a sharp-edged clarity that tormented him whenever he gave his memory free rein. Why did he have to remember that cup, the big nail in the wall where Caroline's saddle húng, the mother-of-pearl buttons on her dress? He dived into the water and stayed under until the images had disappeared from his mind.

When he got back he saw at once that someone had been in his room. The drawer of the bedside table was open, his books were on the bed, his wristwatch lying on the floor. He went into the living room. The policeman was standing in front of the sideboard. Wanda was sitting at the table with her hands over her ears, and little Magda was clutching her teddy bear and crying.

'What's going on?' asked Robert. 'Someone's been searching my things. I'm being spied on.'

'I searched them,' shouted Sergeant Scherz. 'And you're a fine one to talk about spying! What's this, eh?'

He held out a small book and a round object. The stamp! Robert had quite forgotten it. The KGB stamp from Moscow, and his Russian dictionary!

'It's nothing to do with you!' cried Robert, beside himself with rage.

'I'm only doing my duty!' Sergeant Scherz shouted back. 'My duty as a citizen and a police officer! You worm your way into my home without any papers, with no proper notification! And what do I find in your luggage? An official stamp belonging to the Bolshevist secret service! I may not know Russian, but I can tell that much.'

'Oh, Friedrich!' protested his wife. 'Robert's such a nice, well-behaved young man. I'm sure he can explain where he got these things. I mean, it's not a crime to own a Russian dictionary.'

'And where does all this money come from? Can you tell me that?' He waved Robert's remaining three 100-mark notes in the air. Only now did Robert realize that they were missing from his room too.

'You've no right to take my money!' he said, white with anger, and snatched the notes from the man's hand.

'It's his wages, the traitor!' cried the sergeant. 'The fellow's in the pay of the Russians!'

'Oh, this is too much!' said Robert, and he left the room. He threw his few possessions in his travelling bag – shirts, toothbrushes, his money and his other bits and pieces, all jumbled up anyhow, put the door-key on his bed and left the flat. He slammed the door behind him with a sigh of relief. As he went down the stairs he could still hear the sergeant and his wife quarrelling. The man was shouting and his great-grandmother was weeping. Robert had had enough of the pair of them.

He took a taxi to the big hotel near Mr Hirschberg the jeweller's shop. Tomorrow is another day, he said to himself.

But next day the sky was grey and Robert didn't know what to do. He must find new lodgings, but what was the point? Lea had gone away. He had no friends here. Where could he turn? Nobody needed him or took any notice of him. The hotel room was comfortable, but there wasn't even a television set to distract his mind. The year 1930 was definitely not a good choice, he thought – as if he'd picked the destination for himself.

After wasting the morning doing nothing much in his room, he left the hotel. It was drizzling, and he turned up the collar of his raincoat. He felt in his pockets for the old junk he carried around with him: his watch, the toy car, the crumpled Polaroid picture. He didn't take it out; it would only have depressed him. Ratibor had gone out of his life for good. But useless as his souvenirs were he was glad he'd kept them; they were the only tangible proof that he was still himself, Robert.

He came to a small square that was new to him. A rather restless crowd had assembled on the scanty grass in the middle of the square. There must have been about 500 people there, pressed close together in front of a platform guarded by a line of uniformed men. On the platform, a wind band was playing a loud march, and a number of the people were singing along with it. He could make out only a few words, about being 'forced to starve' and 'the last battle'. Then the man in the middle, who was wearing a Chairman Mao cap, began making a speech. He barked out short sentences in an excited manner, and whenever he stopped for breath the people in the first row shouted 'Up with the Red Front!' and punched the air with their clenched fists.

Robert supposed they were Communists, but he could make out almost nothing of the speech. Looking around, he noticed that police cordons had positioned themselves at the sides of the square.

Another band could now be heard in the distance – drums and pipes, coming closer and closer. 'Watch out!' someone shouted. Robert saw a police officer in the background put a whistle to his mouth. The speaker on the platform stopped, and he too called out a warning or an order of some kind to his audience. A number of determined-looking young men made their way through the crowd. The audience turned away from the platform and followed. Robert saw that some of them were armed with wooden cudgels.

Meanwhile the procession with the drummers had reached the police cordon. Its leaders wore light brown uniforms and caps that looked like little wooden boxes. People at the back were chanting in chorus. 'Germany arise! Death to the Jews!'

'Down with Fascism!' the Communists shouted back. They were all raising their arms to punch the air now. Robert, who took no interest in these rowdy fanatics and their slogans, wondered why he kept getting involved in riots. This was the second time; he'd seen it all before in Siberia. Although in Siberia he'd known that right was on the side of the people facing the tanks, whereas here it was just two sets of shabbily dressed people marching on each other, their faces distorted with rage. It looked as if they had nothing better to do than kill each other, and only the police would be able to stop them.

But the first Nazis were already breaking through the cordon, attacking their opponents with cries of 'Sieg Heil!' The policemen drew their rubber truncheons, but they had no chance against this furious crowd. Robert saw one of them flung to the ground, and for a moment he thought he recognized Sergeant Scherz. Perhaps I did the man wrong, he thought fleetingly, but then he forgot him, for the other policemen had taken to their heels, and he found himself jammed in a crowd of people all bashing each other. He, Robert, who always avoided even a harmless scuffle in the playground at school! He had to get out of here, fast!

Robert succeeded in freeing himself from the throng of fighting men, and thought he was out of the worst of it when something struck the back of his head. He lost his balance and fell over. A droning noise inside his skull mingled with the yelling from the street fight. He got to his feet again and ran on.

The owners of the shops around the square had put up their shutters by this time. Robert touched his head, felt something sticky and realized that he was bleeding. He staggered across the street, where just one shop was still open. The shopkeeper, a frail old man, was even standing calmly in his doorway watching the tumult in the square.

Robert ran towards him as fast as he could. He almost knocked the shopkeeper over, but the old man stepped aside and Robert crashed through into the dark shop, which was full of books from floor to ceiling. He clutched a low display case to steady himself. The blood was beating in his ears. He felt sick, as if he were about to faint. Leaning over the glass of the display case, he saw a picture of a bay swarming with little sailing ships, and behind it a small seaside town of little red and white wooden houses set among green hills. An idyllic scene, like something out of a picture book, made up of thousands of little dots and painted in water-colours. The tiny dots began dancing in front of his eyes like a swarm of gnats. Robert rested his head on the cool glass. The last thing he saw was the white church steeple high on top of the hill.

THE FOURTH JOURNEY

When Robert came round he was looking at two large, coal-black eyes, a thin moustache with carefully pointed ends which for some reason, he didn't know why, struck him as French, and a cheerful face with a small dark mole on the left cheek. The man's head was so close to Robert's nose that he saw the cloudless bright blue sky behind the curly hair only at a second glance. It was so dazzling that Robert shut his eyes again.

A soft voice muttered something close to his ear in a language that Robert didn't understand. It was just a singsong that meant nothing to him, though he guessed it might be Scandinavian. Eyes closed, he lay there wondering where he was. And that wasn't the only question! He was by no means entirely used to being suddenly flung from familiar into unfamiliar surroundings, but he knew this wasn't the first time it had happened. This time, however, it was worse. This time he couldn't even remember where he had come *from*. The information had been wiped from his mind like chalk from a blackboard when you wipe it with a damp cloth.

I've lost my memory, he thought, close to panic.

He felt the man raising him carefully, feeling his head with gentle fingers. Opening his eyes a crack, he saw his helper's hand. It was covered with blood.

The man held him firmly and spoke soothingly. This time he tried English. 'You're injured,' he said. 'Don't worry. The wound doesn't look dangerous, but you need a doctor.'

Robert tried to sit up. 'Slowly,' said the man. 'Wait a minute. I'll be back.'

The man was wearing a plum-coloured jacket, much too long and with an amazing number of silver buttons, and close-fitting stovepipe trousers. He looked a little like the doctor in *Struwwelpeter*. Rising abruptly to his feet, he crossed the meadow to a triangular wooden stand and folded it up. What did you call that thing painters used out of doors when they wanted to sketch a landscape? *Easel*. Robert was glad he'd managed to dredge up the word. So his memory hadn't deserted him entirely.

The painter tucked the easel under his arm. He was holding a piece of carefully rolled-up paper in his other hand.

Robert saw a wide panorama of hills and rocky islands behind him. There was a white lighthouse out in the sea, and a small harbour town lay just inland, at the mouth of a river. Its scattered houses, painted dark red and white, gleamed in the morning sun. Robert saw sailing ships and boats anchored in the bay or moored by the quayside. One of them was a three-master. The tiny figures of sailors were clambering around its masts and rigging, reefing in the sails. A white church steeple rose behind tall trees on a hill. He felt he'd seen that steeple with its black weathervane and golden ball somewhere before . . . This whole little world was very bright and clear, and all the rocky islands further out to sea shone in a cool, northerly light. This wasn't an ordinary bay, but – oh, the word was on the tip of his tongue – yes, a fjord, that was it.

The painter put down his easel, got an arm under Robert's shoulders and helped him up. A path wound its way downhill to the first houses. There was a fresh breeze blowing off the sea, carrying the tang of salt. Gulls circled in the morning sky. Robert felt no pain, just a dull thudding at the back of his head, and he made good progress leaning on his helper. A long, narrow wooden bridge across a shallow arm of the fjord led to the outskirts of the little town.

'Nearly there,' Robert's companion told him. 'My name's Mogens, by the way. And you are . . . ?'

'Robert,' said Robert. They went through a gate and into the front garden of an old, low-built wooden house. It looked rather dilapidated; its white paint was flaking, and there were a couple of broken panes in the windows that looked out on the sloping floor of a veranda. Wild roses clambered up a trellis to the roof. The door was open. A single large room almost filled the entire house. It smelled of paint, and of the flowers that stood in tall vases on the floor. A few canvases were propped against the wall. There was a bed in a dark corner, and clothes and empty bottles were scattered everywhere.

'Sit down, Robert, and I'll fetch the doctor. I'll be back in a moment.'

Gradually, Robert's memory was coming back. The odds and ends in his pockets chinked as he took his raincoat off. He felt the rustle of the notes he'd got for his opal. Now he remembered where he had come from: his own home town. The open-air swimming pool. Lea. The Salvation Army, his granny as a little girl. His memory was okay. He felt the back of his head where his hair was all sticky, and then he remembered the street fight, the shouts of *Sieg Heil!*, the blow from behind, his flight into the antiquarian bookseller's small, dusty shop . . .

The doctor arrived, a small man in a dark frock-coat, wearing old-fashioned buttoned gaiters. He was carrying a bulging, shiny black bag. He told Mogens to fetch hot water, and as he washed Robert's wound the two of them talked in low voices in Swedish, or was it Norwegian? Robert guessed what they were saying. 'He needs rest.' 'He can stay here for the time being.' 'Where did you find him?'

Iodine stung Robert's wound, and he leaned back, suddenly exhausted, as if the doctor were a hypnotist putting him to sleep with his soft hands. He felt the man binding up his wound with a muslin bandage, tight and slightly warm on his brow and the back of his head. The doctor would certainly want to know how Robert got here, who had hit him and why, and what he was doing in the town by the fjord this fine spring day, but he was in no mood for questions and trying to find answers. In fact as soon as the doctor left he had a brilliant idea. Amnesia! That was it. Everyone knows that when a concussion victim wakes up he can't always remember what last happened! That would be the simplest solution, if not the most truthful, since he knew perfectly well what had happened to him in his home town, in Australia and in Russia. He just couldn't say so.

But Mogens asked no questions. He picked up the roll of paper he had brought with him, spread it on his easel and examined it critically, eyes narrowed. It was a water-colour. Robert came closer. The picture showed the whole scene once again: the islands in the fjord, the hills, the town in the morning sunlight, the ships in harbour, even the top of the church steeple. But there was a piece of meadow missing from the left corner in the foreground, exactly where the artist had found Robert. And something else was missing from the elegant water-colour too: the thousands of dancing dots Robert had seen before his eyes in the antiquarian's display case back then, or an hour or so ago when he was taking refuge from the fight – it made him feel nauseated just to think of it.

'What will you do with your picture?' he asked. 'Sell it?'

'You don't know the Norwegians!' said Mogens. Ah, good, thought Robert; now he's told me what country I'm in. 'Philistines,' his saviour announced. 'You've no notion how narrow-minded they are! Pious blockheads – skinflints! Take my father the Consul, for instance. The richest man in town, a shipowner, a merchant, a speculator – a proper moneybags, as they say. You think he has any time for art? I could starve for all he cares. I've had to live on dry bread in London and Paris, but I'd rather sleep under the bridges there than waste my time here!'

'They don't like your pictures here?'

'That's about the shape of it! I think we're going to get on, Robert. Would you like a glass of wine?'

Mogens took a bottle and poured some wine. Robert just sipped from his glass and let him go on talking. He didn't really want red wine so early in the day.

'Then what do you do with your pictures?'

'I have to make engravings of them. Look at this.'

He pointed to a table further back in the room. Robert let the artist explain what the tools were for.

'I brought all these back from Europe: the burin, the scraper, the ground roller. The wood-blocks come from Germany. They're made of the hardest woods available, box or pear sawn across the grain. The pictures you get are called end-grain engraving, and if the wood's very hard it's a lot of work bringing out the finer nuances.'

'What do the tools do exactly?' asked Robert.

'I'll show you. First you have to polish the block and prepare it. This white here is for the ground. Then you do the preparatory design. I copy my picture on the block in Indian ink. Views of towns, landscapes with leafy trees — idyllic scenes like that sell best. Then I take the burin, d'you see, like this, and cut the outlines in the wood. I'm copying my own pictures in the sweat of my brow, and very tedious it is too. Once the wood-block's ready I send it to my publisher in Copenhagen, and he pays me eighty talers apiece, cash down.'

'What about the little dots? Where do the little dots swarming all over the pictures come from?'

'I do them with the stipple graver. Thousands of tiny dots — a devil of a job.'

'What does the publisher do with your picture?'

'What, that slavedriver? Oh, he prints off a few hundred and has them coloured in by a dozen poor girls working for starvation wages. Then he sells them quite cheap to folk who hang them on their walls, and he gets rich. In the end he sells off the blocks for a song, and my pictures get into the illustrated magazines. Oh yes, my dear fellow, an artist has to provide what's wanted if he's going to eat!'

And very likely I'll be there some day, thought Robert, in a picture of this Norwegian town: a boy in a meadow, foreground left. Someone will buy the engraving and hang it on the wall, and then the buyer's grandchildren will take it to an antiquarian dealer who'll put it in his display case, and I'll come in with a knock to the back of my head and feel dizzy at the sight of that church tower, and then . . . then I'll end up here with Mogens, who painted the picture in the first place.

By now the artist had almost finished the whole bottle of wine. He didn't notice Robert, who was feeling hungry, consuming an apple and a bread roll, all he could find to eat in this chaotic bachelor household. Mogens waved his arms about and carried on complaining about his father, his fellow countrymen and his home town.

'You'll soon see how narrow-minded they are. Sticking their noses into everything, and since there's nothing, absolutely nothing going on in this dead-and-alive hole they gossip about any stranger. There!' he added triumphantly. 'Out there already, lying in wait.'

Robert could indeed hear voices in the garden outside the house. He looked out of the window. Four men of dignified appearance were lined up there like a reception committee.

'Pillars of society,' muttered the artist. 'And burning with curiosity. The doctor must have told them about you. Yes, there he is, the good Dr Bing. The fat man beside him's our pastor, the Reverend Lørenskog, and the other two are his friends Brox the magistrate and that pill-roller from the town pharmacy.'

The bell rang, and Mogens opened the door, propelling Robert out of it ahead of him, as much as to say, 'Here's your suspect.'

The four men politely took off their hats – one was even wearing a real top hat – and began talking to Mogens. Robert couldn't make out what they wanted. After a while, however, Mogens explained that the pastor was inviting him, Robert, to move into the parsonage for the time being, until the wound on his head healed.

Robert was not particularly keen on this suggestion, but he had seen the artist's house and reckoned that at best he would be sleeping on the floor. As for his host's culinary skills, he'd rather not speculate on them. The pastor, on the other hand, looked very well fed, with his red cheeks, his double chin above his white clerical bands, and his broad, plump hands. Well, thought Robert, why not? And he went with the four men. If they were feeling curious, so was he. Reluctantly,

Mogens accompanied the deputation – 'I'm doing you a favour,' he whispered to Robert, 'to make sure they don't string you up.'

It was an odd walk they took. News of Robert's arrival had obviously got around, for onlookers were staring out of windows everywhere, horse-drawn carts stopped in the street, and passers-by turned to look at Robert and his companions. Talk about running the gauntlet! Robert wondered why they all seemed so surprised to see him. There wasn't anything out of the ordinary about him. Or was there?

He himself was taking a closer look at his new surroundings. There were no proper shops here, and the streets weren't paved. He smelled horse dung and open fires. Not a TV aerial anywhere, or a street light or a car. These people didn't even seem to have bicycles. Perhaps they were so poor that they couldn't afford such things? But the gentlemen walking beside him were clearly not starving, and their clothes looked quite expensive: white silk stocks, black hats gleaming in the sun, silver-topped walking sticks in their hands. And the people in the street could have been straight out of a movie, some kind of costume drama: the young man with the yellow silk waistcoat, the officer in the blue tailcoat with a long sword at his side, the fishwives in their apron dresses. Even the children playing with hoops and coloured tops in the road reminded him of the naughty boys in *Struwwelpeter* being dipped in the inkwell by the great Agrippa.

The whole town looked to Robert like something built with an old-fashioned model kit. No telephone kiosk, no news-stand, no filling station, only a few horse-drawn vehicles and handcarts. And the people had so much time on their hands! This seemed a snug little place, but it was very, very strange all the same.

As they walked past the harbour with its small sailing boats, fishing cutters, sturdy warehouses perched on stilts above the water and tiny grocery stores, it became clear to Robert that he had gone even further back into the past this time. Much further back than 1930! He wondered: what am I going to do? I keep falling further and further back. Back and back. If this goes on I'll end up with the cavemen in the Stone Age.

However, he couldn't stop to think about such prospects now. They were walking along a street of narrow, crooked little houses, going uphill to the church. A crowd of small boys trotted after them in silence until they reached the parsonage, a handsome building in a large garden behind a white-painted fence. The pastor's wife, a thin, middle-aged lady with her hair in a grey bun, was waiting for them at the door, surrounded by five children.

The pastor led Robert and the town dignitaries into a gloomy room. His family had to stay outside; only Mogens was allowed in, although the gentlemen ignored him.

Striking a dignified pose, the pastor made a long speech of which Robert could understand almost nothing except that it was about a 'foreign and unfortunate human soul'. Then the gentlemen, still standing, began a lively discussion. Little Dr Bing became quite heated, the apothecary and the magistrate whispered to each other, and they were all talking about Robert as if he wasn't there at all. His glance fell on a mirror in which he saw a monstrous head swathed in white. It was his! So that was why everyone had turned to stare at him. He looked like a severely injured patient after an operation on his skull.

Then the gentlemen sat down at a round table and his cross-examination began. They asked him, in English, where he came from, what his native country was, what his parents' names were, whether a ship had put him ashore and how old he was. Robert simply shrugged his shoulders. He had decided to stick to his original idea and pretend he was suffering from amnesia. They tried German too – the pastor and the civil servant went to a lot of trouble over the half-forgotten German they had learnt at school – and then they tried French, but Robert remained stubbornly silent, and they had to give up. The visitors left, looking disappointed, but Mogens, who had caught on to Robert's plan, winked at him.

The pastor's wife didn't seem very enthusiastic about her new guest. Looking sour, she led Robert up two steep flights of stairs to an attic bedroom. So this was where he was to stay! The room was hardly bigger than a broom cupboard, and there was no real bed, only a straw mattress on the floor. No sooner had he stretched out on it than a little boy of about five or six came in and sat down on the floor with him. One of the pastor's children. He gravely pointed to himself and said, 'Nils.' Robert copied him, saying his own name. Then the little boy stretched his fingers and counted: 'En, to, tre, fire, fem, seks, syv, åtte, ni, ti.' Robert immediately got the idea, of course, and carefully repeated the numbers one to ten. It was touching to see Nils trying to teach him a few words of Norwegian, and Robert wished he could give the child a piece of chewing gum, but he had none left. What had they told the little boy? Maybe that Robert was handicapped, or anyway some kind of foundling and probably not all there.

Someone on the stairs called, 'Nils!' The little boy took Robert's hand and led him down to a narrow dining room. People here seemed to eat their evening meal in the middle of the afternoon! Everyone else was already seated. Looking solemn, the master of the house recited a prayer. Robert guessed it was the Our Father. Then a very old maidservant brought in the meal. The pastor was given a large tankard of beer and a big plate of soup. His wife came next, then the children in order of size, and Robert last of all. There were only a couple of spoonfuls of soup left for him, and it was the same with the fish that came next. The pastor's wife kept a sharp eye open in case anyone got too large a helping, and only the master of the house could take as much as he wanted. No wonder he was the fattest. But when he saw Robert looking ruefully at the few bones on his own plate, he smiled and passed a large piece of mackerel across the table. 'Here you are, Kaspar!' Robert thought he must have heard wrong. His name wasn't Kaspar. I'm going to have to learn Norwegian in addition to everything else, he thought. If I don't understand what these people are saying, I really will end up crazy.

After supper there was another prayer, and then the pastor clapped his hands and sent the children to bed. Nils showed the guest the earth-closet out in the yard and the water pump, which seemed to be the only way of washing around here.

Robert had never gone to bed so early in his life. The sun was still high in the sky, but that had its advantages, since there was no artificial light in his broom cupboard of a room. In fact he hadn't seen any proper lights in the house at all. How about electricity at this time, whenever it was? When was electric light invented? And if there wasn't any electricity, what did they use instead? It looked as if the people here had to manage with candles. No fridges, no movies, no record players, and so on. Not an appealing idea, but Robert had once been on a camping holiday somewhere in the mountains, with no TV and no bathroom, so he knew that you could get by somehow if you had to.

He took out his souvenirs. They were some small comfort, but he didn't like to think what might happen if the pastor spotted them. All that money, the watch, the pocket calculator: yes, it would look extremely mysterious and extremely suspicious! Proof positive that he didn't belong here. Every item would raise questions. What kind of things are these? How do they work? Where did you get them?

He counted his money, and suddenly realized that in this little seaside town in Norway it wasn't worth anything. Or rather, it wasn't worth anything *yet*! If he stopped to think about it, the notes weren't even printed yet. He'd given up his opal and got nothing at all in exchange. Annoying, but all the same, he didn't want to part with the few things he'd brought. He decided to hide his possessions at the earliest possible moment. Even better, he could bury them. This plan calmed him, and although the straw mattress was prickly and smelled of the stables Robert soon fell asleep.

Breakfast next day was no fun. The pastor wasn't there. No doubt he was preaching over in the church. There was no sign of the children either. Mrs Lørenskog gave Robert a mug of milk and a piece of bread – bread with a taste of resentment about it. For some reason Robert didn't like the way the woman's bun of hair was held in place by three long knitting needles. He saw a newspaper on the table, and read, in ornate Gothic print, the words:

Christiania-Posten
Tirsdag, den 22. Mai 1860

The *Christiania Post* of 22 May 1860 . . . well, thought Robert, so long as there's a newspaper or a calendar I can always find out just when I'm living. A few decades one way or the other didn't bother him any more. He knew by now that the past was the strangest of all countries.

He couldn't stick around the parsonage any more. He

wanted some fresh air! Glancing in the mirror, he was as startled as before by the sight of the grotesque white bandage round his head. Out in the yard, he carefully undid it. His wound was almost healed.

He felt better out of doors in the bright morning light. A handsome brig, fully rigged, lay at anchor, with small boats scuttling hastily back and forth. Sacks and crates were being unloaded on the quay. There was a smell of fish, tar and freshly sawn wood. Robert took no notice of the people who turned to stare at him. He soon found his way back to the house where Mogens lived, and slipped into the garden. He found an empty biscuit tin in the toolshed, emptied his pockets and put his treasures in the tin box, and then he buried it under a lilac bush.

'Hey, what are you doing out there?' called Mogens out of the window.

'Oh, nothing,' said Robert quickly. 'Can I come in?'

His friend and rescuer wasn't entirely sober, even in the morning. 'Well, so how are you getting on with the good pastor and his wife?'

Robert told him, not mincing his words.

'Hmm . . . do you know why Pastor Lørenskog is so keen to have you staying with him in the parsonage?'

'No idea,' muttered Robert.

'Because you're a sensation, my dear fellow. Or so he thinks, anyway. He read a book about Kaspar Hauser, you see – he was boring the whole town with it last year. You know who Kaspar Hauser was?'

'Didn't they make a movie about him? It's supposed to be a good movie too, but I haven't actually seen it.'

Mogens stared at him, tapping his forehead. Robert had made yet another mistake. How would his friend know what a movie was?

'Tell me about this Hauser, then. Who was he?' Robert hastily added.

'Well, nobody knows for sure, that's the point. About thirty years ago a boy who could hardly talk turned up in a town in Germany. Everyone wondered where he came from. He'd just been abandoned, and it turned out he'd been kept shut up by himself somewhere all his life. Very soon there were all kinds of rumours going around: some said he was really the son of a prince and his parents wanted to be rid of him. All Europe was puzzling over the story, and it didn't end happily. I believe an assassin stabbed him.'

'Thanks a lot!' said Robert. 'So what's this story got to do with me?'

'Oh, well!' said Mogens scornfully, drinking from his bottle. 'Our small-town philosophers here have taken it into their heads that you're another fascinating case of the same kind. Pastor Lørenskog fancies himself as the Good Samaritan, our good Dr Bing wants you as a guinea pig for scientific purposes, and the apothecary thinks he'll make a name for himself by writing reports for the national newspapers about the mysterious stranger who arrived out of nowhere, and there's no explanation of how you got here.'

Mogens was convulsed with laughter, but Robert couldn't see anything funny about it.

'Don't let it worry you,' the artist advised him. 'Once those fools see you're nothing special, just a perfectly ordinary schoolboy in search of something new, they'll soon lose interest. Anyway, you won't be able to keep your pretence of amnesia up for long. You'll soon be speaking Norwegian like everyone else. It's not difficult for a German. You do come from Germany, don't you? I could tell that at once. You understand half of what we Norwegians say anyway, even if you don't let on. Norwegian is rather like an old German dialect, only it doesn't do to say so. Guess what this means: *fisk.*'

'Fish,' said Robert.

'*Brød.*'

'Bread.'

'*Katt.*'

'Cat.'

'There, you see? You just have to keep your ears open, and as soon as you start talking they'll realize you're not a prince's son in exile. No one will take any notice of you any more, and you'll have to fend for yourself. Just like me! So far as my distinguished father the Consul's concerned I could starve to death. Only a few days ago he made a terrible scene, just because of a bill of exchange I signed. I'm going to pack and leave, that's what I'm going to do. I'm going to Paris! But I must finish a few more engravings first, to get money for the journey out of that Danish bloodsucker.'

Mogens sat down at the table and picked up his stipple graver. 'If this gets boring for you,' he added, 'you can try your hand with my water-colours.'

'I'm not all that good at art,' said Robert. 'You'd only laugh at my pictures.' But Mogens pushed a blank sheet of paper over to him and pointed to the palette lying on a small board near the easel.

It rankled that his friend didn't think he was anything special. Well, he was right about Robert not being the mysterious son of a prince, but Mogens might have shown rather more imagination. The man thought of no one but himself! Robert wanted to show him he was no ordinary runaway who'd left home because he was afraid of his parents, or just because he wanted to play truant from school. He fetched a glass of water and picked up the brush. With a few strokes, he sketched the apron of an airport, complete with control tower, landing-strip and planes on the ground. If he wasn't careful the paint ran down over the sheet of paper. The aeroplanes looked clumsy, and he couldn't reproduce the silvery shimmer of aluminium. The brush was too thick. He found a finer brush and painted a crowd of tiny passengers. Finally he added a jumbo jet up in the blue sky, coming in to land.

He was so absorbed in what he was doing that he jumped when Mogens, who had risen and was looking over his shoulder, gave a gasp. 'You've taken leave of your senses! What on earth are *those* supposed to be?'

'Aeroplanes,' replied Robert, and said no more. He was pleased to see Mogens standing there, staring in amazement. 'I made rather a mess of the windows in the control tower, I'm afraid. I think water-colour's very difficult. The paints keep running into each other.'

The painter took the sheet of paper off the easel and examined it, frowning. 'Aeroplanes!' he murmured. 'I'm beginning to think you really *are* crazy.'

'Maybe I just have more imagination than you,' said Robert, with a pleasing and rather malicious sense of satisfaction. 'Don't worry! You'll find other things to think about in Paris.'

He wasn't really happy to hear that Mogens was leaving. On the way back to the parsonage he thought how quickly he kept losing his friends. No sooner did he get to know them than they disappeared from his life again. It had happened with Olga, with his little grandmother and with Lea, not to speak of his girlfriend Caroline. And he didn't even know if he really liked Mogens, who was terribly vain, and drank too much. All the same ... As Robert passed a small red house and saw a notice with the words

Kgl. Norsk
Post

he thought of his mother sitting at her mirror putting her make-up on, and suddenly felt an irresistible urge to write to her. But how could he? He stood in front of the letter-box, clutching his head. How long would his letter take to arrive? Over a hundred years! And no postman would find an address so far in the future.

You can get used to *almost* anything. Although life was very austere with his hosts at the parsonage, Robert endured it without complaining. Even the smell of the tallow candles and the dim oil lamps which provided some light after dark didn't bother him any more. Little Nils proved a devoted companion, and the two of them explored not only every corner of the town, the dockyards, the rope-making works and the sawmills but the surroundings of the little town as well. They rowed out to the skerries in the pastor's boat and looked for birds' eggs on the rocks. Robert was soon speaking broken Norwegian.

One Sunday afternoon Pastor Lørenskog came home beaming. In laboured German, he imparted a piece of good news: Consul Garman himself was giving a dinner party, and Robert was invited, along with the pastor's family. Clearly this was an extraordinary event. The big shipowner lived in seclusion on his estate further up the fjord, seldom condescending to mingle with the townsfolk.

Mrs Lørenskog spent a long time wondering what to wear. Robert felt no such anxiety, since he only had the clothes he stood up in, which he had bought in the distant year 1930 and in which he looked like a visitor from another star.

On the evening of the great day, the family drove off in a carriage and pair. Even the horses were decked with little garlands, and everyone was as fine as possible. The pastor's wife smelled of mothballs, and her husband was wearing his wedding tail-coat, which had become much too tight for him over the years.

The Consul's estate did indeed look much grander than the modest houses of the little town. Robert had become so accustomed to the toy-town world in which he had landed that the manor house at the end of the drive, lined with old trees, seemed like a palace. There was a wide flight of steps up to the door, and the master of the house was receiving his guests in the hall. With the order he wore on the breast of his evening coat, and his bushy white side-whiskers, he looked both distinguished and jovial, important and cheerful. A broad staircase led up to the first floor, where a large dining-room lit by candelabras awaited the guests. The table was covered with a fine damask cloth, and a whole battery of glasses stood at every place for champagne, white wine, claret, and port with the dessert course.

The dignitaries of the little town, who usually put on such airs, seemed very shy and awkward here. The stout pastor's manner was quite servile, and his wife looked sour. She was probably totting up the cost of such a meal in her head. The doctor, the apothecary, the head of the fire service and the magistrate hardly dared to open their mouths. Only two sea captains in the shipowner's service and two gentlemen from the capital, with their ladies, conversed easily, while casting curious glances at the silent guest. No one really knew why Robert had been invited.

After the soup course, however, the master of the house tapped his glass and made a speech, trusting that as an old seafaring man, now a shipowner, he might be allowed a frank word. He thought it a pity, he said, nor was it really for the good of the town, that there were so many bores and wet blankets around the place these days, even some who might be described as narrow-minded fanatics, enthusiasts and obscurantists. It couldn't be good for a community that lived by trade and exchange with the rest of the world, he added. Think of the freight trade in wood and fish, coffee and cotton, bound not just for England and for Lübeck in Germany but going all the way to America and the coast of Africa. The fortune or misfortune of his captains and crews depended on it, not to mention the livelihoods of the local woodcutters, sawyers, shipbuilders and sail-makers. He for one must continue in the seafaring trade, not just for the sake of the house of Garman but in all their interests, and he meant to send his sailing vessels all over the world as long as the wind blew and the timber forests grew. Petty feuding and sour faces would achieve nothing, and a little more acquaintance with the ways of the world could do his dear countrymen no harm.

For instance, continued the shipowner, just to cite an example, supposing a mysterious stranger appeared in these parts, they all ought to show their best side. He didn't hesitate to say that such an event was a stroke of luck, and for his part he would happily do all he could to make their unusual guest comfortable. He would take it upon himself to pay the gifted young man's board, lodging and school fees, he'd make sure he had suitable clothing, and he would at least hope the stranger would prove worthy of his good offices. And now, he concluded, he wished to drink the health of his guests in a glass of good claret.

Robert, of course, had understood only about half of this speech, but the main point had not escaped him: most of it was about himself. He also noticed how the face of the pastor's wife suddenly lit up for the first time when the Consul mentioned the money he proposed to provide for their visitor's board and lodging.

At this point, to the astonishment of the whole company, Robert rose to his feet and broke his long silence. With some confusion and in a mish-mash of three languages, but expressing himself with civility, he thanked the Consul for his invitation and the help he had promised. He was not at all mysterious, he told them, just an ordinary boy from Germany cast ashore here. He had kept quiet until now only because he spoke Norwegian so badly; the fanciful tale of his being a prince's son banished from home was certainly untrue, and his case would be of no interest to either science or the national newspapers. He would do his best, he said, not to disappoint the Consul, whose unexpected invitation was a rare honour and was giving great pleasure to all present.

The Consul was pleased with Robert's speech. Only the pastor, the doctor and the apothecary looked reproachful; they were disappointed that the sensational discovery which had looked so promising had eluded them, and annoyed that it was him, Robert, a jumped-up nobody, whom they had to thank for their invitation to this brilliant social occasion.

Robert soon felt the effects. The pastor's wife had no intention of using the Consul's money to improve on the frugal portions she gave him at meals. The pastor too became increasingly morose and monosyllabic, and in the end they both forbade little Nils to play with Robert. There was no getting around a visit to the tailor, though, and soon Robert was walking around the town in a pair of blue-grey trousers, a blue frock-coat and a yellow waistcoat. However, the people in the market and down by the harbour would have nothing to do with him; they looked at him wordlessly, and no one seemed to want to talk to him. He missed the afternoons he had spent in the artist's house, the painter's tirades on art, his sharp remarks about the Norwegians, even his complaints and his vanity – for Mogens had left one day without saying goodbye.

Robert was bored, and could hardly wait for school to begin, for the pastor had put his name down for the grammar school, which was housed in a little yellow wooden building and bore the proud name of Latin School. Yet another language, thought Robert, as if I didn't have enough foreign vocabulary churning around in my head already! Now he'd have to polish up what little Latin he already knew.

But even his fellow pupils were unfriendly. They laughed at Robert's broken Norwegian, viewed his wonderful tailor-made suit with a mixture of scorn and envy, and made it clear that he simply didn't belong. Robert was used to that kind of thing. He was well able to defend himself, and once he had shown them a couple of times that he wasn't putting up with their behaviour they left him alone. He had to reconcile himself to being regarded as an arrogant loner in class, even though it was the others who cut him dead.

However, he was interested in the schoolmaster Mr Tidemand, a thin, pale man who seemed as out of place as Robert himself in this small town of sailors and fishermen, the devout and the self-important, market women and petty civil servants. Emanuel Tidemand always wore the same shabby black suit. You could see he was a confirmed bachelor. But those eyes! He wasn't blind; he saw everything, but the light, silvery gleam of his pupils – Robert had only ever seen such eyes once before, in a woman neighbour who was blind. You scarcely dared look at him. Tidemand ignored the nasty little tricks the schoolboys played, as if they were nothing to do with him. The odd thing was that he couldn't sit still; he seemed to be eternally and compulsively restless. Is he just nervous, Robert wondered, or is he afraid – but what of? Perhaps he was simply impatient for the bell to ring and mark the moment when he could leave the schoolhouse, as if he had more important or exciting things to do at home.

Then, one day, he whispered to Robert, 'Is it the same for you? This is no kind of life! What do these clods know of what really matters? Theirs are deaf ears, Robert! Sometimes I think you're the only one who listens to me.'

Robert was taken completely by surprise. Tidemand was looking at him bright-eyed, as if expectantly, but Robert didn't know what he was supposed to say.

'Perhaps you aren't from around here either?' he asked politely.

'Indeed I am not,' replied the schoolmaster. 'We come from far away, you and I.'

Robert could hardly argue with that.

'But this is not the time to speak of serious matters,' continued Tidemand. 'You may visit me if you like. Number 5 Strandgate, on the first floor. I never go out. It must remain our secret, though. You understand!'

Robert didn't understand in the least, but he said, 'Thank you, Mr Tidemand. There's no one else I can talk to. The pastor and his family will hardly say a word to me. I think they regret taking me in, and if Consul Garman didn't pay them money for my board and lodging every week they'd probably turn me out this minute.'

'Call me Emanuel,' said the schoolmaster, and he put on his black hat and left.

Robert thought about this conversation all day. Why was the man acting so mysteriously? What did he mean by the 'serious matters' he wanted to discuss? And what did he have in mind by hinting that they both came from far away? Did he know more than he was saying?

In one way he liked Emanuel Tidemand, in another he didn't. On the one hand, he was the only person who seemed to have any understanding of Robert, even to trust him. On the other, there was something rather odd about the man. That sallow complexion, the slight twitch around his eyelids, the ingratiating tone of his voice ... Robert asked himself what the schoolmaster's invitation meant, and couldn't think of an answer.

Tidemand did not refer to the conversation again; only an enquiring glance from his silvery eyes showed that he had not forgotten it. In the end Robert's curiosity and the boredom of his attic bedroom overcame his uneasiness, and one afternoon he set off for Strandgate.

The water of the fjord was glittering in the slanting sunlight, and the leaves were taking on a whole range of bright, early autumn colours. For a while Robert forgot that he was living in a kind of exile; he whistled as he walked along and put his worries out of his head. But when he reached the house where the schoolmaster lived his good humour evaporated. The roof was crooked, and it was a long time since the window frames had been painted. Robert hesitated. After a while he opened the door without ringing the bell first. A dwarf-like little old woman with her head tilted sideways on her shoulder let him in. Without a word, she jerked her thumb upwards. Robert climbed a creaking staircase and reached the schoolmaster's lodgings.

'I'm glad to see you, Robert,' said Tidemand, leading him into a gloomy room. There were black curtains at the windows, and a seven-branched candlestick stood on the table. Only once his eyes were used to the darkness could Robert make out the sparse furnishings: the narrow bed in an alcove in the wall, the two high-backed chairs. The room itself was painfully clean and felt uninhabited. However, there were a few signs of life on the table: beside the candlestick he saw an inkwell with a quill pen, and a small pile of neatly stacked manuscripts and pamphlets.

'I know you are the only person worth talking to in this ignorant town,' continued Tidemand. 'I saw that at once. And do you know why? Because you travel between the worlds, as I do.'

'How do you mean, Mr Tidemand?' asked Robert. He had sat down on one of the hard chairs.

'You can tell me Emanuel, after my spiritual godfather, the great Swedenborg.'

Robert shifted about in his chair. He had no idea what the schoolmaster was talking about.

'You don't know who Swedenborg is? Let me tell you. But forgive me – I have offered you no refreshment, and you are my guest!'

So saying, he picked up a broomstick and knocked the floor hard with it, three times.

'Emanuel Swedenborg,' he said solemnly, 'is the Columbus of the spiritual world, discoverer of the heavenly sciences. He knew the secret language of the angels, and fought many a terrible battle with the demons who oppressed him.'

Robert felt the schoolmaster's silvery eyes resting on him, and noticed the twitching of Emanuel's face. 'Do you know what the name Emanuel means? *God is with us!*' cried Tidemand. Robert could make nothing at all of his remarks. He didn't know what the schoolmaster was getting at with his rheumy enthusiasm. He was saved from embarrassment by the old woman, who entered the room, wheezing, and put a tray of tea and bread and butter on the table.

'Please help yourself,' said the schoolmaster, and his voice now sounded quite normal again. Robert realized that he was very hungry, and set to work on the bread and butter, while his host resumed a solemn, singsong tone.

'He who sees spirits knows no difference between night and day. A sense of dizziness overcomes him before he experiences his visions, and spectral lights appear before his eyes, showing distant worlds and past times.'

Robert felt Tidemand seize his arm. 'Will you tell me you are not familiar with such moments? Why, you are almost among the initiates already! If you will entrust yourself to my guidance you will soon be one of those dreamers in whose features delight or pain may be read, depending on whether they see heaven or hell!'

Robert swallowed. What the man was saying sounded crazy, yet he had guessed at something no one else seemed to understand. The lights, the dizzy feeling, visits to distant times – it was all only too familiar. Not that he, Robert, had ever had anything to do with spirits and angels, only with solid flesh-and-blood people: a pharmacist in Siberia, a girl called Caroline who taught him to ride, old Mr Hirschberg who knew about opals, his tiny little grandmother – not to mention whoever had hit him on the back of the head with a cudgel. None of them ghosts, perfectly normal people, good-looking or bad-looking, friendly or unfriendly, just like other people all over the world.

'I see you doubt me, Robert. I am not surprised. For you must know: most folk do not even realize that they have long been living in the realm of spirits. I will show you.'

By now Robert had finished the last piece of bread and butter, washing it down with tea.

'Where does your Mr Swedenborg live?' he finally asked, hoping to bring the conversation down to earth.

'Ah, he has been gone from this humdrum world almost a hundred years. But I speak to him daily, and perhaps you too will soon partake of that favour, if you return and entrust yourself to my guidance.'

'Thank you, Mr Tidemand . . . I mean, Emanuel,' added Robert quickly, seeing the schoolmaster wince slightly in the flickering candlelight. 'But I have to go now, or I'll be in trouble with the pastor.'

'Observe the deepest secrecy!' said Tidemand, laying a finger on his lips. 'For as soon as one begins to frustrate the tricks of the hypocrites and Pharisees one is slandered, suspected of heresy, persecuted! Oh yes, my dear Robert, we must be careful. So not a word to your fellow pupils or the pastor's household. God's blessing be with you!'

Robert was glad to be out in the open air again. Dusk was already falling, and the lights of the sailing ships cast bright streaks across the calm sea. He wouldn't be in a hurry to enter the schoolmaster's darkened room again, that was certain.

Yet Robert couldn't get Emanuel's mysterious remarks out of his head. He thought about them before going to sleep, but he couldn't tell sense and nonsense apart in all this stuff about spirits. Perhaps there *is* something in it, he thought – but what?

A few days later, when the fine autumn weather was over and thick rainclouds lowered above the town, Pastor Lørenskog took him aside. 'Robert, I must give you a warning,' he said. 'It has come to my ears that you are meeting Mr Tidemand in secret. He may be a good teacher of Latin, but he is far removed from true Christianity. I never see him in church, and they say he is in league with evil spirits. Be that as it may, he can only be a pernicious influence on a young man like you. I forbid you – I forbid you, do you hear me? – to see him outside school.'

'He only gave me some tea and bread and butter,' said Robert, but the pastor waved his objections away and walked off.

Robert was far from happy to have the master of the house telling him who he could visit and who he couldn't. If only out of defiance, he decided he wasn't putting up with this. And if Tidemand had things all mixed up, confusing Robert's travels in time with seeing apparitions, suggesting that his private movie show was something to do with angels – well, what business was that of Pastor Lørenskog's? Wasn't the schoolmaster right in saying he was the only person in the whole town who understood? So why shouldn't he, Robert, take the risk?

He spent some time wondering whether to make a second visit, though. It got quite dark early in the afternoon now, and the dense, drizzling rain made the town look more and more dismal. Then, one evening, word ran like wildfire through the sleepy streets: 'The herring are in! The herring are here!' In a moment the whole town was up and about. Men in oilskins and tall boots met down by the harbour, knocking on the storehouse gates. Little fishing cutters hoisted their sails, and the anchor chains were rattling up. Lamps were lit, deals were done, and soon the first drunks were tottering from tavern to tavern.

Next day it rained harder. Stormy gusts tore the leaves from the trees and sent tiles crashing down into the road. No one took any notice of Robert as he set off for Strandgate after school. Once again the dwarf-like old woman opened the door, as if she had been waiting for him; once again he found Emanuel sitting in front of his manuscripts in the darkened room. The broomstick was pressed into service again, and soon there was a teapot on the table with steam rising from it.

'The herring are here!' said Robert.

'The herring too are eternal wanderers,' said Emanuel Tidemand, smiling his thin smile. 'Yet who knows if they have souls? Ours, however, my dear Robert, are divine in nature. They are immortal and seek freedom, but alas, they are prisoners of the body. Pray help yourself, don't hold back!'

Tidemand himself did not eat a morsel. The man looked half starved! He had dark rings under his eyes, which were too bright, and he fidgeted nervously in his chair. There's something the matter with him, thought Robert.

'Do not think you are alone,' the schoolmaster began again. 'I am not unfamiliar with your experience. Purified, freed from the fetters of the body, we shall be reborn, and our souls will journey on until we return to the bosom of God, though it may take a thousand years.'

'How do you know, if I may ask?' enquired Robert politely, although his mouth was full, which did not seem to bother Emanuel, if indeed he noticed at all.

'Don't you remember your past life? Don't you feel as if you had lived on earth before? Have you forgotten everything – your parents in the past, your friends, the towns where you lived, the countryside you knew?'

Once again, Tidemand had hit on the crucial point. How on earth did he know? 'But that is not enough,' he continued. 'Time and space are merely earthly illusions. The inner eye can see far into the distance. Here, in this room, and with God's help, I can even see the Holy Land if I wish it. And he who truly sees can overcome time too.' His left eyelid twitched as he went on, but there was no stopping him now.

'Do not be amazed. It is perfectly common! They call it the transmigration of souls. I can remember my earlier lives quite clearly. Once I was an Icelandic sailor, in another life I was even a woman, and when I think far, far back, I was a high priest in ancient Egypt. Since I know that I shall return again, death holds no terrors for me.' With these words he stood up, blew out a candle and said to himself, quietly, 'Quite the contrary.'

Robert was so confused that he lost all sense of caution. 'No, you're wrong, Emanuel,' he replied. 'This stuff about reincarnation – you've got it all mixed up! It's not like that, and I know what I'm talking about. First, I don't go forward, I go back, further and further back. And second, I'm always the same Robert. I've never been a woman or a high priest and I never will either! It's bad enough being pushed around in past history the whole time – at least I want to hang on to myself and my body!'

By now he didn't care what Tidemand thought. He wanted to get it off his chest, even if his companion thought him crazy. Well, the man was mad himself! Robert stood there red in the face, suddenly not in the least afraid of the mysterious Emanuel Tidemand.

The schoolmaster had shrunk in on himself. 'I don't understand a word. I don't know what you're talking about,' he said at last.

'It's perfectly simple,' said Robert. 'My journey, or the transmigration of my soul, as you call it, began about a hundred and forty years away from here in time, just before the year 2000. And since then I've been going further and further back. No sign of any angels and spirits! I haven't noticed being purified either. All I can tell you is, it's a real nuisance always having to begin again, and everyone thinking I'm mad.'

'You can't be serious,' said Tidemand, in a faint voice. 'Such things don't happen.'

'Why not? You seem to believe in just about anything else. The spirit realm, hell, even television, although you can't possibly know what that is.'

'No,' whispered the schoolmaster. 'No! Robert, I wouldn't have thought it of you. I would never have thought you'd tell me such shameless lies.'

'Oh, so you don't believe me?' cried Robert furiously. 'Then I'll show you! You'll soon see!' And so saying he stormed down the steep stairs without a word of goodbye and was out in the street.

Robert was so upset that it was a little while before he noticed how the rain was lashing into his face. It was pitch dark, and the wind was whistling down across the fjord from the north-west. However, he had only one idea in his head: how to prove his point to his antagonist the schoolmaster. And as usual when it really came to the crunch, he had an idea. He'd have to show the man his things, solid evidence from the future: the money from 1930, the quartz watch, the Polaroid picture of Ratibor in hockey gear ... that would impress Tidemand! He could never have seen a Porsche, let alone a pocket calculator. Transmigration of souls, for heaven's sake! Robert had travelled in time in flesh and blood! His treasure was within easy reach, under the lilac bush in front of the deserted house where Mogens had lived before going off to Paris, the city of his artistic dreams.

It was so cold outside that his teeth chattered. He was surprised to see so many people out and about in the pouring rain. Their dark lanterns wandered like will-o'-the-wisps through the darkness, and they were all in a hurry. The warehouses down on the quay were brightly lit, and their gates wide open. A penetrating smell wafted across the harbour square. When Robert came closer he saw dozens of women and girls swathed in thick clothes, standing in the middle of a sea of shining fish by the flickering light of tallow candles. Knives flashed in their hands as they swiftly gutted herring after herring. Slippery puddles of brine and blood covered the ground as far as the square. Men with shiny black capes stood in the rain, shovelling the dead fish into wooden casks. In the reflection of the lights Robert saw that their hands, their oilskins, even their faces were covered with bright fish scales that shone with a silvery light, like the eyes of the man who saw spirits. He stood transfixed to the spot, until the smell of the fish caught him in the throat, and then he ran on.

Wealth had come to the town, and fear with it. He met sailors bellowing as they walked down the narrow street. Drunks lay in the gutter. By the time he reached the artist's abandoned house he was soaked to the skin, and in the darkness he could scarcely see his hand in front of his face. He dug in the damp earth with his bare hands until he felt the cold metal of the tin box. Picking it up, he heard his treasures rattle inside. They were all still there! Opening the tin, he stuffed his things into his coat pocket, all but the large brown banknotes that Salomon Hirschberg had given him and were worth nothing now. Those he tore into tiny pieces and let the wind carry them away. A pity about his lovely opal!

He was shivering with cold, but the idea of returning penitently to the frugal table kept by the pastor's wife was intolerable. The town that had looked so idyllic in spring now seemed like something out of hell. But was that his own idea, or had Tidemand put it into his head? He had an account to settle with that pale visionary; come what may, he had to prove there was nothing supernatural about his travels!

The rain had slackened off. Robert could see the blinking of the lighthouse far out to sea. But now a cutting wind was howling down the streets of the town. He avoided the bloodstained area around the harbour, and was glad when he reached the schoolmaster's dilapidated house, quite out of breath. This time he had to pull the bell hard before the crooked little old woman opened the door. He ran upstairs. The door to the schoolmaster's lodgings stood open, and the room was darker than ever. Robert took his lighter out of his pocket. Yes, it was still working! He lit a candle and looked around him. At first he thought Tidemand must have gone out; then he saw the man's thin figure on the bed in the alcove. The schoolmaster was not moving. Candle in hand, Robert shone its light into the metallic shimmer of the dead man's staring eyes. The candle fell to the floor, and in the dark he knocked a chair over.

Robert did not scream. Panic tightened his throat. In the darkness, he groped his way to the stairs and ran out of the house. He must get away from here! That was the only thought in his head. Only when the storm wind blew into his face did he begin to wonder exactly what had happened that evening. Had the schoolmaster suffered a stroke? Or was it murder? And who could have murdered Emanuel? Robert remembered the man's mysterious remarks. In his faint voice, Tidemand had said, 'Death is only the doorway to another, better life.' And positively trembling with delight at the thought, he had added, 'Once a man dies, however worn, however desperate he may have been in this life, he returns to the first bloom of youth.'

Had he poisoned himself? Robert hadn't seen any traces of blood on the bed. He shook himself, but the horror remained with him. Once the corpse was found the little town would have plenty of material for scandal. The pastor, who had forbidden Robert to go and see Tidemand, would question him, and then the police would be called, and perhaps they might even suspect him, Robert, of murder.

Without thinking, he had gone down to the harbour again. A three-master was lying at anchor off the quay, and in the light of the ship's lanterns he saw four men rolling heavy barrels on deck over a wooden plank. Other men caught them in ropes and hauled them down into the hold. Several sailors were scrambling around the rigging, but no one seemed to be watching the gangplank. Without thinking, without forming any plan, Robert ran aboard. His pulse was beating hard in his throat. He stood by the rail, looking around. No one had noticed him. Carefully, step by step, he went forward until he found a hatch, groped his way into the darkness inside, intent only on hiding, and went on through the vessel until he found a dry corner between decks, right behind the bowsprit. He could still hear the hollow sound of the casks of herring rolling aboard. Then his eyes closed, and after a while he fell asleep on the hard wooden floor.

He didn't know where he was when a crunching sound roused him from sleep. The floor was swaying beneath him. There was a menacing creaking in the planks and ribs of the ship, and his head was still whirring and droning. He rubbed his numb feet and stretched. When he remembered where he was, he felt trapped. He also felt very sick. The ship must have sailed into a storm, for he heard waves breaking and crashing over the decks, and there were incomprehensible cries and heavy footsteps overhead. With difficulty, he dragged himself out of his corner, stumbling over rope ends and crates. He had never been seasick before. If I'd known what it was like, he thought, I'd have died sooner than set foot on this frightful ship!

A hatch opened somewhere above, and a flood of icy water was thrown over him. 'No!' shouted Robert. 'I don't want to drown! Help!'

In the weak light he saw a burly figure in a sou'wester

clambering down to him. 'What the hell are you doing here?' growled the man in English, taking him under the arms and raising him.

By now Robert didn't care about anything. He felt so wretchedly sick that nothing worse could happen, and he was so unsteady on his feet that two sailors had to drag him into the cabin, where at least it was warm and light. If only all that stamping and rocking and the droning in his head would stop!

A man with a red beard, pale eyelashes and a big nose bent over Robert. 'A stowaway! All we needed! I'd like to throw you straight overboard, you monkey! Here, get him away from me before he throws up!'

No doubt about it, this was the captain. Robert turned his face to the wall and said nothing.

'Where d'you come from? And what's your name?'

'Robert,' said Robert, with difficulty. 'I think I'm dying.'

The captain laughed, so loudly that Robert wanted to put his hands over his ears. 'You don't die that easily, young man. Well, you picked a fine voyage, I must say! Wind force eight, a nor'wester in the Kattegat, that's bad enough, and it doesn't look any better for tomorrow. More likely to get worse before we reach Copenhagen.'

Robert didn't want to hear any more. 'You're from Germany, captain,' he whispered. 'I can hear you are. Please don't throw me overboard.'

'A fellow countryman, eh?' said the captain, and he roared with laughter again. 'Well, well, mercy before justice, then! Seeing I'm in a good mood! I like a storm like this. You can have my berth, young fellow, until I want to turn in myself. Then I'll chuck you out and you get a hammock like everyone else. Here's a towel, so don't throw up on my bed. I must go back on deck and get my men to the pumps. Sleep well!'

Bent double, hand to his stomach and swaying with nausea, Robert dragged himself over to the captain's bunk and fell on it. There was a yellowed copperplate engraving on the front wall of the cabin. It showed ladies in hooped skirts and gentlemen with long wigs dancing in a lighted hall. Robert could practically see them turning in time to the music; his head was turning in time as well, and so was the ship as it rocked up and down, his stomach churning with it, until he felt dizzy and everything went black before his eyes. You don't die that easily . . .

But maybe you do, thought Robert, maybe crazy old Emanuel was right when he said death held no terrors for him. Was he on a ghost ship? Was it a dance of death the elegant ladies and gentlemen were performing before his eyes? 'On the whole people don't even notice that they've been living in the spirit world a long time already.' Who'd said that? The captain? The late Swedenborg? Was this Robert's last thought before he died – or before he finally threw up?

THE FIFTH JOURNEY

Robert was surprised to find that he was *not* surprised. Was he getting used to falling out of one life and into another?

The world had stopped thudding, heeling and rocking around him; instead of howling, creaking noises he heard the music of flutes and violins. All at once, the dim light of oil lamps had given way to brilliant radiance, and only Robert himself still felt dizzy. There was a buzzing in his head, and his queasy stomach was still heaving with nausea.

This time he had come to his senses in an oval hall with a high ceiling and pink marble pillars. Ladies with powdered hair, wearing expensive dresses, and gentlemen in tall, snow-white wigs were revolving like dolls on a shining dance-floor. The musicians were playing in the background, and footmen in dove-grey livery stood by the walls. No one took any notice of him.

Only when there was a pause in the dancing did two servants, tall fellows in knee-breeches and coats trimmed with braid, suddenly pounce on him, holding him so hard that it hurt and beginning to frog-march him away. But one of the ladies, the youngest of the whole company, had noticed. She left her surprised partner and came up to Robert. There was a gleam in her deep blue, slightly slanting eyes.

'What are you doing? Can't you see this man's ill?' she snapped at the two servants. 'Let him go! Take him to my ante-chamber, and call my physician to give what attention he needs.'

'Yes, Serene Highness. Just as Your Serene Highness wishes,' muttered the footmen. The girl, who couldn't have been more than sixteen, looked curiously at Robert, then turned, offered her hand to the gentleman who had followed her, and continued dancing as if nothing had happened.

With an imperceptible shrug of their shoulders, the two servants escorted Robert to an elegantly furnished room and left him there. He sat down on a narrow sofa covered with yellow and white striped silk. As soon as he had partly recovered from his seasickness, the usual questions began going through Robert's head. Where am I? And most important of all, *when* am I? He shooed them away like troublesome flies; he was far too exhausted to think about it now. At least he didn't seem to need a foreign language here, although the German spoken in this place sounded very stilted.

The doctor appeared, a morose and grey-haired man. He did not wear a white coat or a dark suit, but a brown uniform laced with silver that made him look rather like a hotel door-man. He gave Robert a cursory examination, felt his forehead, put an ear to his chest, shook his head, and muttered to himself, 'Nothing the matter. Needs a little rest, that's all.' And taking no further notice of Robert he minced out of the room.

Perhaps a couple of hours later – and Robert remembered afterwards that he had been lost in all kinds of confused dreams – he was startled into waking by a soft laugh. He saw the lady who had spoken up for him enter the room, followed by a stiff, haughty looking gentleman also wearing a uniform, but much more magnificent and with more gold braid on it than the physician's.

'Well, and how is the young gentleman who dared to burst into our ball?'

'Better, much better,' said Robert. 'Thank you for helping me! Those two louts would have thrown me straight out.'

'You are at court now, young man. You should address Her Grace the Princess of Herrenlinden as "Serene Highness",' said the man with the gold braid, casting Robert a reproving glance.

My word, thought Robert, here I am talking to a real live princess who has to be addressed like royalty the whole time, maybe even in the third person! 'Will Her Serene Highness allow me . . . ?' and so on and so forth. What a palaver – and no easier than Norwegian or Latin. And who might this other man be? A major-domo? Or would he have some grander title, like Lord Chamberlain?

'May it please Her Serene Highness,' he said, trying out this new language, 'I'm a stranger here and I don't know your rules and regulations – I mean Her Serene Highness's rules and regulations.'

'Never mind all that,' said the Princess. 'We're talking in private here, and as for court etiquette, you'll soon learn it. I like you, and I feel curious about you. Tell me your name and rank! Not so shy, please!'

'My name's Robert, and as for my rank . . .' But here he began stammering, for with the best will in the world he couldn't say what his rank was. 'Well, I think I'm not out of the very top drawer, but not right at the bottom either,' he said at last.

This reply made the Princess laugh.

'Then I'll confer rank on you, if you like,' she said. 'That ought not to be too difficult. What do you say, my dear Massenbach?' she continued, turning to the dignitary who had come with her. 'Don't you think he'd make a passable page? Not in those ridiculous clothes, of course. See that he's properly dressed, and give him accommodation in the castle. And then we'll see about the future, young Robert.'

The chamberlain didn't seem too keen on carrying out these orders, but what could he do? He bowed and led Robert out, down echoing corridors and up broad staircases, until they reached a stuffy attic room where a grey little man was in charge of a number of large cupboards. He received Robert with much bowing and scraping, while the Lord Chamberlain, or High Steward or whatever the self-important man was called, cast him another chilly glance, and then left.

Trying on the clothes the tailor brought him lasted ages. The old man kept fetching more from his chests and his closets, and he never seemed satisfied with their fit. But at last, looking in the mirror, Robert saw a fine gentleman he hardly recognized. This person wore a wine-red brocade waistcoat with silver buttons, a lace stock at his throat, peach-coloured silk stockings, a satin coat with frilled cuffs and, incredibly, a powdered pale blond wig. He almost rubbed his eyes, but remembering what that could lead to he refrained.

Such fantastic costumes existed only in Hollywood or illustrations to fairy-tales. Or had he gone back even further in time? He thought of those boxes of Austrian marzipan sweets with pictures of Mozart on the lid, and he remembered an opera he'd once heard in some castle park in summer. Baroque or rococo? He wasn't entirely sure, but he definitely had the impression that this time he was roughly two or three hundred years in the past. His mother would have liked this place. She loved watching royal weddings on TV, and she knew everything there was to know about the royal families of Europe. Robert wasn't so keen.

But now, still slightly bemused by his new surroundings,

he was handed over to – and had to take orders from – a rather less important chamberlain. This man was a surprisingly uncouth character who put on fine airs, but was careful to stand aside and look servile when he met anyone of higher rank. The chamberlain gave Robert a room in the side wing and showed him where he would eat at the end of a long table with the other court pages. At least the accommodation here was better than in his Norwegian lumber-room, and compared to the frugal meals served by the pastor's wife the food was lavish. But Robert soon found out that Herrenlinden was no paradise, for his training as a page began the next day.

'What, you can't fence? Never been hunting? What a spine-less ninny! Are you a good dancer? No? Must have been reading too many books. We can do without that kind of thing here. And your manners! If you want to rise at court you have a great deal to learn. You needn't think the protection of the Princess will do you much good either. We know all about that! Wheedled your way in, didn't you? Wait until His Serene Highness the Prince hears about it. A difficult customer, His Serene Highness, and he guards his only daughter like the apple of his eye. You don't know anything about life here, do you? Well, can you at least ride?'

Yes, Robert could. But he did not enjoy his lessons from the fencing master, and he felt a fool going about all day wearing a sword-belt. The drinking sessions with his arrogant new companions were hard going too. He discovered that they stank. It obviously wasn't usual to wash every day in this castle, and when Robert asked for a bar of soap he got nowhere. The courtiers wore the same shirts under their magnificent velvet waistcoats for days on end, until they were as grimy at the edges as their owners' fingernails.

But the worst of it was that he couldn't come up with any

ancestors. People here were constantly talking about their family trees and who they were related to, directly or by marriage. It was awkward as well as deadly boring. Robert knew it would be no good mentioning his grandmother. Even apart from the fact that she wasn't even born yet, her name was plain Magda Scherz and she had no aristocratic title whatsoever. These people set great store by titles. They dropped noble names all day long: 'My father the Baron von Ensingen'; 'My distinguished cousin'; 'My aunt, a member of the Saxe-Gotha-Altenburg family'. But Robert was just Robert: practical, but rather a nuisance in the long run.

And he had trouble with the way you talked at court. He had been relieved when he first arrived and thought that at last he would be able to speak his own language again – but too soon. It wasn't as simple as that. For instance, you couldn't just say, 'The Prince wants', or, 'The Prince would like'. You had to say, 'It pleases His Serene Highness to decree.' Sometimes Robert felt as if he were living in a French lesson, for he had to bone up on words he'd never heard before. How was he to know what a gavotte was, or an *assemblée*, a privilege-holder or an entail? Even ordinary things had names Robert didn't know. A sitting room might be a salon, a boudoir, a withdrawing room, a cabinet or even a *salle de compagnie*. In time, however, he discovered that he only had to keep his ears open, and after a few weeks the native manner of speech flowed easily enough from his lips.

Robert was beginning to fear the Princess had forgotten him when a lady in black beckoned him over to her one afternoon, after the dancing lesson.

'I see you are beginning to acquire some manners,' she said. 'Her Serene Highness Princess Sophie Amalie wishes to see you. I am Madame von Erk, her lady in waiting. Pray follow me.'

Robert obediently trotted along after her. The Princess's apartments were on the side of the castle facing the garden. 'Wait here,' the lady in waiting told him, and she disappeared. Robert was uncomfortable in his new clothes. The brocade waistcoat felt tight across his chest, and he was sweating under his heavy wig. He saw that the door was left ajar, and impelled by curiosity and impatience he pushed it open and entered the antechamber. Then he listened.

He could hear the Princess speaking. 'I don't know what you have against him. I think he's delightful.'

'To be sure, Ma'am. But think of his origins! What will His Highness your father say when he learns you have taken him in? And the young fellow is said to be very pert.'

'Oh, he has his weak points, but the boy's attractive, you can't deny it. Now, pray help me, my dear. How tight this bodice is!'

'If you will permit me to say so, Ma'am, the boy is growing into a man.'

'Yes, indeed,' replied the Princess.

Robert felt that this was quite flattering. Quietly, holding his breath, he pushed the door handle and cast a glance past the heavy velvet curtain just inside it and into the Princess's dressing room. She was sitting in front of a large mirror, with Madame von Erk attending her. Her powdered face glowed in the looking-glass. She had a black beauty spot shaped like a half moon below one of her slanting blue eyes, and her lace chemise had a deep *décolleté* which showed her velvety skin. The lady in waiting was kneeling in front of her, loosening her garter.

At this moment their eyes met in the mirror. The Princess saw that Robert was looking at her, and Robert saw that she had seen him.

'Oh, see who's stolen in here!' she cried. 'A thief!'

Madame von Erk looked around, startled to death. Robert came further in, fell to his knees at the Princess's feet, caught her hand and kissed it. 'I beg your pardon, my lady!' he said quickly. 'I couldn't resist discovering what you think of me.'

Princess Sophie Amalie broke into a peal of laughter, but the lady in waiting was angry. 'Never mind, my dear Erk!' said her mistress. 'One must make allowances at his age. And at least he evidently has the courage to pay the tribute due to our sex!'

'Courage, do you call it, Highness? It looks more like impudence to me.'

'Well, we will keep silent about this impulsive behaviour, or the outcome might be unfortunate, don't you agree, Robert? And now you must wait outside until I have finished my toilette. Then I want you to accompany me. Privy Councillor Treibnitz is waiting for me in the garden, our most learned man, a philosopher of high degree, and he is giving me instruction in the sciences.'

The scholar, a thin man of about sixty accompanied by a servant carrying a long case of some kind, was already waiting for the Princess at the foot of the stairs. 'Pray let me introduce my protégé,' said the Princess. 'His name is Robert, and he seems to me to have a lively mind. You will like him. I want you to be well disposed to him.'

The Privy Councillor inspected Robert with his short-sighted eyes, and offered him a cold and rather bony hand. Then the little party went out into the park. The whole garden might have been divided up into regular patterns with a pair of compasses and a ruler; even the shrubs were clipped to look like diagrams from a geometry textbook. The roses in the flowerbeds had all faded by now, and the first leaves were drifting down to fall on the white statues that cast their shadows on the gravel paths.

'Summer is over,' the Princess began. 'We shall soon have to leave Herrenlinden and go back to town, where our boring cousins are expecting us. I always feel melancholy when the leaves fall.'

'You are wrong to do so, Highness,' said the philosopher. 'I am invigorated by the approach of autumn. Is it not extremely strange that no two leaves falling from the trees are ever the same?'

'I can't believe that!' said the Princess.

'Go and bring Madame as many leaves as you can carry,' Treibnitz told his servant, and the man scurried about collecting fallen leaves and brought them to the Princess, who picked them up, leaf by leaf, and compared them.

'You are right,' she admitted at last. 'But how could you know that no leaf would be exactly like another?'

'*Nihil fit sine causa sufficiente*,' said the philosopher in his faint and hesitant voice. When Robert saw that the Princess didn't understand, he supplied the translation. 'Nothing happens without due cause.'

'Correct,' said Treibnitz, nodding. 'A principle also known as the law of sufficient reason. It follows, therefore, that all things in the world must be different from each other, for if there were already one thing present, there would be no sufficient reason for the existence of another of its kind.'

Princess Sophie Amalie clapped her hands and laughed. 'You are always able to amaze me, dear Treibnitz. But tell me, what's in that fine case you have brought us?'

The servant opened the case she had been pointing at, and a telescope gleaming with brass appeared.

The scholar bowed. 'Am I to discuss philosophy with the most enchanting person in the world in this beautiful garden, when the moon is already in the sky?' he said. 'No! Let me entertain you instead with this new instrument I ordered from

Holland. See, the evening star has already risen in the west. Would you not like to look at it?'

'Oh, yes,' cried the Princess. 'I love the stars, and blame the sun for hiding them from us.'

'What you see there is Venus, a wandering star like our own Earth, like Mars and the other planets. They all pursue their courses around the sun, which is far worthier of that honour than our little Earth. It used to be thought that all the heavenly bodies revolved, instead, around us, but since a very learned man from the kingdom of Poland called Copernicus destroyed the notions of the fixed sky held by the ancients, there's nothing left of our old heavenly train but the moon, which does indeed run around us in its orbit. You can see through this telescope that the moon has seas and mountains, just like the earth.'

The Princess was delighted. 'Well, I'm glad that the moon at least keeps us company, since the planets don't care for us. Perhaps, when the people of the moon have become as skilful in the art of making lenses as the Dutch, they'll look down on us with as much amazement as we look up at them.'

'Er . . . I don't think that's very likely,' said Robert.

'Your young companion seems to know something of astronomy.' The philosopher took real notice of Robert for the first time, and asked, with an ironic smile, 'But how do you know there are no stargazers on the moon?'

'Because the moon has no atmosphere, and there can't be any life without air.'

'Well, perhaps one day we shall know more of these matters. For the art of flying is still in its infancy, but with time it will become so perfect that we can fly to the moon.'

'Good gracious me!' cried the Princess. 'What can you be thinking of?'

'As a matter of fact, the first men really *will* land on the moon in a couple of hundred years' time,' said Robert.

'You speak like someone who can see into the future, my friend.' She didn't believe a word of it, but Robert could see that his boldness pleased her. 'However, I fear that your voyagers to the moon will break their necks!'

'It may well be that our young soothsayer is right,' said Treibnitz, 'for great as the distance to our pale satellite may seem to you, it is nothing by comparison with the magnitude of the cosmos as a whole. If only we had telescopes powerful enough to look into the depths of the universe, then we would see that the fixed stars above us are suns themselves, many of them even greater than our own heavenly body.'

'How small and unimportant you make us seem, dear Treibnitz! But you needn't believe I feel humbled by your teachings,' said the Princess, laughing. 'I assure you I think just as well of myself as before.'

'And very right you are to do so, Highness. We don't guard our rank in the universe as jealously as we do our precedence at a social gathering. But wait until it is dark, and then you will see a bright cloud in the firmament by night. That cloud is the Milky Way, and through the telescope we may see that its light proceeds from thousands of suns.'

'May I say something?' asked Robert.

'Pray do!' replied the philosopher, with a small smile.

'As far as I know our Milky Way is only one of many galaxies. Each of the distant nebulae that look so small through the telescope consists of millions of other stars, racing away from us at enormous speed.'

'Stop, stop, Robert!' protested the Princess. 'You make me quite dizzy. What do you say, Treibnitz? Don't you agree that he's going too far?'

'He certainly doesn't lack imagination. And who knows, there may be some truth in his suppositions. Has it not always been said that the stars never change? Yet we no longer see some of the fixed stars that were observed in antiquity. It appears as if the suns may be extinguished, and even our own will not last for ever.'

'That's right,' said Robert. 'I've heard it may be swallowed up in a black hole some day.'

'Now that *is* going too far,' said the philosopher, and his mild voice assumed a sterner tone. 'You have much to learn yet, and meanwhile you had better guard your pert, forward tongue. Black holes, indeed! What nonsense!'

Robert thought it wiser not to contradict him, and in fact he wasn't too sure himself exactly what black holes were; he had only read about them in the newspaper.

'Do not be alarmed, Ma'am!' continued the scholar, and his voice was calm again, the voice of a schoolmaster. 'It takes a great deal of time for a world to wear out, and meanwhile, that's enough for today. I ask your leave to withdraw, and wish you a peaceful night.'

It was not the last time the Princess asked Treibnitz for tuition in some subject or other, and she always took Robert with her. While to outward appearances he was a docile listener, it was hard work not showing the philosopher what he knew; exile in the past meant not only stress and strain, but a certain inevitable sense of superiority. He felt the thrill and temptation of his secret power. He could so easily have astonished the Princess, if he wanted, by telling her about satellite telephones and Jupiter probes. But it wouldn't have been fair. He realized that the philosopher's pedantic manner concealed a brilliant mind, and he liked Treibnitz and didn't want to hurt his feelings.

The first gloomy days of autumn came, and the castle and its inhabitants were in the grip of restless hurry and bustle. The Master of the Waterworks turned off the park fountains, maids filled huge trunks with clothing and brocade tablecloths, horse-drawn carts were loaded up with barrels, and an old valet packed silver goblets away in caskets and wrapped coarse sacking around pictures – still lifes and small landscapes.

One day, after a last lesson from the Privy Councillor on the language and writing of the Chinese, the Princess drew Robert aside and led him to the white-walled hall. Little remained now of the brilliant balls that had been held there; all the furniture was covered with hessian, and the walls were empty.

'I'm sure you must have noticed that the court is about to leave, Robert,' said the Princess. 'We're going back to town and the Old Castle, a dismal fortress of a place where they'll imprison me again, bore me to death with tedious ceremonies and try to marry me off to some distant cousin. All my pleasure is in the arts and sciences! The pictures that hung on these empty walls were my own collection, although I'm afraid you scarcely gave them a glance.'

'I had eyes only for you, Madame,' replied Robert. By now he was so used to the courtly manner of speech, that most foreign of all foreign languages, that the gallant compliment sprang easily to his lips.

The Princess smiled. 'I fear we shall have fewer opportunities to speak together in town. Take this souvenir as some small consolation. And remember that I wish you well; you mustn't doubt that.'

She beckoned to her servant, who produced an album bound in red morocco leather with a series of drawings glued into it.

'This one is in sanguine,' Sophie Amalie explained, 'and this one a pen-and-ink drawing, highlighted in white with a brush, and at the very end there is a landscape by Paul Bril, a Flemish painter who once lived in Italy.'

Robert was impressed by the Princess's enthusiasm and indeed her expertise; he wouldn't have expected her to know so much about art. He thanked her sincerely for the gift, and was dismissed with a soft glance from her slanting eyes.

Early next morning a long procession set out from Herrenlinden, with armed guards riding ahead. They were followed by the princely family's gilded state coach, other coaches carrying the courtiers and the open carriages for the servants, and the rear was brought up by a baggage train of carts, open and covered, heavily laden with furniture, casks and trunks. The procession came to a halt outside the capital city, and to his amazement Robert saw two swineherds driving a grunting herd of pigs through the gate. In fact the capital didn't seem to him much like a city at all. There were piles of manure at the roadside, and when the coach in which Robert was sitting rattled over the wooden bridge outside the castle a horrible smell rose from the branch of the river that divided the city in two.

Robert now had to share his room with a young Danish squire who spoke only broken German and whom he did not much trust; he soon realized that his room-mate was an envious snob and a gossip. 'So what's your Princess like at close quarters?' he asked with a knowing grin, and it was only when Robert scored a hit to his throat on the fencing ground one day that he stopped making such insinuations. Even then, Robert was on his guard, thinking it quite likely that the Dane was spying on him.

Whatever happened, he thought, the possessions he had kept throughout his strange travels mustn't fall into the Danish squire's hands. And why would he want to carry a little toy Porsche or a Russian dictionary around with him here in the Old Castle? They'd only make trouble for him if they were found, arousing suspicion and causing people to ask questions he couldn't answer. Yet he didn't want to part from them; they were the only solid evidence that Robert really was Robert and not some changeling. When he discovered a secret compartment in the long-legged chest of drawers where he kept his clothes he hid his treasures there, including the album the Princess had given him.

Sometimes, on free afternoons when he could be sure that no one would disturb him, he took it out, looked at the pictures and day-dreamed. There were views of Roman palaces, little landscapes with rivers, shepherds and ruins, nymphs bathing, knights drawn in sharp outline fighting one another with spears. His favourite picture was a water-colour drawing of an attack on a travelling carriage. Robbers were advancing from the outskirts of a little wood. The coach-horses in their red velvet saddlecloths were rearing, and the footmen in sky-blue livery had already made off. A wheel was lying on the ground; it had come off the carriage, which was now tilting at an angle across the road. A bandit was aiming his shotgun at the travellers, while another man, who wore a plume, was holding a spear and aiming it at an armed guard who was turning to flee. A gentleman in a fur-trimmed cloak lay on the ground bleeding, and a finely dressed lady with an elegant little hat was bending over him. There was a second woman there too, climbing carefully out of the coach with her back turned to the viewer. Robert was particularly fascinated by this figure, which reminded him of Princess Sophie Amalie. Surely that was exactly her figure, her way of holding herself and moving? Or was he just imagining it? The picture must be at least a hundred years old, so it couldn't possibly show the Princess, yet sometimes, when Robert half-closed his eyes and fell to day-dreaming, he thought he saw her before him.

No sooner had the court settled in than more festivities

began. First there was Sophie Amalie's birthday to be celebrated. Some distinguished guests were attending, the cousins from Ratzeburg and Gotha about whom Sophie Amalie was so unenthusiastic although – or because – her father had great plans for them. His bodyguard met the foreign visitors at the city gates, and their travelling coaches entered the capital to the ringing of bells and the sound of trumpets.

The assembled court was waiting for the princely guests in the great hall of the castle. The Lord Chamberlain struck the floor with his staff and announced, in a loud voice: '*Son Altesse, Monseigneur George Auguste, le Prince de Ratzebourg-Herrenlinden, Comte de Ammerfeld et Hardeck, Seigneur de Kalkum, Schoepf et Entenhausen.*' Robert wondered why this string of titles had to be recited in French, since most of the ladies and gentlemen present couldn't even speak educated German properly and preferred to converse in their own rough dialect. After the guests had seated themselves, with a good deal of noise, poor Treibnitz had to step forward and recite an endless poem of welcome stuffed with Latin quotations, which fell on deaf ears. Then dinner was announced. Robert was sitting far down the hall with his companions, who on this occasion were acting with perfect propriety. 'How old *is* the Princess?' he asked his neighbour at table. 'You should know best!' the young man whispered. 'Wait a moment – she was born in 1685, so she's seventeen today.'

Aha! 1685 plus 17 made it 1702. At last Robert knew what time he was living in.

A banquet of formidable proportions was served, a bewildering array of lark pasties, fish soup, haunches of venison, partridges, pickled cabbage and ox tongue. There seemed no end to all the dishes, and Robert, trying to keep up with all the

166

toasts being drunk, was soon quite dizzy with the burgundy, Moselle and Tokay wines that accompanied them.

After dinner the whole company moved to the court theatre, where an Italian opera was performed. No one seemed to listen to it. The ladies and gentlemen talked in loud voices in their boxes, ignoring the singers.

In the middle of the second act Robert, who had only standing room on the ground floor of the theatre, felt someone pluck his sleeve. It was the stiff and starchy chamberlain who had shown him around that first evening after the ball. 'It pleases His Serene Highness to summon you to his box,' he whispered in Robert's ear.

The Prince, a corpulent man of sixty, was sitting alone in a tall, gilded chair with his back to the stage. He had a goblet in one hand, and seemed to be deep in thought. Robert waited. At first he thought the Prince had drunk too much, but when His Highness turned to him and looked at him, with slightly bloodshot eyes, their glance beneath the heavy lids was cold and alert.

'Well, well,' he murmured. 'So you're the young fellow Robert that everyone's talking about, whether they speak good or ill of you. A prodigy, according to Treibnitz, but then he's an oddity himself. My court preacher, although he's a blockhead, warns me against you and says you are a black magician who can see into the future. You don't look as dangerous as that to me. I hear, however, that you don't always show princely persons all the respect due to them. I am sure you know what I mean. In future I wish you to avoid such foolishness and pride. Mark what I say! I see that you are of good family, some runaway sprig of an old line, the family of some turnip-headed Prussian count, no doubt, or even a bishop's son, teehee!' The Prince bleated with laughter.

'Yes, you've probably run away from home like the Prodigal Son in the Bible.'

He stared at Robert, who stood in the doorway of the box without venturing to answer. There was a pause while the singers on stage performed an endless quartet. Robert was beginning to think the Prince had lost the thread of his train of thought when His Highness finally announced his decision in surprisingly loud tones.

'I shall keep an eye on you, and if you behave well I'll make you a squire of my chamber. And now get out of my sight!'

Robert had not spoken a word throughout this audience, but news that the Prince had summoned him spread like the wind, and his noble companions, including the Dane who shared his room, took good care not to annoy him from now on. The days went by in a routine of fencing practice, dancing lessons and riding, and the only work he did was to render the chamberlain a small service now and then, carrying a confidential letter or escorting a distant relative of the princely family when she went to Mass.

But what occupied his mind most, and hurt him too after a while, was that he hardly ever saw the Princess any more. He hadn't even been able to offer good wishes on her birthday. All she granted him was an occasional slanting glance on the great staircase, or a small smile as she climbed into the coach. Robert didn't intend to be shaken off so easily. First he tried to win the confidence of Sophie's lady in waiting, but Madame von Erk was not forthcoming. 'A little more reticence would suit you better,' she said, thin-lipped. 'Her Serene Highness has better things to do than talk to you.' In her high-necked black dress she looked very forbidding, but Robert guessed that she knew more than she would say.

So he decided to stake everything on a single throw. He had long ago found out where his girlfriend had her apartments –

for he wouldn't let anyone persuade him that the Princess was *not* his girlfriend. Hadn't she spent whole afternoons talking to him about the distant stars, or any ridiculous little matters that came into their heads? Why had she given him that wonderful album if she wanted no more to do with him?

He was only waiting for a good opportunity to visit her in secret, and one evening, when the Prince was out hunting with his retinue and not a soul was stirring in the castle, he summoned up his courage and crept up the servants' back stairs to the wing where Sophie Amalie lived. The full moon cast bright bars of light on the marble slabs paving the vaulted galleries and corridors of the castle. He knew he was breaking the rules, and when he entered the dark anteroom his pulse was beating hard in his throat. But it wasn't the first time he had ventured so far. He opened a second door, and found himself in the kind of small room called a cabinet. This room too was dark, but he could hear voices next door. It was the Princess – he recognized her laugh – and the muted reply must come from her lady in waiting.

Cautiously, Robert pressed down the handle of the boudoir door until it opened just a crack. The Princess's hair, which she had loosened, shone like a halo in the candlelight. She was sitting at her mirror in a dressing-gown. Robert remembered the scene in Herrenlinden, but this time he did not intend to be discovered on any account. He stayed back in the shadows and listened with bated breath to the conversation.

'You do very well to avoid him, Ma'am,' he heard the lady in waiting say. 'He's an impertinent fellow, and there have already been wicked tongues wagging at court, telling silly tales of some secret liaison between you.'

The Princess seemed to find this funny. The fire on the hearth was burning so brightly that it was very hot in the room. 'But my dear,' she said, fanning herself for air, 'you know he was only a plaything! A charming plaything, it's true, and without him I'd have perished of boredom out there in the country.'

'However, Ma'am, it is always best to keep up appearances, if I may venture to say so. He was pestering me only recently, and you should have seen his look of dog-like devotion as he begged me to take you his inane compliments. He really imagines that . . .'

'Let him imagine what he likes,' cried the Princess. 'Although now that I come to think of it, if those fools are spreading such rumours they could be useful to me after all.'

'Highness, what do you mean?'

'My dear Erk,' replied Sophie after a moment, 'you know I can hide nothing from you. You are the only person I trust, and I need your help. Young Baron Lövenstierna –'

'The Swede?'

'Yes, the Swede.'

'Out of the question! I implore you – the Baron has nothing to his name but debts, and his reputation is not of the best either.'

'What do I care for his debts?' The Princess jumped up, throwing her fan aside. 'I like him, and he's madly in love with me. So there! You must make sure he can come and go to visit me unobserved. He'll be waiting at midnight at the little gate by the stables. If necessary, give the guard money and kind words.'

'But Serene Highness, I beg you! If the Prince your father should hear . . .'

'I know you. You won't let me down.'

'You'll reduce me to beggary!' said the lady in waiting, but Robert could see her eyes shining. Such an adventure excited the old spinster's imagination, and she was certainly ready to dare anything for the sake of her mistress.

'Nonsense! My father wants to get me into bed with my dreary cousin, that boring greybeard with his stinking breath, and why? To get the Gotha cousins on our side at the imperial court. I've no intention of being sold like a brood mare.'

'But if His Highness your father should see that you favour the Swedish baron . . .'

'We won't let it come to that. It won't be difficult to hoodwink him, and little Robert is just what I need. You'll send him up to my rooms – the more often the better – and everyone will be talking about it. And meanwhile I can please myself with my dear Lövenstierna undisturbed.'

Robert had heard enough. He was so angry that he felt like slamming the door, but he controlled himself and tiptoed away. Your own fault, he said to himself when he was in bed, too furious to sleep. Why had he gone along with the Princess's little game? This ridiculous little princely state into which chance had flung him was very far from being a fairy-tale place. He told himself he would never again fall for the sidelong glances of a spoilt, capricious bitch – for he was in such a temper that the word 'bitch' sprang to his mind, and only the snoring Dane beside him kept him from venting his disillusionment out loud.

When Madame von Erk approached him next day in the castle courtyard she was entirely changed: graciousness in person. He pretended to have an urgent errand, and rode out for miles, past turnip fields and meadows, until his anger died down. After that he withdrew entirely from the company of the other pages. He spent his time reading all kinds of books from the castle library: long-winded, old-fashioned novels, travel books, impassioned treatises showing him that the natural sciences were still in their infancy.

These were monotonous days. He avoided the Princess's lady in waiting, and although he would have liked to talk to Treibnitz, the Privy Councillor had been sent to Vienna on a secret mission and was still away.

In early November, on All Souls' Day, Robert woke late. His room-mate wasn't there. Sleepily, he looked out of the window. The first snow had fallen, and there was nothing moving in the castle courtyard. The world seemed to be packed in cotton wool. Even the bells ringing from the city church sounded muted. Footmen scurried along the corridors, and there was no laughter to be heard in the kitchens. It seemed as if no one dared speak out loud. The whispering did not begin until late in the afternoon, when dusk was falling.

Then the coachmen and grooms put their heads together. Someone said a guard had been posted outside the Swedish baron's house, and the door had been broken down and all the rooms searched. Under the seal of secrecy, another man repeated what his brother-in-law the cloth-worker had told him: the night before, he said, he had seen two men swathed in cloaks dragging a heavy sack away behind the stables and throwing it into the dyers' ditch.

Late that evening three of the squires met in the room next to Robert's, and he could hear them through the wall in loud conversation over beer and schnapps. The Dane was particularly outspoken, shouting, 'Serves the fellow right! These damn foreigners should be drowned. I'd have done the same in her father's place!' So saying, he threw his glass at the wall, and the other two agreed with him.

No one dared ask where the Princess was. Not until next day were there whispered rumours, after church, that she was being kept confined to her room. No, said someone who seemed to know better, a troop of armed men had taken her away to Kalitz, a remote fortress to which His Serene Highness was banishing his only daughter as punishment. It was also said that the Princess remained obstinately silent, but her lady in waiting, Madame von Erk, who had disappeared too, had already confessed everything about the Princess's secret love affair with Baron Lövenstierna.

Robert listened to the backstairs rumours. Had they really murdered the Swedish baron? He could hardly believe it. The whole of this court struck him as a bunch of lunatics, beginning with his room-mate and including the entire puffed-up set of Chamberlains, Privy Secretaries and Presidents of the Chamber, right up to His Serene Highness in person. It was like some kind of soap opera. The only person he was sorry for was the Princess. She might have played cat and mouse with him, but she didn't deserve to be imprisoned by her own father. There was only one person left in the entire principality with whom he could exchange a sensible word, and that was Treibnitz.

Treibnitz was back from Vienna now; Robert saw him in the snow-covered castle courtyard one icy winter morning. Two men were carrying him to the porch in a sedan chair. He got out of it grunting, supported by his servant.

'May I speak to you, Excellency?' Robert made haste to help him, for he saw that Treibnitz was suffering from gout again.

'Ah, Robert, our young prodigy,' said the philosopher. 'How have you been keeping? I'm glad to see you.'

'Can you spare me a minute?'

'Not now. Not here. The walls have ears in this place. We could go for a sleigh ride this afternoon if you like.'

And so they did. Treibnitz, wrapped in a heavy fur coat, drove up after the midday meal in a small sleigh drawn by a single horse. Robert sat beside him, and let the driver give him a thick travelling rug.

They went out over the broad, bare plain, past lonely farmhouses with chained dogs yapping outside them. There wasn't a soul in sight, and only the smoke rising from the chimneys showed that the area was inhabited at all. It was quarter of an hour before the philosopher broke his silence.

'I'm giving up this nonsense,' he began. 'I've wasted enough of my time at court. I used to think one should try to wrest the bright opal from the mine, the gold from the mud, the light from darkness. I set myself the aim of promoting the general good. And a fine aim it is, too. But there's nothing to be done about the stupidity of princes and their turbulent passions.'

Robert had never seen the philosopher so angry before. The mild tones in which he used to speak in the park at Herrenlinden were entirely gone! The old man had talked himself into a fury; his face flushed red, and Robert had a feeling that he had completely forgotten who was in the sleigh with him.

'They threaten violence!' the old man went on. 'They'd like to break my neck! The Prince is out for revenge. He seeks scapegoats, and who knows, he may have fixed on me. It would be dangerous to stay here. Since he disowned the Princess I have lost my last comfort. There's not a human soul here now who is capable of any higher idea. Every wish for knowledge has died away.'

After this outburst, Treibnitz closed his eyes and fell into a doze that lasted some time. When he opened his eyes again, his glance fell on Robert.

'And what about you? Believe me, you can expect nothing but malice and ill-will from the court of Herrenlinden.' His voice had resumed its usual gentle tone. 'If you like I'll take you with me to my small estate in Westphalia, where I shall be safe from the slander and persecution that I face here. You are rather too high-spirited, but clever, and you could help me. I'm exhausted, and I need an assistant. If you have fluent handwriting and know a little Latin, you'll do.'

Robert assured him that he did have a certain amount of knowledge, and by the time the sleigh stopped outside the castle again their deal was done. The philosopher shook hands as they said goodbye, and whispered, 'Wait for me in the Wood Market, then, just before sunrise tomorrow. Pack your things, but let no one guess your intentions.'

Their journey was more like flight. The philosopher had secretly bought a travelling carriage and loaded it up overnight. Robert brought nothing but a bundle of clothes and a little linen bag containing the Princess's album and his possessions from the old days. They had a long journey ahead of them, and there were no paved roads. The carriage jolted over corduroy roads made of logs, and rutted tracks through the fields. It got stuck in a snowdrift more than once, and the driver, swearing, had to wield a shovel. Treibnitz cursed the bad horses; he was in a bad temper anyway because of his gout. They had to spend the night in a gloomy inn where there was only bread soup for supper, and they travelled through the second night without stopping, resting only briefly in the morning at a posting station where they changed horses. It was not until nearly evening, when they reached the long avenue leading to the Privy Councillor's country house, that Treibnitz's face brightened.

Their journey ended outside a handsome half-timbered building. An old manservant, hardly less frail than his master, and a kitchen-maid came running out to greet the philosopher. Soon the fire in the stove was raked up, and pots and pans were steaming on the range. Robert was given a chilly room with green wallpaper and a four-poster bed. Supper was chicken broth, smoked meat and cabbage. Treibnitz poured a glass of Tokay for his guest and one for himself, saying he was glad to get away from the pointless life of the court.

The biggest and most comfortable room in the house was the philosopher's study. The very day after their arrival his table was groaning under the weight of papers and bundles of documents. Folio volumes bound in parchment or calfskin stood in long rows in the bookcases. The scientific instruments the scholar had collected gleamed in a tall display cabinet: a valuable astrolabe, compasses of all sizes, a sextant and a brass telescope. They were surrounded by minerals, shells and fossil finds, and a large globe was enthroned on a stand in the corner.

Robert had a small table beside the stove, and his first task was to copy a long legal treatise; he could barely understand half of it. He also had to learn how to handle a quill pen. The sharp tip of the feather was scratchy, and wouldn't hold the ink. By the time you had finished a page the wretched thing was so blunt that it had to be sharpened with a little penknife. Robert ruined several sheets of fine vellum with his clumsy writing, and he kept making mistakes as well, so that it was a week before he could produce a manuscript to anything like his master's satisfaction. But Treibnitz still did not approve of Robert's handwriting. 'What a scrawl the boy has,' he muttered. 'All askew, no grace to it.' He found a manual of calligraphy, and after a while Robert became used to writing a chancery hand with all its arches and curlicues.

Even worse was the fact that Treibnitz never went to bed. He sat over his papers until late at night, and didn't seem to notice that Robert, like most other people, needed eight hours of sleep. He made his assistant work long hours by candlelight. The slight scratch of the pen on the paper was the only sound in the room, which smelled of leather, dust and the smoke from the stove. Sometimes Robert stopped and fell into an idle day-dream, until the old man looked up and commented, 'It seems to me your mind is often somewhere else. What are you thinking of, Robert?'

Robert was thinking of Sophie Amalie's dark blue eyes, of Olga in the cold of Siberia while he was here in frosty Westphalia, of being a noodler in Australia and of his friend Ratibor – what would Ratibor be doing now? But the philosopher knew nothing about all this, so Robert just said, 'My eyes hurt. I'd like to go to bed.'

'Rest,' said the philosopher, looking at him sternly, 'rest is a staging post on the road to stupidity. One must always be aware of how much there is to be done, to be thought, to be planned. I thank God such awareness has been granted to me! At last I can return to my projects, and indeed I have no time to lose. I have spent far too long over the Prince's documents, poring over his archives, prying about the capitals of Europe for him.'

'I didn't notice any of that,' said Robert quickly. He was wide awake again, and glad that Treibnitz was ready to talk to him. 'Listen, the fact is I really got to the court of Herrenlinden by mistake. At first, out in the country in summer, I enjoyed it. And your conversations with the Princess were interesting and exciting. I thought we could live like that for ever, but then . . .'

'You thought so only because you know nothing of life on the stage where the great lead their lives. Vanity of vanities, all is vanity. Titles, claims, inheritances, alliances, military campaigns! Merely to get the better of their neighbours and gain a few villages! Why, the battle of Schwarzach against the French alone cost seven hundred lives, and what was the war good for, when it was nothing to do with us? It was started only so that the Emperor in Vienna would sign a piece of paper and subsidies from Saxony would go on flowing. Thirty thousand ducats! And what thanks did I get for my services as mediator? The Prince was too tight-fisted to support my plans to improve the mines and build an observatory. Believe me, Robert, no air is more poisonous than the air of a court. We have seen how far malice can go there.'

As far as murder, both were thinking, but neither said so aloud.

'I don't feel any of that here on your estate,' said Robert. 'But copying all the time does make me tired. Why, the treatise you gave me is all about marriage contracts too, and boring legal arguments about inheritances!'

'You are right, my young friend. I have neglected my duties as your teacher, and there's no other tutor to be found for you anywhere near. I shall try to make up for it tomorrow.'

And with these words Robert was dismissed, and could finally get into his warm bed.

Directly after breakfast Treibnitz began to fulfil his promise. He seated himself ceremoniously in his armchair. 'Now, if you are not afraid of mathematics I will teach you some of my ideas. The science of mathematics is my comfort, for it gives one a wonderful insight into the divine idea. Does that surprise you? Let me tell you: God had only to make his calculations and perform them, and the world was created! And I believe that in my own studies I am following him who cares for the good of the whole – for it is all one to God whether we humans acknowledge his care or not.'

Trust Treibnitz, thought Robert. Like all scientists, he thinks he can compete with God. He wouldn't work for anything less, and when his fellow men don't understand he feels hurt. But Robert kept these observations to himself, and assumed his most attentive expression. With a philosopher like Treibnitz, you never knew if he might come up with some fabulous new idea next moment, and Robert thought he would like that after all the boring copying he'd done.

Sure enough, the old man suddenly asked him, 'Do you know what prime numbers are?'

Robert could answer that one straight away. 'Only you never know in advance whether a number is a prime number or not,' he continued. 'Perhaps you can explain that to me. And how often do they occur – is there any rule about that? My maths teacher at school kept avoiding the question when I asked him.'

The old man was pleased. He looked at Robert with his short-sighted eyes as if seeing him for the first time. 'I don't know either,' he said. 'It is one of the great riddles of the world. The best of mathematicians have been unable to solve it.'

The treatise on the laws of inheritance was forgotten. Gradually, Treibnitz told his pupil what he knew about prime numbers. He seemed positively reinvigorated, and filled a whole sheet of paper with hastily scribbled proofs. Then he began complaining about the decimal system.

'Nothing but an old habit,' he assured Robert. 'We use ten different numbers merely because we have ten fingers. It would be far simpler and more elegant if we made do with two. All you need is one and zero. Nothing in the world can better demonstrate the power of Almighty God, which is to say his creation of all things out of nothing, than this manner of deriving all numbers from 0 and 1.'

'You mean the binary system?'

Robert had certainly hit the target with this bold reply. Treibnitz stared at him as if he had some kind of mathematical genius in front of him. It was nothing special, thought Robert, in fact it was rather a cheap trick to surprise his master with the maths he was learning in Class Nine. All the same, he went on to show the philosopher how easy it was to calculate with the binary system:

$$1 = 1 \times 10^0 \qquad \text{corresponds to} \qquad 1 = 1 \times 2^0$$
$$10 = 1 \times 10^1 \qquad \text{corresponds to} \qquad 2 = 1 \times 2^0$$
$$11 = 1 \times 10^1 + 1 \times 10^0 \qquad \text{corresponds to} \qquad 3 = 1 \times 2^1 + 1 \times 2^0$$
$$100 = 1 \times 10^2 \qquad \text{corresponds to} \qquad 4 = 1 \times 2^2$$
$$101 = 1 \times 10^2 + 1 \times 10^0 \qquad \text{corresponds to} \qquad 5 = 1 \times 2^2 + 1 \times 2^0$$

and so on

'For instance, 53 can just be taken apart into powers of 2, 32 plus 16 plus 4 plus 1, which is 110101, and of course then it's easy to add and subtract because you're only dealing with those two tiny numbers.'

This did just what Robert intended: the philosopher entirely forgot that he was not talking to one of his colleagues from Leyden University or the Paris Académie, but a starving if involuntary tramp who should be glad of a bed and a plate of soup in a country house in deepest Westphalia.

Robert was pleased to see the old man taking him seriously, but he soon had to admit that there were disadvantages to it, for there was no holding Treibnitz now. His explanation of what a constant function was, and which series 'converged' and which did not, wasn't the worst of it, since if Robert paid close attention he could just about follow. But then came the theory of enveloping curves, and finally Treibnitz started on his hobby-horse.

'Here, my young friend,' he said, throwing a huge manuscript on the table. 'The fruits of my labours, the results of my thinking! Study them hard so that we may discuss them. Few know this work, but you shall be one of those few!'

Robert's heart sank. He had understood about as much of the enveloping curves as he did of the complicated intrigues of the Herrenlinden princely family – nothing at all. And now he was supposed to wade through the old philosopher's mathematical bible, full of mysterious formulae and written in Latin at that:

Nova Methodus

pro Maximis et Minimis, itemque tangentibus, quæ nec fractas, nec irrationales quantitates moratur,

and so on and so forth. He couldn't even understand the title, so he simply said, 'I'll try, but heaven knows if I'll make anything of it. Honoured sir and master, I am no learned scholar.'

Perhaps Treibnitz realized that he had gone too far. He simply nodded, but his disappointment was obvious. Robert felt a fraud. He did try, gradually, to decipher the manuscript. It seemed to be something to do with the calculation of differentials, but you didn't get to them until Class Twelve at school, and he didn't see why he should have to learn them in Latin as well. In the end Treibnitz just asked him to write out the text in a clean copy, which was no light task, since the old man's scrawl was difficult to read.

In the long run it became too much for both of them, shut away there in the study. Robert's eyes hurt, and he found the philosopher sitting in his armchair one morning in January looking worn out, in dressing-gown and night-cap, trembling with exhaustion and temper.

'What's the matter?' he asked. 'I'm afraid you need a doctor.'

'It's nothing. Only the gout, a little fever, and a sense that it is all too much for me. Just when I have my freedom back I feel my powers diminishing. As for a doctor,' he added with a scornful laugh, 'you wouldn't find one within fifteen miles of here.'

He rose, with difficulty. 'I have thought about it,' he continued, gravely, 'and I have decided to tell you a secret. To whom else can I confide it? There's no one in this country able to judge the true worth of my invention. But for my enemies I could present it to the Royal Society in London, but they'd only rob me of it there. Come with me!'

Picking up a candlestick, he lit the candles in it and led his pupil to a door in the wall covered with wallpaper and so well disguised that Robert had never noticed it. A windowless room lay behind it, and there, on a rostrum covered with velvet, stood a heavy, shining object made of brass, two yards long and one yard wide. The machine had two cranks with wooden handles, a number of gearwheels and metal spirals, and a graduated roller.

'That is a calculating machine,' said Treibnitz proudly, 'and moreover, it can calculate in all four branches of mathematics. Anyone can use it, without the need for thought, to add, subtract, multiply and divide.'

'May I try it?' asked Robert.

'Better not – the device is sensitive. One wrong move and you could ruin it.'

The temptation was too great. Robert couldn't resist it any longer. 'Would you wait for a moment?' he asked, and left his surprised master where he was. He ran upstairs to his room, reached into the little bag containing his possessions, and hurried back to the room where Treibnitz, looking rather irritated, was waiting for him.

'Here,' said Robert, handing him his pocket calculator. The philosopher turned it this way and that, read the airline's advertising slogan out loud, shook his head and gave the little device back.

'What is it?' he asked.

Robert showed him how the calculator worked. 'You just have to touch the keys,' he explained. 'The black area here is a solar cell. The sunlight, or if necessary the light of your candles, feeds the calculator with energy. This is the storage key, and you can use it to work out percentages.'

Treibnitz snatched the calculator from his hand again, and began trying it out.

'It's only a simple one,' said Robert apologetically. 'For a bit more money you can buy one that will work out logarithms, sines and cosines and so on, and roots and powers.'

He ought not have said that, for the old man was speechless and indeed frightened. 'A marvel!' he breathed. 'A marvel.'

'But, master,' Robert tried to soothe him, 'you yourself said once: "Marvels do not make me marvel; they are less unreasonable than we suppose."'

'Go!' cried Treibnitz, beside himself with excitement – or was it anger? 'Leave me alone! I must be alone.'

Robert did not see him again until the evening, when the philosopher would eat nothing. He sat at his desk, bending over the pocket calculator, muttering confused words and filling sheet after sheet of paper with his illegible handwriting. Now and then he crumpled a sheet up and threw it away. Robert felt sorry for him. I shouldn't have shown him the thing, he thought. But it was too late now.

Two days later Robert woke with a headache and swollen eyelids, and Treibnitz, who had not appeared at breakfast, lay in bed with a fever, suffering hallucinations.

The old servant scratched his head. He couldn't remember that his master had ever called in a doctor, he said. Then the kitchen-maid intervened: two villages away there was a barber-surgeon, she told Robert, and he was said to be very skilful. Robert got her to tell him the way, took the only horse in the stables, and found the man sitting over his breakfast of bean soup, still half asleep. He was a strong, muscular fellow who didn't want to be disturbed, and went on with his meal unmoved. 'It's very urgent,' said Robert, and finally he persuaded the barber-surgeon to get up behind him on the horse with his knapsack, which he clutched tightly.

They found the philosopher asleep. The barber-surgeon looked at him, felt his forehead and pulse and shrugged his shoulders. 'The Privy Councillor won't last long,' he said. 'No, when you get the intermittent fever along with the gout, it's a bad business.'

Robert felt guilty. The frail old man had been brooding over the little pocket calculator for nights on end, getting more and more distraught the less he could manage to work out how it was made. Could it be his feverish study of it that had weakened him to this extent?

'But the case isn't hopeless yet. If the gentleman isn't suffering from the flux . . . For the moment we'll leave him to sleep, that's the best thing. But now to you, young sir. It's the eyes with you, I see.'

Bending over Robert, he muttered to himself. 'Aha . . . pressure of the blood, reddened conjunctiva, swollen lids. Do you feel any itching? Headache? Dizziness? We'll soon deal with that.'

Wearing only shirt and trousers, Robert had to lie on his bed while the barber-surgeon produced the tools of his trade from his knapsack. He held up a jar with a dozen whitish worms wriggling at the bottom of it. 'Never fear,' he said, 'it won't hurt. We'll just bleed you a little.' Using a pair of wooden pincers, he skilfully hooked the first leech out of the jar and put it in a small glass. With disgust, Robert felt him tilt the glass against his left temple. When the creature bit he sat up with a jerk, crying, 'What are you doing? I can't stand the sight of blood!'

'Keep still,' snapped the barber-surgeon, pushing him back on the pillows with his powerful arm. Firmly, he applied more leeches to both temples, right and left of Robert's nose, even behind his ears. When he set one to suck at an armpit Robert, who was squinting sideways at the leech, watched the creature slowly swell, becoming plumper and plumper and taking on a reddish tinge. Sweat stood out on his forehead and tears rose to his eyes. Dizzy with revulsion, he closed them. He was already half unconscious, and in a kind of semi-dream he saw the Princess standing before him, giving him the album bound in red morocco. He looked for the picture in which he fancied he recognized her, and when he had found it he saw the scene with such exaggerated clarity that the sunbeam on the spear of the robber wearing the plume dazzled him, and he thought he felt the breath of the wind stirring the foliage of the oak under which a man in a helmet was sheltering. It seemed to cast a flickering shade. And then he heard the shot.

THE SIXTH JOURNEY

At first he saw only what he wanted to see: the Princess. Her back was turned to him as she clambered cautiously out of the coach: not an easy task, since the body of the vehicle was tilted on three wheels and threatened to tip over completely at any moment.

Only it wasn't Sophie Amalie at all! When the woman turned, Robert saw a stranger's face covered with suppurating pustules filled with dark blood. The woman was weeping. She had smallpox – or could it even be bubonic plague?

Robert realized that he had fallen into the deep well of time yet again. The picture frozen on the leaf in his album had come to life, and was now in movement before his eyes. Although the attack lasted only a few minutes he noticed every detail as clearly as if it were all happening in slow motion: the acrid smell of powder rising to his nostrils, the coach-wheel that had rolled across the road, the whinnying of the coach-horses, the man with the helmet in the undergrowth, the screams of the victims, the robbers shouting. He caught a few words that sounded German, but others were unfamiliar. Perhaps they were thieves' jargon or some dialect he didn't know. At least I haven't landed in Spain or America, he thought briefly, watching the man with the plume driving the coachman ahead of him with his spear, its tip glittering in the sunlight. Another man was standing behind a forked branch, propping his musket in the fork. It must have been he who fired the shot. His victim, the man in the fur-trimmed coat who had drawn his sword to defend himself, was lying on the ground, bleeding from a wound in his throat. There was no sign of the travellers' servants; they had evidently made their escape by now.

The third robber, a muscular, red-haired man, was holding a finely dressed lady in his arms. She was shouting and struggling as hard as she could. It was the woman in the elegant little hat who had been bending over her husband as he lay motionless on the ground. Robert watched as she narrowly avoided rape, buying herself off by offering the man her pearl necklace and her purse. He snatched them from her hands and she fled across the fields, stumbling and weeping.

The red-haired man watched her go, unmoved. He was rocking back and forth on the balls of his feet as if the whole scene were nothing to do with him. When he turned his head, Robert saw that the man was smiling. And it was Ratibor. Robert could hardly believe his eyes. The robber was undoubtedly a little taller and a few years older than his friend, but otherwise he was the spitting image of Ratibor. The way he grinned, the way he carried himself, the way he put his hands on his hips – no doubt about it, this was his friend Ratibor to the life.

Robert wanted to run over and say something, but he stood there frozen with surprise and alarm, unable to move from the spot. The man he thought he knew so well uttered a piercing whistle. Immediately a fourth robber, who had been waiting under the oak in the bushes, broke out of his hiding place holding the bridles of two horses. Ratibor swung himself up on one of them, a dapple-grey, shouted another order to his men and galloped away.

The robbers who had been left behind picked up two heavy chests that were lying in the ditch behind the coach, took the neighing coach-horses out of the shafts, mounted them and set off after their leader, along with their loot and their weapons.

It was suddenly so quiet that Robert could hear a cuckoo calling in the distance. The sun was already low in the sky, and an evening breeze was ruffling the leaves of the trees. He realized that he was shivering; he was wearing only a thin, billowing undershirt and close-fitting breeches. He never seemed to have the right clothes for these crazy journeys, he thought, because he never knew where he was going to end up! At least it wasn't as cold and windy here as in Siberia.

His glance fell on the man lying on the ground in front of the empty coach. Reluctantly, he went over and took a closer look. The shot had hit an artery and the man was dead. There was a trickle of blood running down over the fur collar of his coat. Robert hesitated, but then plucked up all his courage and pulled at the dead man's boots. The corpse was heavier than he had expected. As if moving in a nightmare, he turned it over and removed the coat. He took the man's sword and its sheath as well. The corpse looked at him with glassy eyes. He turned away quickly with his booty, and sat down in the grass on the outskirts of the wood to think.

None of the robbers had noticed him. But surely Ratibor ought to have recognized him! Robert felt his mind must be going.

He had no idea where he was, and he owned nothing in the world but a shirt and a pair of trousers. The little bag with the Princess's album and his other possessions were left behind in the philosopher's house. Not that they'd have been any use here anyway, he told himself.

He passed a hand over his eyes. The swelling had gone down, and he felt no burning any more. Had the barber-surgeon's blood-letting done him good after all? He pushed back the collar of his shirt and found a small dark mark on his shoulder. When he looked more closely, he could even see the leech-bite. A row of tiny dots showed where its little teeth had pierced Robert's skin.

Well, he had to do something before nightfall. Reluctantly, he picked up the dead man's coat and put it on. It fitted perfectly. When he tried to button it up he realized that it was actually a cape, with ends that you simply threw over your shoulder. As he was adjusting the fur-trimmed hem he felt something in the pocket of his breeches, something hard and round. The little object he found there was his car, the toy Porsche he always carried around with him. How ridiculous! He almost threw the stupid thing away, but he couldn't bring himself to do that. It was his last souvenir, a talisman, an amulet. Clutching the toy in his breeches pocket, he found something else there too. A piece of stiff, crumpled paper. He extracted it and smoothed it out. In the middle of this deserted place, he was overcome by such a sense of happiness that he almost wept. It was Ratibor, Ratibor in his hockey outfit in front of the wall of ads with the cigarette advertisement showing the Wild West! The photo was bent here and there, but when he held it close to his eyes to check every detail he was even surer than he had been before. It wasn't just the red hair. The Polaroid also showed the bold glance, the strong hands, mouth and nose of the robber who had ridden away on his dapple-grey only a quarter of an hour ago.

Robert made up his mind. He put on the tall, wide-topped boots of soft yellow leather that he had taken off the dead man; he stood up; he stowed the photo and the little car carefully in the pocket of the cape, he slung the sword around his waist and then he set off. It was obvious which way to go: after the red-haired horseman, even if he didn't know exactly where he had gone or how to find him. He would just have to trust to luck.

The road didn't look exactly inviting. He walked up hill and down dale, and when a stream crossed the path he was lucky to find a rotten wooden bridge over it; usually he had to wade through deep puddles. Back at home Robert used to feel indignant about the great swathes the motorway builders cut through the countryside, but toiling on like this over stony places and deep potholes was no fun either. At least he was glad to have acquired a pair of high boots, or he wouldn't have got far.

Dusk was falling. He didn't feel cold in his warm cape, but his stomach was grumbling. He had eaten nothing since breakfast in the philosopher's house. Now and then he passed a deserted farm. There was not a light to be seen anywhere, and when he passed through woodland he felt uneasy. He didn't want to fall into another ambush.

He began brooding again, which made him forget the danger. Sooner or later he'd find out where he was this time. He remembered every detail of his earlier journeys. But what had actually happened to him in between them? Where had he been during all those years that lay between his Norwegian adventure and his arrival in the castle of Herrenlinden? Had he existed at all?

And now this encounter with Ratibor! Incredible! He couldn't make any sense of it. He remembered the unfortunate Mr Tidemand who had killed himself in the hope of a wonderful life next time around. How long ago that seemed, and how far away! The silvery-eyed schoolmaster believed so firmly in reincarnation. Perhaps there was something in it after all? Nonsense, said Robert to himself. It wasn't Ratibor's soul that had travelled in time but his nose, his hands, his red hair. No wonder he hadn't recognized Robert. Not only because he was fully occupied during the attack on the coach – that had been no children's game – but how would Ratibor know that he *was* Ratibor, the same Ratibor whose picture Robert was carrying about on a crumpled Polaroid in his pocket? It would be a few centuries before his friend sat next to him at school . . . a tangle of time that couldn't be teased out. Or was he simply imagining the whole thing? Was the robber captain simply Ratibor's double, someone in the past who happened to look just like him?

Robert shook himself and pushed these thoughts away. Just now he had to concentrate on finding something to eat and a bed for the night, and puzzling over such a weird idea as reincarnation wouldn't help.

After he had been walking for two hours a village came into sight beyond a wooded hill. The place was in darkness, but of course Robert knew there'd be no electricity or proper lights here. At best, the villages might have a few candles or some dim lamps, and even in Norway those had been used sparingly. So perhaps this place wasn't entirely deserted.

Sure enough, as soon as he came closer the dogs began barking. That was a good sign. He listened. There were cattle moving restlessly in the outbuildings, and he could hear sounds coming from one of the low, thatched houses. Robert stepped cautiously through the gate into its yard. Something was moving in the dark stable there. He peered inside, and once his eyes were used to the darkness he recognized Ratibor's dapple-grey horse and knew he had come to the right place.

Groping his way back to the road, he found the entrance

to the house. When he opened the door a babble of voices met his ears. Inside the smoke-filled, dimly lit room a quantity of dishes and tankards were all jumbled up on the table. Some six or seven men bawling at the tops of their voices fell silent as he came in, and they reached for their weapons, but a brief glance at Robert was enough. They turned their attention back to their beer, banging on the table, calling to the maidservant for more and patting her bottom.

Robert hesitated, but the smell of roast meat rose to his nostrils, and he felt quite weak with his craving for food. He looked around for Ratibor. The robber captain was leaning back in the largest chair without touching his food, his back turned to Robert. Robert recognized only three of the others: the man who had driven off the coachman with his spear, the murderer who had fired the shot – he had now leaned his gun up against the wall, ready to hand – and the groom who had held the horses. None of them looked clean, but the two men he hadn't seen before were even shabbier and dirtier than the others. Plain-clothes robbers, he thought, irrelevantly, but the idea was apt enough here.

The only one who didn't look like a bandit was Ratibor, whose neighbour at the table dug him in the ribs. Ratibor turned to look at Robert and cast him a strangely intent glance – enquiring, or suspicious, or examining him in some way? No, none of those things. The robber captain seemed to be on the track of some idea. He shook his head in annoyance, pulled himself together and beckoned Robert over. 'A chair!' he ordered, and the ugly little maidservant dragged one up at once.

'That's a fine cape you have.' These were his first words, and Robert recognized his voice at once. He almost shouted 'Ratibor!' and hugged him, but just in time he realized it might be wiser to keep his mouth shut.

'Got some blood on it, though,' said the robber captain. 'Look, on the collar there. You seem familiar to me, friend.'

'My name's Robert.'

'Aha. So you were one of the travellers and made off when things got hot.'

'No,' said Robert. 'I just came on the scene by accident.'

'Oh yes? So where are you from?'

The others had fallen silent and were listening to the conversation, their faces impassive. Robert thought for a moment. Then he decided to tell the truth. He didn't really mind now whether Ratibor believed him or not.

'Herrenlinden,' he said. 'I was a page in the castle there.'

'A page, in those shabby clothes? That's a lot to expect us to swallow, friend. And where may Herrenlinden be? Anyone know a Herrenlinden Castle?'

There was a general shaking of heads and murmuring.

'Seems to me more likely you're a tramp, and a starving tramp at that.'

'Starving's true enough,' said Robert. 'I haven't had a bite to eat all day long.'

'More food here!' cried Ratibor, if it was indeed Ratibor, and Robert was immediately served with a piece of meat on a wooden platter, half a loaf and a mug of beer. He thanked the robber and fell on his meal, while the others began talking and shouting again. Robert couldn't follow their conversation, which was conducted in thieves' jargon, although now and then he caught a word in French.

'I like you, young fellow!' said Ratibor, pushing the cape off Robert's shoulders and feeling his upper arm. 'If you weren't such a lanky beanstalk and had a little more muscle, maybe I could use you.'

'I haven't learnt your trade,' Robert protested.

'Oh, it doesn't take long. Wait until they send you off to

war as a common musketeer! They'll work you to death and starve you until you run away. The great lords pocket their soldiers' wages themselves, and you're even supposed to put the countryside to fire and the sword and do their looting for them. Anyone with his wits about him is going to say: might as well do that on my own account! See him over there?' He indicated the man with the gun, who had a pointed beard. 'His name's Erik, and he's from Sweden. Now he's joined us. He limps to this day because his colonel made him run the gauntlet after the battle of Sennheim until he fell senseless and was left for dead. And Krawat there – he doesn't have any Christian name, we just call him Krawat –' here he pointed to the man with the spear – 'he barely escaped the gallows. They'd have strung him up merely because he's a Catholic. As for me – well, never mind that.'

'Is your name by any chance Ratibor?' There – it was out.

The man looked at him in surprise. 'Well, something like that,' he said. 'How d'you think you know my name? It's Radomir, and I come from Bohemia.'

So he wasn't really Ratibor. But what was he, then? A ghost? A twin brother, lost somehow in the wrong century?

'It must be hard to make yourselves understood around here,' said Robert, who had eaten well and was already on his second mug of beer. It was hot in the tavern. He was already feeling a pleasant weariness in his limbs. 'Those two over there seem to be talking French, the other one's a Swede, you're from Bohemia, and heaven only knows where Krawat comes from.'

'The lands of the Austrian emperor, blockhead, where they speak their own gibberish. We talk with our hands if it can't be done any other way. He understands me all right. And Silent Jacob there can't speak a word, not since a hussar slashed his throat with his sabre. But he only has to grunt and

the horses listen as if he were speaking their own language.'
So that was the man in charge of the robber band's horses.
The two who kept putting their heads together and whispering
were the Frenchmen, but they were apparently of rather low
status, since Radomir didn't think it worth the trouble of
mentioning them by name.

'*Er du svensk?*' Robert decided to try out his rudimentary
Norwegian. His neighbour on the left, the man called Erik,
was pleasantly surprised to hear his question, but answered
with a torrent of words very few of which, unfortunately,
Robert could understand. However, he had aroused Radomir's curiosity.

'You know Swedish?'

'Not really. A bit of French and English, and some Latin.'

'A scholar! Just what we need!'

'But in all this turmoil I don't know if I'm on my head or
my heels.'

'It's the same for us all, my dear fellow. The war's thrown
us together and taught us our trade. There's no going home
for the likes of us any more.'

By now the others were brawling drunk and beginning to
fight each other. The low-ceilinged room echoed to the sound
of curses, but when Krawat drew a knife and made for one
of the Frenchmen Radomir put a stop to it with a single word.
It sounded something like *Kush!* The robber captain spoke it
very quietly, yet so sharply that peace was restored in a
moment. Just like Ratibor when his hockey team got out of
hand! Robert took another surreptitious look at Radomir.
Not only did the man look like his friend, he even had the
same kind of way with him. It was enough to make your head
whirl – although Robert was careful not to say exactly what
was going on in his head.

'That'll do for today,' Radomir ordered. Reluctantly, his

companions put down their tankards, rose to their feet and trotted out. 'You stay here,' he told Robert.

Robert was unused to the beer, which made him feel sleepy, and Radomir seemed to be sunk in thought. They sat opposite each other for some time without speaking. 'Well, wake up,' said the red-haired man finally, 'and pay attention to what I say. I don't know why, but I've a feeling you might be useful. There's no trusting those Frenchies; a foxy pair, they are, just waiting for a chance to betray me. What I need is a scout with some brains in his head. Only a fool follows our trade at random – it's dangerous, and it doesn't pay off either.'

Robert was pleased that Radomir seemed to have confidence in him, but he hardly felt it was justified. 'I've never done anything like that before,' he protested. 'I mean, when I chanced upon your last robbery I just stood there gaping. I didn't know whether to run away or watch, and then next moment it was all over and you were off with the loot.'

'Oh, that was just a small affair! We happened to be on the road, we seized our chance. And what did it bring us? Just a load of old junk apart from the pearl necklace, and the Jew in Strasbourg will give me twenty guilders for that at the most.'

Robert pricked up his ears. Strasbourg – that was in Alsace. Well, now he knew where he was again.

'You have to discover the lie of the land in advance to find good plunder. Come and join us, then! You won't regret it.'

And so Robert became one of the robber band. He didn't have much choice, without money or a roof over his head, right in the middle of a war, and when the only person he knew was Radomir, who was the image of his friend. 'All right,' he said. 'I'll give it a try.'

They set out very early next morning. Erik the Swede flung him some clothes – baggy breeches tied at the knee with ribbons, a felt hat and a doublet with slit sleeves – and Silent Jacob found him a mare to ride. The landlord, a crooked, shifty-looking fellow, saw the little band off with much bowing and scraping when Radomir pressed a few gold pieces into his hand.

They rode across country for a good hour, towards the green hills. Those must be the foothills of the Vosges Mountains. Robert wished he had his atlas with him; a scout without a map was about as much use as a fork with no prongs. He took particular notice of the way they were going. The robber band stopped in a dense wood of fir trees, where they had their camp in three abandoned charcoal-burners' huts standing in a shallow valley. Radomir had evidently taken possession of one of them for himself, and his men had to share the others. The kiln was no longer smoking, but there was plenty of charcoal around, and they immediately lit a large fire over which the two Frenchmen roasted a couple of chickens. They ate sitting on rough wooden benches at a table made from a door wrenched out of its frame.

That afternoon Robert was sent out on his first scouting expedition. 'But be careful,' Radomir warned him. 'Don't linger anywhere, say little, look for fine carriages standing in a yard and well-dressed women, and if you see any soldiers turn back. We don't want to get involved with soldiers; they're the worst looters of all, and butcher anyone who gets in their way.'

The mare proved a good, obedient ride, but Robert looked in vain for prosperous houses. All the villages he passed through had been burned down. Once, feeling thirsty, he went to drink from a well, but the stink of carrion rose to his nostrils; the looters had thrown dead cats and dogs into the water, and maybe even the corpses of their victims. Robert moved on in a hurry. From the top of a hill he saw a band of armed men approaching in the distance, and turned round. At last, as evening was beginning to fall, he found an isolated mill standing among meadows, proud and intact as if it were peace-time. He noted the spot and rode back to the robbers' camp.

'Ah, millers, they're never short of money,' said Radomir. 'A miserly set of folk, they are, taking a third of the farmers' corn when times are bad. We'll see if there's something for us there tomorrow.'

But Robert was not happy with the idea of bloodshed. He led the band to the place, and when they could see the mill from the outskirts of the wood he told Radomir the plan he had thought up. He suggested sending two men off to close the weir in the millstream and bring the waterwheel to a halt. No sooner said than done. Soon the miller came out in haste, with two of his men, to see what was up. He was a stout fellow with a long face like a hare's. Silent Jacob and Krawat, who were already lying in wait, leaped out of the bushes and seized the three of them, and then Radomir, who had been watching with a smile from the top of the rise, rode down with Erik and Robert to search the house at their leisure. The miller's wife was hiding in the attic. She wrung her hands and assured them that there wasn't a penny in the house. Down in the living room Radomir and Erik searched chests and boxes, but they found nothing. Robert discovered a worn book dusty with flour on a small shelf below a crucifix:

The Husbandman's Historical Calendar for the Year 1638

With the General Practice of Agriculture, the Seasons of Fertility, the Weather to Come, the Hours of Darkness, the Saints' Days and Church Festivals for All the Year

Unobserved, he pocketed the 'calendar'. Then he whispered something to Radomir. When Radomir nodded, Robert went over to the miller's wife, who immediately began weeping, blindfolded her, took her gently by the hand and led her all over the mill, keeping a finger on her pulse. On the grinding-floor, he felt her give an involuntary jerk. Looking more closely, he pointed to a crack between the planks. The Swede forced the concealed trapdoor open, climbed down, and came back with a heavy, iron-bound chest that had something clinking inside. They had found the miller's hoard. The band freed the whimpering man, mounted their horses and made for home. Robert was glad the raid had passed off so smoothly.

That evening Radomir invited him into his own hut, which stood some way from the others. 'You did well, friend,' he said. 'I reckon you could even teach us a few cunning tricks!' Robert scarcely listened, for he was entirely absorbed in the little book calling itself a Husbandman's Calendar. He had almost given himself away in sheer surprise when he found out what period he had landed in. He was right in the middle of the Thirty Years' War!

He could hardly say so, of course. The war wasn't over yet, and how were Radomir and his men to know it would last thirty years? Robert was the only person here who had ever heard of the Peace of Westphalia that would bring it to an end. Back at home, his history teacher had shown them a map hanging on the blackboard. It was amazing to think of that patchwork of duchies and small states and Free Imperial Cities being Germany; it just looked like a mess. There were small crossed swords drawn all over it, showing battles involving the Hungarians, the Spanish, the Swedes and the French, but unfortunately Robert had forgotten what they all wanted and what the real reason for the slaughter was. The teacher had spent a good deal of time explaining the disputes between

Protestants and Catholics; apparently the war had something to do with the service of Holy Communion, though Robert could hardly believe it. The whole thing seemed to be just a lot of indiscriminate fighting, with various bands of robbers at odds, burning villages and looting one another, and what that could have to do with God was a mystery to him. He remembered a little verse he had heard once in the playground at school when he was little:

> Down came the Swedes,
> Took more than their needs,
> Smashed our windows and doors
> And pissed on our laws.

Well, thought Robert, you could substitute just about any other group you liked for the Swedes in this rhyme. Radomir watched as his friend leafed through the Husbandman's Calendar he had stolen. It was not the kind of 'calendar' that Robert's father kept on his desk, which was more of an engagements diary, but a collection of all kinds of curious facts. The book gave a weather forecast for the whole year in advance, and not only that: it told you about comets and witches too. One chapter gave detailed instructions for bleeding a sick person. Robert almost threw up when he saw the disgusting woodcut of the leeches, and swiftly turned the page. After a while Radomir asked him, 'Can you really read, then?' His tone was incredulous, as if it were a rare talent.

'Of course,' said Robert.

'Anything about the future in there?'

'Yes, listen to this. "According to Precise Calculations, Opinions and Conjectures, there shall be Wretched, Sad Conditions, with Wars and Great Bloodshed, the Death of Princes, Pestilence, Famine, Earthquake and Many Other Ills, as already Prognosticated in the Year 1630 by Twenty Astrologers, and described by Doctor Herlicium, Mathematician of Greifswald." Want to hear any more?'

'To be sure, but tell me how *my* stars stand. My sign's Sagittarius.'

Robert had not the faintest idea of astrology, but to please Radomir he muttered something or other. 'Wait a moment ... I see a conjunction of Mars and Saturn in the sign of Scorpio ...'

'And what does that mean?'

Robert didn't want to land himself in trouble – and who knows what might come of it, he thought, if I try casting Ratibor's horoscope? Perhaps his stars don't look too good, and if so I wouldn't want to be the bearer of bad news.

'I'm not sure. Well, the next few months don't seem very promising for you, but that's not so surprising in your trade, is it? Let's go out and join the others,' suggested Robert. 'They're already round the table drinking wine.'

He was in high spirits: the raid had gone well, and Radomir had praised him.

'Listen, everyone, I can tell you what the future holds,' he began when they had joined the other members of the band. 'Not just tomorrow or the day after tomorrow, there's nothing special about that – I can tell you what the future holds in a few hundred years' time. You'll never believe it!'

'Go on, then, what *does* it hold?' asked Erik the Swede.

'Amazing things!' said Robert. 'For instance, you could be here and still talk to your children in Sweden without moving from the spot, that is if you have any children. You could just speak into a little black tube, and they'd hear what you're saying in Stockholm.'

The men slapped their thighs, laughing. 'Just hark at his nonsense!' cried one. 'Our Robert here's a fine liar!'

'Braggart!' shouted the others. 'Layabout! Trickster!'

But there was no holding Robert now. 'And that's not all,' he went on. 'People will be able to travel from here to Paris faster than the fastest coach can go, and fly through the air quicker than any bird, and see what's happening at the other end of the world without a telescope, just by switching on a little box.'

At this point Krawat jumped up, clenching his fists. '*Ludost!*' he bellowed. '*Varalica!*' Robert didn't know why he was so agitated; perhaps he was jealous because Radomir was showing a preference for him, the newcomer.

'Look, I'll show you.' Putting his hand in his pocket, Robert brought out his toy car. Radomir took it from his hand at once, turned the little thing back and forth, wrinkling his brow, and whistled quietly through his teeth. 'Amazing,' he said.

'Of course the real thing's much bigger,' Robert explained. 'You get in at the front here. The driver sits behind this steering wheel, and there's an engine stronger than a hundred horses under the bonnet here. You can drive at ... at over thirty miles an hour in it.' This figure was plucked out of the air at random, since Robert, used to thinking in kilometres, had no idea just how far a mile was. His friend looked at him doubtfully, but he pulled himself together quickly and said, smiling, 'If we had two of them here we could have a motor race.'

Krawat, sitting at the other end of the bench, could obviously stand it no longer. He rose with a menacing look, as if about to attack Robert. '*Lazac!*' he hissed through his teeth. Robert wound up the little Porsche, put it down on the bench and set it going straight towards the other man. Krawat stared at the growling thing as if it were a poisonous insect. When the car fell to the ground and went on buzzing with its wheels turned upward, like a beetle, he yelled and flinched back. Then, when the clockwork ran down, he stamped on the Porsche until it was wrecked, and drew his sword. 'Come on, then, if you dare!' he shouted.

There was no alternative: Robert had to draw his own sword to defend himself. Krawat was a dangerous adversary, but he had drunk more than he could carry, and besides that he was blind with rage. The many hours Robert had spent on the fencing ground in Herrenlinden came in useful now. While the others watched intently, he skilfully parried Krawat's attack, and after a couple of cuts he succeeded in feinting, struck the blade from his opponent's hand and put his sword to Krawat's throat. Growling, the big, heavy man had to admit himself beaten.

This skirmish won Robert the respect of the entire band. Radomir winked at him, as if saying: I knew you could cope with him – we understand each other.

A few idle days passed by, with card-playing and hare-coursing, until one morning Radomir summoned his men and made a small speech. First, he shared out half the loot from their last raid, and each man got a handful of guilders from the miller's hoard. Then Radomir announced his next plan. 'I shall ride to Strasbourg today,' he said, 'to do business with the money-changer and buy powder, provisions, and a couple of casks of wine. I don't want you all idling around meanwhile. A couple of days ago, while the rest of you were sleeping, Robert spotted a manor house in the Wasgau area where there's plenty of stuff to be had. He'll lead you there. Mind you don't fall into any ambushes on the way. Colloredo's regiments are at large around here, and they'll make short work of honest folk like us. Robert will lead you this time. I want to see if he's made of the right stuff!'

Krawat looked sour at these orders, nor did the others seem enthusiastic at the idea of taking Robert, a mere beginner as a robber, as their leader. However, none of them dared contradict the captain of the band, who swung himself up on his dapple-grey and rode off without another word.

That night the rain began. It was cold and damp in the charcoal-burners' huts, and no one felt like setting out on another raid in such weather. After a week there were deep puddles of standing water in the roads, and when the rain refused to stop morale in the camp sank to its lowest point. Secretly, Robert hoped Radomir would come back soon and take the business in hand himself. But there was no sign of the robber captain. Robert began to worry: where could Radomir be? He remembered the horoscope he had dreamed up so lightly. What might the conjunction of Mars and Saturn in Scorpio mean? He hadn't the faintest idea. The Frenchmen were already whispering, spreading the rumour that their captain had made off and left them in the lurch. At this point Robert decided to act, and next day, when the rain slackened, he gave orders to set out.

The manor house that the band reached that morning seemed to have survived the war intact. Corn was being threshed in the barn, a stable-maid ran across the yard, and there were children playing on the steps as if it were peace-time. A warlike ruse would get them nowhere here. Robert ordered his little troop to surround the house. Erik the Swede fired a couple of shots, the servants came running up, and the lord of the manor came out of the door with his wife. The inhabitants of the house were herded together, and Krawat began beating the manservants until Robert told him to stop. Just then a young man appeared at one of the first-floor windows, raising a musket. Before Robert could warn his men a shot rang out, and one of the Frenchmen, hit in the arm, uttered a scream. The Swede returned fire at once, and the marksman at the window fell dead.

The blood shot to Robert's head. The lord of the manor fell to his knees before him, begging for mercy for himself and his wife. All of a sudden he, Robert, had powers of life and death. A very unfamiliar feeling came over him – what was it? Desire for revenge, anger, sheer enjoyment of cruelty? He wanted to shout, 'Cut them all to pieces! Burn the roof over their heads!' He, who hated the sight of blood!

Krawat had seized the lord of the manor by his hair. 'Where's your money?' the Swede shouted, putting the point of his sword to the man's chest. 'The fellow won't talk. Shall I cut his tongue out?' he asked Robert.

The lord of the manor, a grey-haired, well-nourished man with large ears, whimpered and swore he had no money in the house. Robert waved his excuses away. Suddenly the brief madness that had come over him was gone, and he felt very, very tired. 'Let him go. Shut the whole household in the pigsties and keep a watch on them while we turn the place over. It'll be an odd business if we don't find anything.'

They broke open chests and crates, lifted doors from their hinges, slit open mattresses. There were cries to be heard from the stables where Krawat and Silent Jacob had fallen on the maidservants.

But the raid was a failure, a fiasco. They found no silver, no jewellery, no gold or treasure, and in the end the lady of the house told Robert, in tears, that some of the imperial troops had been there a week ago, a wild band of hussars, and fearing fire and the sword her husband had given them everything they wanted.

On the way back none of them spoke to their leader. The wounded Frenchman kept apart from the others, sticking close to his fellow countryman, and the pair of them cast dark glances at Robert.

Once they were back at their camp he flung himself on his makeshift bed and could hardly close his eyes, overcome as he was by terror. Who am I, he asked himself, who am I really? The Robert who took shelter with Olga; Caroline's lucky friend who found that shining opal; the Robert who took lodgings with his own great-grandmother; the foundling in Norway; the page at Herrenlinden Castle, assistant to the gout-ridden philosopher; the bloodthirsty highwayman who had very nearly given orders for the massacre of a whole family – could they be one and the same? He was now one person, now another, and seemed to be tossed back and forth like a cork on the sea until he didn't know who or where he really was. This couldn't go on; if he went on just drifting he'd come to a bad end.

He rose, took his sword, threw his heavy cape around him and went silently over to the other hut; he could hear his companions snoring inside. Cautiously, he approached the enclosure where the horses were asleep and untied his mare. Then he rode away, in flight from himself.

Once he saw torches and flares in the distance. In the nocturnal silence, he heard guards calling out and dogs barking. He described a wide arc around the army camp that had been pitched near a small river. Later, he crossed a mountain pass and looked down at a peaceful plain below. The stony path led downhill through carefully tended vineyards. Storks were nesting on the roofs of the farms. He did not meet a soul until dawn.

When the sun rose, a large city with tall towers and walls lay before him. There were men on guard at the gate. They asked him where he came from and what his business was, and even wanted to see his bag; he began to suspect that they would take his money, but they simply waved him through. Without meaning to, Robert had come to Strasbourg. All he had in the world was twelve and a half guilders, a sword, an historical calendar and a crumpled photograph. He had no idea what he was going to do next. He wondered where to look for Radomir; there must be a money-changers' quarter. He could ask for information there about the captain who was so curiously like his lost friend Ratibor.

Strasbourg seemed to him a very fine place. As if by some miracle the war had spared it. A little river with weirs, locks and subsidiary tributaries wound its way through the city. It smelled of leather and decay, and the water was reddened and dirty; this was a place where tanners and dyers plied their trade. Three fortified towers guarded wooden bridges made of planks that swayed slightly as you crossed them. On the banks men covered with white dust were unloading sacks of corn and barrels from broad barges. As Robert walked on he passed stately buildings with dark porches. They were not exactly shops, but there was lively activity in the trading yards, and once again he saw men dragging sacks and crates about. The streets were swarming with bustling people. In the market place he marvelled at the stalls where women sold wine and ham, geese and pickled cabbage, butter and dozens of different varieties of cheese. The area behind the cathedral with its tall tower was crammed with shops where you could buy brandy, embroidery and Brabant cloth. After his wanderings through the devastated countryside, Robert was overwhelmed by so much wealth. He felt he had arrived in a great metropolis, although the old city of Strasbourg was really smaller than his own home town – but his home town now seemed to him as faded and far away as a place in an old photograph.

But it was the cathedral that impressed Robert most. His first intention was simply to rest in it briefly, but once he was seated on a bench he noticed a vast structure in a side aisle. When he came closer he saw that it was a clock – but a clock nearly twenty metres tall! He stood in front of it for a whole hour. The entire front of the structure was lavishly painted with scenes showing the Creation of the World and the Resurrection of the Dead. There were automata everywhere: an angel turning an hourglass over, a rooster spreading its wings and really beginning to crow, and the Four Ages of Man moving past the waiting figure of the Grim Reaper with his scythe. But most amazing of all was the clock itself, for its many brass discs, hands and faces not only told the hours and the minutes, the date and the day of the week, but gave the festivals of patron saints, the length of days and nights and the date of Easter, and anyone able to interpret the gilded spheres could see the position and movements of the sun, the moon and all the planets. The whole thing was a gleaming, gigantic computer standing in the middle of a church! Robert could scarcely tear himself away. And the clock seemed to be telling him something else, a message not shown on any of its faces: whatever the year, human beings were capable of anything, the worst of evils and the greatest of wonders.

He found an inn in a dark side street not far from the market place. It was a Gothic half-timbered building with bay windows and painted beams, rather like something out of a tourist brochure, and he encountered a very friendly welcome. The landlady asked no questions but immediately led him up a steep, narrow staircase to an attic room. Robert was surprised to find that in the middle of the Thirty Years' War there were still courteous innkeepers and beds with clean sheets. He even found a barber to cut his hair just around the next corner.

He asked the hunchbacked barber where the money-changers did business, and the man sent him to Jews' Alley, which seemed a very run-down street. Robert was surprised, being used to banks that had their premises in the best parts of town. None of the moneylenders in their small shops could tell him anything about Radomir. He lost his way among the tangle of little side streets, and when he asked a cobbler the way the man sent him to the Palace Square. 'What, you don't know the Palace? Biggest square in town! Keep going straight ahead, turn left after a hundred paces and you can't miss it.'

The square was swarming with people. There was such a crowd that Robert couldn't make out what was happening, but it seemed to be some sort of ceremony. A kind of platform had been erected in front of the fine building looking out on the square, and a crowd of armed men stood on guard by the decorated railings of the platform, keeping the crowd back.

'What's going on?' Robert asked a woman. She looked at him in astonishment, and replied, 'You don't know? Why, they're going to carry out the death sentences!' And now Robert saw red-robed judges standing in the portico of the fine building with the city councillors. He heard a roll of drums, and a black cloth was spread over the wooden floor of the platform. The spectators craned their necks, and total silence fell over the square.

Six guards armed with halberds led the condemned men, who were bound with ropes, to the scaffold. There were three prisoners, and the man in the middle was Radomir.

'Radomir!' cried Robert. People turned and stared at him suspiciously. He couldn't help himself; he lashed out, trying to force his way forward. Luckily for him, however, the crowd was so dense that he could not get through, or the armed guards would surely have seized him. Helplessly, he watched the ropes being removed from the first of the prisoners. The court bailiff read out the verdict, broke a white staff over the condemned man's head and told the executioner to step forward. Another roll of drums, and the first prisoner took off his coat, knelt on the black cloth and said a last prayer. The executioner raised his sword and cut off first his right hand and then his head.

Robert had seen enough. When Radomir's turn came he closed his eyes. The drums rolled again, and once again first a murmur and then a sigh of excitement ran through the crowd. Robert didn't wait for the third execution. He forced his way out of the crowd, and afterwards he could not have said just how long he spent wandering aimlessly through the city.

He passed a sleepless night at the inn. Somehow, he felt he was to blame for his captain's death, although he didn't understand why he should, for *he* hadn't betrayed Radomir. Perhaps the money-changers had given him away – or could the two Frenchmen have had a hand in it? Radomir had never trusted them. Now he was dead, and perhaps his head would be put up on an iron spike – Robert knew that was a barbaric custom in use at this period, to serve as a deterrent or so that people could mock the dead criminal. Well, he had got away scot free himself. Maybe that was why he felt guilty.

He lit a candle, took the crumpled photograph out of his pocket and looked at it again. He knew now that Radomir had come to a sticky end – but didn't he have tangible proof here before his eyes, proof in colour too, that the same person lived on a few hundred years later? Radomir, Ratibor, Radomir, Ratibor . . . the names went round and round in his head like a mill-wheel in some old folk-song. Perhaps it was just his imagination; perhaps Radomir and Ratibor had nothing at all to do with each other. A school friend of his at home, a robber in the Thirty Years' War – surely it was the thinnest of threads that linked them. Not that the idea was any comfort.

When he came to think of it, they were his only friends, and now he'd lost them both! Even though he was exhausted it was a long time before he could get to sleep.

He sat down to breakfast next day still feeling weary and dispirited. But he hadn't eaten for twenty-four hours, and he fell ravenously on the ham and eggs the landlord's daughter served him. Then he leaned back and looked at the Husband-man's Calendar. Sure enough, under 18 September, yesterday's date, he found a warning: 'Beware of thine Adversaries, for Saturn ruleth the Hour, and being in the Fifth House bringeth Misfortune.'

'I see you can read and write. Are you a scholar, sir?'

An elegant gentleman was addressing him; he wore a white doublet with a sash and a lace collar, and he had silver spurs. Robert closed the book and stood up.

'I am Captain of Horse in the service of Duke Bernhard of Weimar. Pray forgive me for disturbing you.'

Robert invited him to sit down, and the officer soon made his intentions plain; he had come to Strasbourg to recruit men.

'As for the war, sir,' said Robert, when he saw what the man was after, 'as for the war, I've had my fill of it, and I see no reason to put my life in danger.'

The Captain of Horse laughed. 'I see you're no ordinary musketeer,' he said. 'But what we need is a capable regimental clerk, and you look to me just the man. Twenty talers isn't bad pay. What do you say – will you try it?'

Robert thought for a while, and then agreed. After all, he must do something. He wanted to leave Strasbourg as soon as possible, for he didn't in the least want to see Radomir's bloody head stuck up on a pike somewhere, and he had no idea where else he could earn a living. So he took the money that sealed the bargain, ten silver talers, and received orders to make his way to the area around Kolmar, where the regiment was encamped.

'Oh, and one more thing,' said the Captain of Horse. 'Forgive me for being blunt, but you'd do well to hold to your side of the bargain, or else . . .' And he put a hand to his throat and jerked it to one side. Robert knew what that gesture meant. In this war you had a choice between being stabbed or strung up.

On the way south he kept well away from the main road, which seemed to him too unsafe, and rode along lonely bridle paths through the foothills of the Vosges Mountains. In the afternoon he came up behind the army's baggage train in a densely wooded river valley. Obviously the little army had already struck camp, leaving only a small rearguard to secure their backs. On being challenged by a sergeant, Robert brandished his commission and said he wanted to see the colonel. They let him pass without more ado. The rear of the procession consisted of the sutlers' carts with the women and children, and next he overtook thirty baggage wagons containing powder, fuses, spades, ladders, flour and other provisions. There was even a copper stove and a cart full of pots and pans with the army cooks. Then he rode past teams of powerful horses pulling heavy cannon behind them. He stopped and asked for his colonel, but the artillery officer, who was Italian, didn't understand him. The man's companions, a Hungarian ordnance officer and a Bohemian gunner, spoke little German themselves, and it was only now that light dawned on Robert. This was not the right army!

He had fallen in with the other side. This was the imperial army, or a part of it anyway, marching on Kolmar, probably in order to attack Bernhard of Weimar. Robert still didn't understand what all the slaughter was in aid of, nor did he really mind which side he served. He didn't belong with any of these bands of men claiming to be regular armies. He didn't even know what a regimental clerk was supposed to do. What mattered now was for him not to give himself away by some thoughtless remark, for as soon as the Habsburg officers realized he was in the other side's pay he would be treated as a spy and get short shrift. And he knew only too well how easily you could end up on the gallows or the scaffold in these unpleasant times.

It struck him that the safest place to be was with the advance guard; it would be easier to escape from there, he thought, if anyone came after him. So he rode on. No one took any notice of him, and he had soon reached the head of the procession.

Then a trumpet signal sounded from the heights to left and right, and horsemen with drawn swords burst out of the woods. It was not a spontaneous attack. The imperial regiments had fallen into a trap. Behind the enemy cavalry, their infantry was advancing with fifes and drums, led by an ensign.

Robert had never seen a battle except in movies. What surprised him most was the noise: the neighing of the horses, the screams of wounded men, the rumble of the cannon, the rolling of drums, whistling, trumpet calls, the clash of spears and swords. Soon the lines broke up, merging with each other. In spite of the confusion Robert managed to maintain a clear view. He realized that the heaviest of the fighting was in progress behind him, for the attackers were concentrating on the main body of the troops, aiming to split them up, cut off their retreat, and then slaughter them as mercilessly as everyone did everything in this war.

Only the rearguard and vanguard of the procession had any chance of escape, as the cavalrymen whom Robert joined had quickly realized. Without a thought for their comrades, they spurred their horses on and galloped away.

Riding in loose formation, they made off up-country,

towards the mountain range. The company consisted of five or six Hungarian hussars, who took no notice of Robert but did not seem hostile either. As dusk was beginning to fall they came to an isolated house. It seemed too handsome for a farmhouse, but it could not be a nobleman's residence, for the roof was thatched with straw. All the shutters were closed, and no smoke rose from the chimney. One of the Hungarians hammered on the carved door while the others waited, swords drawn, to see if anything moved inside. But there was no sign of any human presence. The Hungarian broke down the door with the shaft of his spear. The hussars led their horses into the main room of the house and tied them up to the window gratings. They were too tired to loot the place, and simply stretched out on the floor. Looking around, Robert saw a table with an inkwell and papers on it, and found out that they had taken up their quarters in the house of a count's forester and steward of his estate.

In the kitchen he found a loaf of bread going mouldy, some dried meat and a few apples, which he shared with his chance-met companions. He was exhausted, and this time he slept like a top until well into next morning. No one asked him who he was and where he came from, which made a pleasant change; he was sick and tired of inventing stories.

The Hungarians took it easy for a couple of days, amusing themselves by smashing up the steward's furniture and hunting down a few chickens left behind by the inhabitants of the house. Robert took care not to cross them in any way, intervening only when they drew their swords to attack a large painting on the wall of the main room. He was only just in time to prevent them from slashing the canvas; as it was, a small slit on the left edge was the only injury the picture suffered.

Robert had taken to this painting at first sight. He had never seen anything like it before, and stood in front of it for a long time, examining it closely and enjoying the painter's meticulous depiction of details. It wasn't really a single picture but a whole picture gallery: an inexhaustible collection where you could see landscapes, gods, biblical stories, still lifes of fruit, shipwrecks, portraits, scenes of war and fishing expeditions, naked girls, empty churches, bonfires, delicious meals – in short, it was a whole world in itself.

In this picture all the smaller pictures hung in a hall with tall windows through which light fell on the portrait of a man clad in black, obviously the owner of these painted treasures. A few visitors were gathered around a table upon which stood a globe and some open books. A Moor was coming in through the pillared porch to serve them wine, and a fluffy young dog lay on the floor yawning.

The picture itself and the many pictures within it were painted with such a fine brush that Robert could have done with a magnifying glass to see the tiny figures more closely. One painting which hung on the wall of the rich collector's house exactly at eye level – it was about the size of a dessert plate – was of particular interest to Robert, since it showed a painter's studio. Perhaps, he thought, the artist had painted himself here as discreetly as possible. Perhaps he was that figure in front of a large canvas wearing a flowing green cloak and seen from behind, while an apprentice with a neat cap on his head knelt on the floor in front of him grinding or mixing paint on a small bench. But what was the artist painting? Robert went closer, to scrutinize the picture in the picture in the picture. Was it the actual painting in front of which he himself was standing? But closely as he examined the little speck on which the painter was working, it was hardly the size of a thumb-nail, and its subject remained the artist's secret.

His companions the Hungarians had other things on their

minds. After they had searched the whole house and turned it upside down without finding any money or other loot, they became reckless enough to go out raiding in the surrounding countryside. Robert had had enough of thieving, and stayed behind. There was plenty of fruit and vegetables in the garden, as well as nuts and berries. He even found a little bookshelf in a room next to the ruined hall: it held a Bible, a few Latin tracts, and a very strange old text in verse, called

Hunt the Fleas — Hunt the Women
The Amazing and Comical Dealings of
The Fleas with Women:
A New Diversion and Pastime
And a Sovereign Remedy against
the Fleabites of Tedium

This entertained him for a while, if only because it wasn't at all easy to guess what the crazy writer was actually going on about.

One day, at about noon, two of the Hungarians came back galloping hard and calling out to their companions who had stayed behind. It sounded something like: '*Vigyazat, veszelyes!*' Robert didn't realize what was happening until they all snatched up their weapons, led the horses into the house, barricaded themselves behind the windows and aimed their guns. Again, no one paid him any more attention than if he had been invisible. He ran to find the sword he had left hung up somewhere, to defend himself if he must.

Next moment the pursuers arrived, a band of horsemen cautiously approaching the house. Their leader raised a hand. They stopped and waited until some foot-soldiers armed with muskets came up. Then the horsemen surrounded the house

217

at a safe distance. Not a shot had yet been fired. The horses were prancing restlessly. For a moment everything was perfectly quiet. Then the youngest of the Hungarians, a tall fellow with a long mane of hair, could stand the strain no longer. He aimed his gun at the leader of the besieging party and fired. It was a mistake, for he missed, and the musketeers instantly returned fire. No one in the house was hit, but then Robert, looking through a hatch, saw several of the attackers doing something with long black sticks. First one, then two, then three bright lights flared up. A giant of a soldier took the first pitch-soaked torch and flung it at the roof of the house. One of the Hungarians fired again, this time at the man who had thrown the torch, and again he missed. Robert realized that they were in a trap, and their attackers would butcher them without mercy. An acrid smell rose to his nostrils. He sniffed. The smoke was coming from above, thick swathes of it drifting into the hall from the stairs. A crackling and snapping told Robert that the rafters had caught fire, and now the Hungarians realized too. Two of them made a break for it, rushing forward and out of the house with drawn swords. They were running straight into enemy fire; they fell and lay still. The others retreated to the kitchen. The horses in the drawing room scented the fire, snorted and reared; a bay broke free and raced for the open door, whinnying, only to be struck down by a bullet. Now the attackers moved towards the house, step by step. The thick smoke inside took Robert's breath away, and his eyes were beginning to stream. He withdrew to the back of the main hall.

Which was better: to be cut down or burn to death? Robert could no longer think straight. There was a bit of soot in his left eye. He blinked. Rubbing his eyelid with his forefinger, he tried to get out the soot that was making his eyes water, and gasping for breath, he staggered towards the wall. To keep his balance, he supported himself by leaning both hands on the frame of the big painting he had saved from the swords of the brawling Hungarians.

He thought he could already feel the heat of the flames licking around the picture. The tiny painting in the painting grew darker and darker until it was all charred. But that was probably only because, yet again, everything had gone dark before Robert's own eyes.

THE SEVENTH JOURNEY

The next moment he was away from the war. It was quiet and warm in the large room where he found himself. A curious white light lay over the painter's studio, and there was nothing to be heard outside but the sound of a horse's hoofs, so muted that the animal might have been trotting over a carpet of cotton wool. Robert's glance fell on the tall window, and through the streaky bull's-eye panes he saw that it had been snowing.

The painter sat at his easel in his leek-green cloak, just as he had been sitting in front of the tiny picture within the picture that Robert had studied in the steward's burning house heaven knows how long ago. But since his broad back concealed the painting itself, Robert still couldn't see what he was working on. The little workbench with all the tools of the painter's trade was neat and tidy: Robert saw a cloth, brushes, compasses, sponge, a brown bottle and a couple of boxes containing pigments. Even the little dog was there – a brown and white spaniel, lying sleepily on the floor and licking its paws. Only the apprentice whom Robert had seen in the picture was missing.

The painter was so absorbed in his work that he never noticed the intruder. Robert didn't want to disturb him.

Holding his breath, he tiptoed out of the studio and stole down the steep, narrow staircase. When he reached the tiled entrance hall he stopped to admire the heavy carved furniture and the big hearth with a couple of beech logs glowing on it. The walls were covered with tapestries. The whole house seemed a solemn but not an uncomfortable kind of place. A picture in a gilt frame showed a Moor with fair hair. Only when Robert moved did he realize that it was a mirror, and the blackened face he could see there was his own. He swiftly stepped out into the street, picked up a handful of snow and rubbed the soot away, although there was nothing he could do about the dirt that the smoke from the fire had left on his clothes.

The little street, bordered by elms, ran beside a frozen river, but the opposite bank of the river looked exactly the same, like a reflection. It too was lined with trees. The buildings were tall and narrow, with delicate brick gables. Robert was used to guessing where he was by now; in fact he quite enjoyed this kind of mental quiz, and today it took him only a moment to find the answer to the puzzle. He wasn't looking at a real river; it was a perfectly straight canal running through the middle of the town, with small, high-arched bridges leading from one bank to the other. He remembered a postcard someone had once sent him on his birthday. Aha! he thought, and the two words the invisible quizmaster in his head was asking for immediately occurred to him: *Gracht* and *Amsterdam*. Amsterdam was the capital of the Netherlands. *Gracht* meant 'canal'.

The sun penetrated the thin veils of cloud only with difficulty, yet the city was bathed in the dazzlingly bright, diffused light reflected from the snow. Still feeling rather bemused and dazed, Robert walked on. In the distance he heard laughter and shouting, and when he came to the next bridge he saw a colourful crowd enjoying themselves on the ice where the canal flowed out into a wide expanse of water. Was it a harbour basin, or the sea? There were people skating, walking in pairs, children, dogs – even a carriage had ventured on to the ice. It was a cheerful, exuberant scene, and yet again he was the only person standing outside it, with no part in this chilly carnival atmosphere. He looked more closely at the clothes the people were wearing. He couldn't have gone too much further back into the past this time, for these Dutch people – and he now felt sure they were Dutch – were wearing costumes not unlike his own: brightly coloured doublets, wide knee-breeches, lace collars, fur-trimmed capes. Only the hats were taller, and many of the gentlemen were dressed entirely in black.

Going closer, he heard a nursemaid scolding a small boy. Yet another language he didn't know! But it sounded a little like Low German. A number of the words were almost like English, and here and there he picked up a phrase or so that reminded him of his sketchy Norwegian.

He wasn't at all bothered about this new journey into the unknown, nor was he tired; on the contrary, he felt fresh and well rested, as if he hadn't just gone through the arduous process of toppling out of a burning house and into another world. He simply felt curious and ready for any adventure, and as for the foreign language – well, this wasn't the first time he'd had to manage by stammering out broken phrases. Languages were like clothes, new suits which you had to put on; they only felt stiff and uncomfortable at first, until you got used to them. If it's true that clothes make the man, thought Robert, you could say the same of foreign languages. You moved differently in them, changing yourself until you felt right; you almost became another person. The prospect of having to begin all over again held no terrors for Robert now. He was well accustomed to guessing, stammering a few words, and then imitating what he heard.

He spent the whole day wandering around this unknown city as if in a waking dream. Amsterdam was considerably busier, wealthier and finer even than Strasbourg. The harbour was swarming with ships. East Indiamen anchored here with their cargoes of spices, silks and tropical woods, and there were whalers from northern waters and barges unloading their freight on the quay outside tall warehouses. Heavy crates and bundles were hauled aloft by block and tackle and disappeared inside the storehouses. On the other side of the harbour basin, to Robert's surprise, he saw whole armies of windmills turning. So they did exist in real life and not just on picture postcards!

The hurry and bustle in the narrow streets of the inner city was overwhelming. Robert strolled past herb markets, vegetable markets and pig markets in his warm coat. And this time he even had money on him: the golden guilders and silver talers that he had brought from Alsace. He bought a fried fish at one of the stalls and ate it with a piece of bread as he walked along. He met grave, black-clad gentlemen with huge pleated ruffs, probably merchants or town councillors. In one broad street, goldsmiths and diamond cutters were sitting bent over their work in their windows. A rabbi wearing a broad hat trimmed with brown fur passed with his followers. His young, black-robed pupils had let the locks of hair at their temples grow long. Carts and carriages rattled past, stall-holders cried their wares, peals of bells rang from the towers. The churches were surrounded by beggars, cripples and musicians.

Amsterdam was an industrious city. Robert admired the wharves, the drawbridges and the canal locks, but what impressed him most was the feverish building activity. New canals were being dug far beyond the ramparts of the city itself. Tall scaffolding surrounded half-finished churches and towers. There were architects, carpenters, masons, roofers and glaziers at work everywhere.

Robert found an opportunity of studying a plan of the city in the window of a map engraver's shop on the Damrak. Among the engravings fresh off the printing press was a large coloured picture of Amsterdam, a panoramic view of the whole city seen from the sea and bearing the proud inscription:

AMSTELODAMUM TOTIUS EUROPÆ EMPORIUM
CELEBERRIMUM HOLLANDIÆQUE PRIMARIA URBS
DELINEATA ANNO DOMINI 1621.

'The most famous market place in all Europe' – not a modest claim, but perhaps it was accurate. Anyway, now Robert knew not just where but when he was living. He'd gone back a mere seventeen years! Well, he'd experienced more vertiginous falls back through the trapdoors of the past before.

But when dusk fell, and the people in the streets began hurrying home, his cheerful mood faded. He knew no one in this whole city, and he didn't fancy going to one of the many sailors' taverns where he heard raucous women's voices and the babbling of drunks. He knew nothing about brothels except from television, and to be honest, he shrank from the idea of them.

A much more enticing prospect was the only place he knew from the inside: the painter's house. By now he knew his way around the tangle of streets well enough to get back there without any difficulty. In the moonlight, the canal lay as still as a stage set without actors or audience. Robert saw a small relief of an ox's head above the door. On his wanderings through the city, he had already noticed that the houses had names instead of numbers, and the little pictures above the doorways were a kind of address. He climbed the short flight of steps, and stopped outside the green-painted door with its brass knocker. Through the window, he could see the big living room with its tapestries and the pillared fireplace. How warm it was in there, and how the big mirror gleamed in the candlelight! However, there was no sign of the inhabitants of the house.

He jumped when someone spoke to him from behind. A woman's voice, asking, '*Wat blieft u, Mineer?*' He turned, and saw a lady of about forty carrying a heavy shopping basket. Her large brown eyes were looking at him enquiringly, but not in an unfriendly way. Robert, feeling he had been caught unawares, stammered out an apology. Realizing that he was a foreigner, she repeated her question in German. 'Can I help you, sir?'

'I don't want to trouble you,' he said, 'but I was wondering if I could be apprenticed to your husband? It would be a great honour for me. I want to be a painter, you see.' He himself couldn't have said how this idea suddenly occurred to him.

The lady said it wasn't quite as simple as that. She seemed to be thinking, and Robert made haste to relieve her of her heavy basket. She smiled slightly, took a heavy key out of her pocket, and when the door was half open she said, 'Would you like to come in and speak to my husband yourself?'

Robert stood there rather awkwardly as the lady of the house called, 'David!' Well, at least he now knew the first name of the painter who came down the steep stairs, groaning slightly. He was a stout, red-cheeked man of at least fifty, with a head going bald and side-whiskers. He barked out a question that Robert didn't understand to his wife, in a rather surly tone. It was she who acted as interpreter during the little conversation that followed.

Robert explained that he was from Germany; he was afraid he didn't speak Dutch, but he did know Latin and a couple of other languages. No, he had no experience as a painter, although he'd learnt a little drawing at school. But he had a good pair of eyes and a good memory; once he had seen something he didn't forget it in a hurry.

It seemed to Robert that the master of the house listened to him with great suspicion, but his wife appeared to be persuading him to agree. Robert could make out a few words of the discussion they now conducted, because they were very like words meaning the same in German; the painter and his wife seemed to be saying something about an *apprentice*, and the word *died* followed. What did that mean? Were they talking about the boy on the little bench who had been grinding pigments for the painter in the little picture within the picture? Robert found no trace of him in the studio. Had he died so young? Or had Robert mistaken what he heard?

There was a pause. He remembered the little bag he was carrying with him. 'If you take me on as an apprentice, sir, I'm ready and willing to pay you the proper fee,' he said, taking out his bag and showing the master a couple of gold coins. This worked; the painter's eyes lit up, and his wife gave him a little nudge. However, he still did not seem completely happy. He picked up one of the coins – an imperial guilder of the year 1630 – shook his head, and then, much to Robert's surprise, put it between his teeth and bit it. The result of this test seemed to satisfy him, for he nodded and said, '*Ik wil het met hem proberen. Wij zullen zien.*'

Robert was relieved. He had understood; the painter was going to give him a try. The artist gave him his hand, said something to his wife, and disappeared upstairs again.

'That's just his way,' said the woman. 'Short in his manner, but he means no ill. He says you're to make all the other arrangements with me. My name is Agnieta, by the way. You pay fifteen guilders the first year, ten the second year and five the third year. In return we give you board and lodging, and you'll be registered with the Guild of St Luke, the artists' guild. If you are content with that, then I'll make out the contract tomorrow. And now, come to the kitchen with me! You must be hungry.'

So Robert entered upon yet another new career, so unexpectedly that he felt almost alarmed by his good luck.

When someone knocked on the door of his little room at the back of the house to wake him next morning, it was still pitch dark outside. The kitchen-maid had knocked, bringing him a coarse linen shirt and a green apron which she put down on the bed. His own clothes were already in the wash, for the lady of the house would tolerate no dirt. Everything had to be sparkling clean, not a speck of dust must lie on the furniture, no spots of paint must stain the floor. You began the day's work here on an empty stomach. Robert had to sweep the yard, carry an endless number of bundles of firewood into the house and then stack them neatly. Breakfast wasn't until nine, and when it came it consisted of bread, cheese and beer. Then a junk dealer appeared with his cart. The attic store-room was to be cleared out, and Robert's next task was to tie up the lumber it contained in bundles and let them down to the street on a rope looped around the roof-beam, manoeuvring them carefully past the gable. This was not the way he had expected to learn painting.

Before the midday meal they sang a psalm, and the painter read a passage from the Bible. Robert had fallen in with pious Protestants who never ate a morsel without praying first. You ate with your fingers here, too, just like Radomir and his robber band in Alsace. Robert had in fact seen a large meat-fork in the kitchen, but at table people managed with a knife and a spoon. Supper was always porridge: porridge, porridge and more porridge. After saying evening prayers to give thanks to God, the good people of Amsterdam went to bed at dusk, probably to save on lights.

Out of doors, the snow had begun to thaw. The weather was gloomy and misty, and a constant drizzling rain darkened the bull's-eye panes in the windows. Robert gritted his teeth and did not complain. He knew he should be glad to have found someone to help him out of a difficult situation once again; hadn't he spent the whole of the last year stumbling out of one muddle and into another?

But Robert wasn't used to the kind of daily routine that seemed customary here. When he got into his narrow bed quite early in the evening he couldn't drop off to sleep, and he had nothing to read but a Dutch Bible. He took out his crumpled photograph and looked at his friend's picture by the stump of a candle. A consuming longing overcame him – not just for Ratibor and his mother, but for the bath-tub at home, his TV set, even underground railways and super-markets. All the things they didn't have here suddenly seemed to him immensely valuable: paper tissues, light bulbs, choc-olate ice-cream . . . And most of all he missed his own bed, as unattainable as paradise.

Hesitantly, his master gave him some sponges and two palettes to clean, but Robert had to do it in the scullery. Two weeks later he was allowed to enter that holy of holies, the studio, for the first time – in slippers, of course, because Agnieta kept it scrupulously clean. Woe betide the little spaniel if he brought in a smear of mud on his paws! It was wiped away immediately. The workshop was the best-lit room in the house, although now that the sun was showing its face again it didn't shine straight in. Robert remembered old Winziger at school saying that real painters always worked in a north-facing light.

Now, at last, he was able to watch his master at work. The painter sat as his easel, to which he had pinned a pen-and-ink drawing with a clothes peg. The drawing was of a large table with jugs, cabbages and a dead cockerel. A very young, very attractive maidservant in a white cap and apron, whose eyes seemed to follow the observer as they looked out of the painting, was holding up a fish on a thread dangling from her fingertips, as if asking whether she was to cook it for supper. There was something flirtatious in her expression. Robert wasn't quite sure what to make of the girl's challenging look.

The painter had already laid out the basic structure of his picture on the oak panel, which was quite large and covered with a chalk-white ground. Only the painting of the maidservant and the fish were far enough advanced to show his art. The fish in particular stood out from the dark background, its scales shimmering and golden. Its red-rimmed eye looked so real that a small shudder ran down Robert's back.

The painter gave him no time to immerse himself in the picture, but indicated the narrow bench at the back of the studio. Robert had to set to work at the low table where his predecessor had once sat. He knew what had happened to the apprentice now; Agnieta had told him in response to his persistent questioning. 'It was the burning yellow sickness,' she said, weeping slightly over the board on which she was chopping onions. Whatever the burning yellow sickness might be, Robert felt sorry for the boy. 'He didn't suffer long. We buried him after a week.'

His master was meticulous about keeping his tools clean. David explained the difference between broad and pointed brushes and the brushes for painting small figures, showed him fine brushes made of marten, squirrel and bear hair, ran his finger over the stiffer hog bristle brushes, and pointed to the bottle of Strasbourg turpentine. Then, grunting, he turned back to his easel and went on with his work, propped on his painting stick and taking no more notice of Robert, who went on washing the brushes until they did not leave a trace of colour on the paper.

Robert felt proud when David finally allowed him to prepare pigments for the first time. His master spent an hour showing him how to crush the small crystalline pieces of mineral in the mortar, and then spend hours grinding them with clear water on a polished surface, using a long flat crusher stone that fitted well into the hand. It was a test of patience. As soon as the powder had dried it had to be ground again, this time with oil or a solution of size. Only when Robert had learned how to handle brown and green earth pigments was he allowed to treat the more expensive colours: carmine, azurite and malachite. Many of the substances were so poisonous that the apprentice had to cover his nose and mouth to avoid breathing in any of the dust as he ground them. The pigments must not be pounded too coarsely or too finely, so that the crystals would retain their brilliance. The finished paints, freshly made every day, were kept in small dishes or shells before the master put them on his palette. He also showed Robert a vessel containing a translucent, deep blue mineral. He let Robert know this was much too precious for an apprentice; Robert was forbidden to touch this little bottle! Ultramarine made from lapis lazuli was the most wonderful of all colours.

It was not difficult for Robert to understand most of what the painter said; he was beginning to find that Dutch came quite easily. He had soon found out that many words were very much like their German and English equivalents. For instance, there was no problem with *rood*, *groen*, *bruin*, *blauw* and *wit*; they meant red, green, brown, blue and white. He soon became familiar with the words for 'brush' and 'drawing', 'painter' and 'picture'. He just had to get used to the funny rasping sound of the Dutch language.

One day Robert happened to spill a dish of zinc yellow, and David was furiously angry. His cheeks grew redder than ever, he swore like a trooper and threw his apprentice out of the studio. Robert took refuge in the kitchen. When the painter's wife came in he could see that she knew all about it, for she was holding a cleaning cloth stained with yellow.

'Dear me, Robert, did he scold you dreadfully?' she asked. And when Robert didn't reply she went on, 'You mustn't take it to heart so. He has a hot temper – oh, the tales I could tell you! – but he's a good man at heart.' And she gave Robert a plate of apples and nuts with a sugared pretzel as consolation.

'He only pretends not to understand German, you know; he doesn't want to make any mistakes because he's so particular, not just over his painting. Now, tell me,' she said, changing the subject and looking at Robert in a way that reminded him of Lea, 'tell me what really happened to you in Germany. They say the place is in a terrible state, and this war seems endless.'

So Robert told her his adventures. I must just be careful not to get my periods muddled up and talk about a future that hasn't begun yet, he thought. He decided it would be better not to mention his career as a robber either, since Agnieta was such a devout lady.

'Thank the Lord we've had peace here in Amsterdam these last twelve years,' she said, 'and even before that it wasn't too bad. But David had a hard time as a child. He was born in Flanders, you see, where the Spaniards ravaged the countryside. Anyone who defended himself was killed on the spot, or brought before the courts and condemned to be hanged, quartered or burnt alive. Most Protestants had their possessions confiscated just because of their beliefs. Many were driven out of the country, and David had to escape to Holland with his parents.'

Robert was glad to be taken into her confidence, and he understood now why his master was not a very cheerful man.

It was spring before David let him hold a palette-knife or use a brush. First he showed Robert how to prepare an oak panel. A ground of chalk, bound with size and a little egg-white, had to be applied in several layers, and once dry it was smoothed with a wet bunch of horsetail grass. The process was repeated until the ground was perfectly smooth and white.

But the real art of painting began with the next step. In April David took a copperplate engraving from his files, gave his apprentice a sheet of paper and some black chalk, and told him to copy the engraving. In fine, delicate script, the words under the picture said:

Die Terugkeer van de Verlooren Zoon.

Cornelis de Gheyn invenit Adriaen Visscher excudit

The subject seemed familiar to Robert. Hadn't old Winziger brought an engraving like this to painting class once? When he looked closely at a little rectangle at the very top of it, the wording there, in tiny script, read:

FILIUS MEUS MORTUUS ERAT, ET REVIXIT, PERIERAT, ET INVENTUS EST. LUCÆ XV.

Reading it, Robert remembered the Bible story of the Prodigal Son, who was tired of his home; how he amused himself abroad until his money was all gone and he ended up envying the pigs who at least had something to eat while he went hungry; how he came home at last, ashamed and shabby, and how his father, beside himself with joy, gave him everything he could desire. The old painter seemed to have a special liking for this story.

Robert looked closely at the engraving, put it on one side and began to draw. His master, frowning, said, 'You must keep the print before your eyes all the time, fool!' But he was wrong, for Robert didn't need a model, and David watched in surprise as his pupil copied the engraving from memory, right down to the smallest detail: the two maids bringing the ragged son a brocade doublet and shoes with silver buckles, the menservants slaughtering a calf for the feast, the father in his billowing cloak embracing his lost son, even the guests dancing in the background and the two peacocks on the garden wall.

It was no great work of art that Robert produced. The figures looked stiff, the calf's head was much too big, and the delicate clouds in the original engraving loomed over the scene like a heavy white curtain. But it was Robert's memory rather than his skill that impressed his master. 'I only need to look,' Robert explained, 'and then I remember everything.'

'Well, that could be very useful to you some day, my boy,' said the painter, 'for the first principle of art is to know and imitate your models.' He picked up a pen and corrected Robert's drawing with a few powerful lines, so that his apprentice could see exactly where his outlines were wrong. That same afternoon David opened a cupboard and showed him the treasures inside it: stacks of engravings, sketches and freehand drawings that served him as models, frames ornamented with tortoiseshell or carving, and two finished pictures that he had painted to keep in stock. They showed all kinds of delicacies, delicious things that never appeared on the table in the painter's own house: oranges, figs, large crabs with shining red shells. Curious, thought Robert, the contrast between the man's frugal, economical way of life and the luxury he portrayed in his paintings.

Before going to sleep that evening Robert leafed through the Dutch Bible that Agnieta had put in his room. He soon found the passage he wanted: the Gospel according to St Luke, chapter 15, verse 20: 'And he arose and came to his father. But when he was yet a great way off, his father saw him, and had compassion, and ran, and fell on his neck, and kissed him. And the father said to his servants, Bring forth the best robe, and put it on him; and put a ring on his hand, and shoes on his feet: and bring hither the fatted calf, and kill it; and let us eat, and be merry: for this my son was dead, and is alive again; he was lost, and is found.'

Robert rather doubted whether *his* father would be quite so delighted if he came home; he would undoubtedly have something more important to do. But it was a good story, and in fact the Bible wasn't so bad at all if you had nothing else to read.

From now on his master took him seriously. Patiently, he explained how to apply colours to the palette and hold the brush, he taught him to handle linseed oil, egg yolk and resin, let him watch as he made the preliminary sketch and painted the background, and initiated him into the mysteries of varnishing and the play of light and shade. He said as little as ever, but Robert realized that he felt a certain wary confidence in his apprentice. After a few weeks he allowed him, for the first time, to paint a small part of a picture he himself had sketched out. Robert bit his lip and made a great effort, and to his own surprise the little patch of ground in the bottom corner, sketched for him in advance by David, looked quite passable. His master nodded and corrected it with a few rapid brush-strokes. 'Tomorrow,' he said, 'I'll introduce you into the Guild.'

It was a fine June day when they set off. Robert was wearing his best clothes from Alsace, which didn't look as showy as they used to. Agnieta had sewn up the slits in the sleeves of the doublet and changed its collar, so that Robert no longer resembled a mercenary soldier but seemed like a good citizen of Amsterdam.

On the way to the Guildhouse building, his master unexpectedly began letting off steam, but not about his apprentice. On the contrary, he spoke to Robert almost as if he were a colleague. The Painters' Guild wasn't what it used to be, he complained. Instead of doing something about the wicked competition so rife these days, the officials of the Guild just put up with it, and now any dauber could offer his wares for sale at fairs and from stalls. These wretched bunglers even tried to get rid of their work through lotteries, and then there were the traders importing cheap pictures from Brabant, and all the foreigners making themselves very much at home in Amsterdam.

Timidly, Robert pointed out that David himself hadn't been born in Holland, but had sought refuge from the Spanish there, and found it too. But his master stopped in the middle of the street and thundered, 'I am a well-respected man; I've gained citizenship of Amsterdam! His Majesty the King of Denmark buys my pictures! Sixty-eight guilders he's paid me!' When he had calmed down again, he told Robert how frauds would cheat with their pigments. 'They claim that the cheapest blue is lapis, and then they mix it with yellow because they can't handle the verdigris to make that tricky colour, Paris green. No wonder the green fades, the blue shows through, and the foliage in their pictures looks as if it had been raining skimmed milk!'

Only when they had reached the place in the New Market where the old weighing scales stood did David resume his usual dignified manner. The Guildhouse was an old defensive tower with five pointed turrets. Each guild had its own entrance and its own assembly hall in this building, and the door of the Painters' Guild had St Luke above it, with an ox's head. Most of the Guild members were already seated on their benches. Robert had to sit right at the back. He understood very little of the solemn opening ceremony, and his master's turn to speak didn't come for another hour. But then he introduced Robert, and the apprentice's name was entered in the Guild book. In honour of the occasion David stood him a fish dinner, and even gave him two guilders and the rest of the day off.

It was weeks since Robert had been out of the house. Now at last he could stroll about for a few hours. He passed the fine palace of the Admiralty, and watched the coming and going at the arsenals where the war fleet was being equipped. Prostitutes waiting for customers accosted him in the alleys around the harbour. On the Rokin, the main street through the middle of the city, he slipped past the guard carrying a halberd and into the inner court of the Exchange where money dealers called out their rates. The huge building straddled a small river that disappeared under the paving stones and came into view again on the other side of the Exchange. Robert watched as a small barge laden with vegetables and flowers emerged from the dark vault, and called a greeting to the sailor. Then he crossed the Singel to the Herengracht, and spent some time watching the builders on their scaffolding, constructing magnificent dwelling houses for the officers of the East India Company, bankers and rich arms dealers.

All was very quiet in the courtyard of the Beguine lay sisterhood on the other side, where just a few old women sat in front of their tiny cottages, knitting. A street further on, in the Rasphuis, you could see through an open gateway into a prison yard. A prisoner was in the stocks there, and two guards were whipping him with birch twigs. Others were standing at workbenches, pushing heavy files over tree trunks, back and forth, back and forth. He asked one guard what they were doing, and the man told him they had to grind Brazilian wood to a red powder which made good material for the Dyers' Guild. Strange how the people of Amsterdam managed to reconcile luxury and strict morality, religion and loose living, indulgence and punishment, bringing them down to a single common denominator!

It had been a good day for Robert, a successful day, but all the same he felt discontented. His apprenticeship was hard work, there was no end to it in sight, and although David seemed pleased with him, Robert entertained no illusions. He would never be as good a painter as his master. He was too inconsistent, and probably not gifted enough. Those highlights on the fish, the glaze of the Chinese porcelain, the seductive gleam in the maidservant's eye – he didn't think he would ever be able to paint like that. He couldn't even have painted the creamy dots that were the florets of David's cauliflower. And anyway, what was he doing in the busy city of Amsterdam? He tossed and turned on his narrow bed that evening, and fell asleep with these unhappy thoughts in his head.

That very night Robert hit upon the answer to his problems. The idea came to him in his sleep; he would never have come up with it just by thinking. The dream began in a very ordinary way. He was standing at his classroom door; inside, the biology lesson had been going on for some time, and Robert was late again. 'Where on earth have you been? Where were you, Robert?' asked Dr Korn. She was holding a burning torch in one hand, and was about to throw it at him. Everyone in the class had turned to watch with malicious glee. But then his faithful friend Ratibor jumped up and snatched the torch from the teacher's hand.

Robert ran away as fast as he could go, stumbled on the stone stairs and fell down them. Then, all of a sudden, he was lying on a stretcher covered with a white sheet. Two paramedics were carrying him to an emergency ambulance waiting at the gate, blue lights flashing. They hastily shoved him inside. The interior of the ambulance was dazzling white, and he lost consciousness. When he came to his senses the space had shrunk, so that he was crouching between the white walls, curled up like an embryo. It was icy cold in that tiny cell, and he heard a soft humming. Then he realized he was in a fridge, because there were plastic compartments inside the door holding tubes of mustard, boxes of cheese and a few eggs. He opened the door, and stared in surprise: he was in his parents' kitchen at home! Everything looked just as usual: the bars of sunlight falling on the wall cupboards, the stove with the pans on it, the Venetian blind over the balcony window. Even the kitchen clock still said three minutes to nine. But the strangest thing of all was that he saw himself too, sitting on his stool at the counter, wearing his old blue linen jacket and watching television. Instead of a ham roll, however, this second Robert was holding a big brush with red paint dripping off it and falling to the floor. Was it really paint or was it blood, his own blood? Robert felt terrified. War or no war, he couldn't stand the sight of blood.

He woke, bathed in sweat. But no sooner had he realized where he was – in the painter's house in Amsterdam, in the summer of 1621 – than he also knew what he had to do. He must paint his own kitchen, paint it exactly as he knew it, with every plate, every kitchen drawer, the coffee machine, even the TV set with the flickering black and white picture of the Siberian street on screen. It would be difficult, horribly difficult, but it was his only chance.

Robert waited for weeks for a good opportunity. He was quivering with impatience inside, but he took good care not to let it show, and followed his master's instructions to the letter when he was allowed to copy a small picture for the first time. Robert had to keep painting over places where he went wrong, or retouching mistakes. But in his heart a subject very different from the cherries and glasses in the picture he was copying hovered before his mind's eye.

At last, at the beginning of September, his master went away. The King of Denmark's Amsterdam agent had invited him to Copenhagen, to visit the court where he hoped to get new commissions. At the same time his wife Agnieta was invited to a christening near Mecheln, where her family lived. Robert and the maidservant were left in charge of the house. They were told to be very frugal, to be careful with lighting fires, to keep the place clean, to do all their duties. But no sooner had the master put Agnieta on the travelling coach to Flanders and gone on board a schooner bound for Copenhagen than Robert took possession of the studio, found a panel of the best oak in the painter's stores, sat down at the easel and began to sketch his kitchen. The maid dared not ask what he was doing. She was glad that he left her alone and didn't mind where she spent the night.

His master should be pleased with him, thought Robert, for he was conscientiously following the principles David had taught him, grinding pigments, grounding the panel, designing the underdrawing in black chalk, and since his head held as precise a picture of the kitchen as if it were on a photograph in front of him, the design stage went well. But the painting itself, when he began it, turned out to be very arduous. Instead of applying layer after layer with confident brush-strokes, Robert had to keep wiping out what he had done, shaving it off and over-painting it – and still the curlicues cast by the sun on the lacquered surfaces of the wall cupboards didn't have the right gleam.

Robert spent days on end in the studio, often not even stopping to eat. However much trouble he took, his work seemed to him incompetent. But did he necessarily have to create a still life of the kitchen that would bear comparison with his master's painting? No. It just had to look accurate, absolutely accurate down to the smallest detail. He mustn't forget a single spoon, or the handle of the fridge where he had crouched in his dream a few weeks ago. The big hand on the clock must stand at exactly three minutes before the figure twelve.

What about Robert himself, though? The photographic memory he was so proud of let him down when it came to his own face. He simply couldn't picture it. Perhaps he ought to use a mirror to help him? Or would a back view do? That was how he had been sitting, after all, lounging casually on his stool, eyes on the TV screen, ham roll in his hand and a glass of iced tea on the counter in front of him, still half full. He mustn't get anything wrong.

With the utmost care, he painted the little bit of pink ham looking out between the two halves of the roll. A tiny yellow dot would do for the butter. The black TV set with its knobs and the small red glow of the light diode succeeded first go, but the picture on the screen presented problems. How did you show it flickering? He had to use the finest marten hair brush and a magnifying glass, and he spent hours painting in all the little grey strokes to suggest the picture of a snowy street in tiny graduated shades.

He went on painting eagerly even on Sunday, although the pious folk of Amsterdam forbade working on the Lord's day. In the evening he lit a couple of candles, which his master had strictly forbidden because of the danger of fire. But he had sense enough to clear his picture away every evening before he went to bed, and remove all signs of his secret activities.

Agnieta was the first to come home, laden with good things that her family had given her: a goose, a large cheese, and all kinds of delicacies from the south.

'I want to finish the copy the master told me to do before he comes back, to show him I haven't been idle while he was away.' This was Robert's excuse for spending all day in the workshop. Once Agnieta nearly caught him, but with the cunning he had now learnt he always had a half-finished copy within reach, and before she approached the easel he quickly substituted it for his own picture. The painter's wife was feeling a little lonely and would have liked some conversation, but after a few minutes, realizing that he was impatient and thinking only of his work, she left him alone.

The kitchen was almost finished now. He could see nothing missing from it. Admittedly the glasses could still have done with some reflected highlights, and the Venetian blind at the window had a very clumsy look. Nor was Robert happy with the effect of depth he had achieved. But time was running out; David could come back any time, the days were getting shorter, and now that Agnieta was home again he dared not put the finishing touches to his picture at night by candlelight. She would soon have discovered what he was up to. Now or never, Robert told himself.

He sat before the picture, plucked up all his courage, and began to rub his eyes. He didn't feel happy about what he was doing. He was glad that the other Robert, the Robert in the picture, had his back to him. How would he have looked at him – would his expression have been baffled, ironic, reproachful? He imagined Agnieta searching the whole house for him, calling him, only to realize at last that he had vanished without trace for ever. And what about David? He would come home, make haste to his studio, and what would he find there? A painting of subjects he would be entirely unable to understand: a coffee machine, an electric clock, a refrigerator, and his runaway apprentice Robert lounging on a stool, staring at a black box . . .

He dismissed these ideas, he tried to concentrate, he rubbed and rubbed at his eyes until tears came into them. Nothing happened. Robert stayed where he was. No leap back to his own time, his own home town, his own kitchen! Disappointment struck like a blow in the pit of his stomach. What had he done wrong? He didn't know. His weeks of work had all been for nothing.

And now, he thought, now I must spend the rest of my life as a painter in Holland – and only a run-of-the-mill painter at that, an artist who can't even paint the picture of a kitchen that functions the way a real kitchen ought to.

Close to tears, he hid his pathetic effort behind the other panels in the store-room and joined Agnieta, who was sitting in the kitchen, rather downcast herself and wondering whether some accident had happened to David on his travels, since he wasn't home yet and had sent no message.

That evening Robert fell to brooding once again, and once again, between waking and dreaming, inspiration came to him. It wasn't a breadknife or anything like that missing from his painting, it was himself. He had painted the wrong Robert, the Robert who spent the nights tossing on his bed here in Amsterdam. Two years had passed since he first set off on his involuntary travels. He had shot up in height; he looked much older now. That was the crucial mistake. He must paint himself younger, two years younger, if he was to get home again exactly as he had been when he disappeared.

David had once told him the word painters used when they corrected a mistake in the composition of a picture. They over-painted it, and called the concealed mistake a *pentimento*, an Italian word meaning 'repentance'. Robert certainly felt repentant now.

But before he could try again his master came back, cheerfully excited after his long and successful journey. His royal patron had proved himself to be a true art-lover, had assured the painter of his high regard; there would certainly be some good commissions from Denmark coming his way next year. Agnieta was glad to have her husband home. Only Robert was on tenterhooks. How was he to carry on with his picture now, under his master's watchful eye?

And David soon noticed a difference in Robert. 'What's the matter with you?' he asked. 'You look tired, and you haven't taken much trouble with that picture I told you to copy either. Do you know how you strike me? Absent-minded, as if you weren't with me at all. I ask myself what you've been doing all this time while I was out of the house.'

He was right. Robert was *not* with him; he was thinking of nothing but how to get home as fast as he could, and his teacher and master was simply in the way. David seemed to have some suspicion of Robert's secret thoughts and ulterior motives. One day he sent him off to the paint dealer to buy some chalk and linseed oil, and when Robert came back with his purchases he found David in the big living room, red in the face and ready to interrogate him. He held a piece of paper in front of his face. 'So what's this?' he asked, threateningly.

Robert saw at once that it was his crumpled old Polaroid photo of Ratibor. He had feared that his master had found his picture of the kitchen in the store-room, but no! He had simply been snooping around Robert's room to find out what his apprentice might have been up to while he was away, and in the process he had come upon the photograph. He now held it out to his apprentice as if Robert had committed some terrible crime.

'That's my friend Ratibor from Germany,' said Robert, but his master dismissed this information with a furious gesture.

'Who painted it, and how?' he cried. 'That pigment was never made in this world! And do you mean to tell me the diabolical monster in the picture is your friend?'

Robert had to admit that in his helmet, his shapeless gloves and his knee-guards Ratibor did look rather like some sci-fi character – but how could he explain to a man living in Amsterdam in the seventeenth century that his friend was wearing a perfectly ordinary sports outfit?

'And look at this!' bellowed the painter. 'I cut the picture to see what that black coating on the back might be. And see what came out of it! A disgusting, shimmering broth. This is no painting – it's the work of the devil, it's alchemy, you've been brewing poison! I want to know where you got that picture – tell me this minute!'

Stammering, Robert assured him that it was a present from a man he had met in Alsace; he himself didn't know how to make such pictures, and his friend's costume was probably some kind of armour to protect him from the blows and thrusts of the Croats who were ravaging the countryside.

His master didn't believe a word of it. He evidently regarded the photograph as an insult. 'It may look brilliant,' he muttered to himself, 'but it's shockingly badly painted – must be the work of some wretched dauber.'

'Then let's just throw it away,' suggested Robert, sorry as he would be to lose the photo. Secretly, however, he still hadn't given up hope of seeing his friend again soon, so he did not wince when David, with a nasty smile, threw the Polaroid into the fire on the hearth. 'Be careful, my young friend,' he said. 'For if you don't do well you can't stay here any longer.'

Robert felt as if time were really running out now. Instead of improving his own picture, he had to carry on copying under his master's stern gaze. But however much trouble he took with the glasses in the little still life, they looked dull and blurred, and even the skins of the peaches didn't have the same bloom as in the original. Because his mind wasn't on what he was doing he made mistake after mistake, until the picture was ruined, and David took it away from him, growling with annoyance.

'I was mistaken in you,' he said. 'I thought you might come to something, but you're too impatient, too absent-minded. You'll never make a painter.' He sounded more sad than angry, and Robert himself was sorry to have disappointed the old man's hopes. Even Agnieta, who had always protected him from his master's complaints, was more reserved now. She didn't like the way Robert just stared ahead of him in silence after the Bible reading at meals, instead of joining in the prayers. She was right. He wasn't good company.

And so it went on until the last few days of October. Dark was falling earlier every day; in the studio, David was already having to put his brushes away in the afternoon. He was surly, and gave Robert nothing demanding to do any more, but simply set him to grinding pigments, cleaning palettes and washing brushes. It was like the first days of Robert's apprenticeship.

Robert's own patience was coming to an end. One Sunday morning, when the whole house was still asleep, he stole into the studio, got his picture of the kitchen out of its hiding place and set to work. He knew he was risking everything on a single throw, and his heart thudded in his chest with fear and excitement.

He began by painting over the picture of himself. At first he couldn't get the outlines of his younger self right. The proportions were all wrong. How small he had been then! He had to apply the pigment for his shirt quite thickly so that the old outline wouldn't show through. A good thing it was only a back view; at least he didn't have to paint his past face, the face he couldn't remember. Finally, he retouched his shoes and tried to paint the pattern of his socks as well as he could.

The picture was almost finished. This time he wasn't leaving anything to chance, so he checked the places that still weren't clear enough, went over the strips of the Venetian blind, added a few golden-brown highlights to the glass of iced tea, completed the pattern of floor tiles, forgetting himself and entirely absorbed in his work. Suddenly it all came right. It was as if an invisible hand were guiding his brush. He stepped back and looked at his work. Yes, it would do. He had caught the moment of his disappearance, right down to the last curlicue cast by the sun on the toaster. But there was something missing from the counter in front of the TV set. Some small detail. He blinked, trying to remember. Something long and red that didn't really belong in the kitchen. The glove! The long, red silk glove his mother had forgotten when she left. That was it!

Made reckless by delight, he picked up his brush, dipped it in the pot of scarlet madder, and was about to apply the paint when disaster struck.

'What on earth are you doing?' It was his master's voice, trembling with rage and indignation. Robert turned, and there was David in his night-shirt, fists clenched, mouth open, his incredulous gaze on the easel. Robert was so alarmed that he couldn't move a finger. The brush in his raised hand, he stood there with a single thought in his head: *It's all over, it was all for nothing, I'll never get away from here, this is the end . . .*

Tears shot into his eyes. He couldn't see his master any more. Hardly knowing what he was doing, he turned back to the picture as if he could go on painting, as if he could add the missing glove to the gleaming, oily surface that blurred before his eyes, to the place where another, younger Robert was looking at the flickering TV screen. And then he saw and heard no more. He wasn't there any longer; he had disappeared.

EPILOGUE

That dizzy feeling, that brief whirlwind sensation in his brain, deep behind his eyes – he recognizes it. It's nothing new for a traveller like Robert!

Or no, it is, because this time everything is quite different. This time Robert knows where he is. Not in some desert, or the middle of a war, or a princess's bedroom, but at home. This time he could shout, yell and dance for joy and relief!

Because everything here is exactly as it used to be before his long wanderings, just as if he'd never fallen into the past. This is *his* stool that he's sitting on, it's *his* fridge humming away there. How warm and familiar the kitchen seems, how *real* it is! And the same old black and white picture is flickering on *his* TV screen ... but Robert doesn't look at that, he doesn't rub his eyes, he has no intention of doing any such thing! One visit to Siberia is enough to last him a lifetime. He turns the TV set off, and the snowy street is gone for ever. Then he looks at the clock. It still says three minutes to nine, exactly as it did two years ago. Only when Robert looks at the big hand does it jerk a small step forward.

You might think he'd merely dreamed it all, but Robert can only laugh at such a stupid idea. He knows better. He knows very well that a moment ago – well, about four hundred years ago – he was somewhere entirely different. For he is holding not a ham roll but a brush, and the stuff that looks like blood dripping on the kitchen floor is scarlet madder from a dish belonging to his master David, who has been dead for a very long time indeed by now.

What ought he to do? He must mop up the red stains at once. It wouldn't be a good idea for his mother to notice anything! If he isn't careful she'll start questioning him again. 'Where were you, Robert?' she'll ask. 'Where have you been?' And so on.

Then he'll be in a hole, because he can't answer those questions. She'd only shake her head and say he was crazy.

Robert knows how to deal with paint, however. He fetches turpentine from the broom cupboard and finds a rag. Soon the kitchen floor is as spotless and shining as if the cleaning lady had only just left. Now there's just the brush. Robert hesitates. Perhaps he ought to throw it in the bin? No, he can't bring himself to do that. He wants to hang on to the brush. He needs it, or some day he might find himself wondering whether he'd really and truly been in Amsterdam. He wraps it carefully in a piece of polythene and then runs upstairs to his room, where he hides his evidence in an old rucksack behind the suitcase on the top shelf of the cupboard, a place where no one will ever look.

Now he is back on his stool in the kitchen. He has to think what to do next. He's mopped up the red stains, but that was the easy part. The more he thinks, the more problems he sees ahead. At school, for instance. From now on Robert is going to be two years older than everyone else in the class. No one will notice, of course, because he painted himself two years younger. But if it ever comes out, then he really will be in dead trouble.

Also, he knows too much. When the history teacher starts going on about the Thirty Years' War Robert will have to be very careful not to burst out laughing, because of course he knows better than any teacher what it was like at the time. And in painting lessons he'll have to act stupid, or old Winziger, who is no fool, will see there's something wrong – he'll realize that Robert is suspiciously knowledgeable about pigments and can use a brush rather too well.

So he sits on his stool, thinking hard. It's no good. Robert knows what it's going to be like. In future he will be an outsider, an oddity, with some kind of mystery about him . . . In one way it will be quite fun to be cleverer than the others, but in another way, he doesn't feel comfortable about it. It's as if there were two Roberts, not just one. It's a weird idea to think of going about like your own double.

A sound startles him out of these complicated thoughts. Wasn't that the front door? He hears his mother call, out in the passage, 'Robert? Are you still up?'

Of course Robert is still up. His mother comes in, and – this is strange! – she kisses him with tears in her eyes, which isn't like her at all. 'Oh, I've had such a funny feeling the whole evening,' she says, hugging Robert hard as if it were several months since she last saw him. 'I don't know why, but I suddenly thought: "What's happening to Robert? Maybe he needs me!" Silly, really! Anyway, the reception was deadly dull, so I called a taxi and came home. What about you? What have you been doing? I hope you haven't been goggling at the box all evening. I don't want you ruining your eyes. Not that I want you to think I'm forbidding you to watch TV either. I expect you know best what you're doing – after all, you're not a child any more.'

No, indeed, thinks Robert. Poor Mother, she doesn't know how right she is! Then she exclaims, suddenly 'Oh, what on *earth* do you look like?' and pushes him away from her as if he had some horrible skin disease. 'You're covered in paint!'

Only now does Robert realize that he has forgotten something. His clothes! He looks down at himself. Sure enough, there he is in his shirt and stockings and his green Amsterdam apron, which has spots of paint all over it and looks as if some abstract artist had been working on it.

'Don't worry, Mother,' stammers Robert. 'The paint dried ages ago.'

'Are you sure?' asks his mother. How elegant she looks! No wonder she's anxious about her black moiré dress. As she runs a finger carefully over his apron to make sure none of the paint comes off, the only reasonable excuse occurs to him. 'I was wondering what it would be like to go to art college and learn to be a painter. So I put on the things I always wear in old Winziger's painting class.'

She dumps her handbag on the work surface, takes off her long red glove and notices something. 'Oh dear, I've lost the other one,' she cries. 'What a nuisance! Or did I leave it at home here? Have you seen my glove?'

'No,' says Robert. My second lie already, he thinks, and it won't be the last! But what else can he do? He knows very well that the red glove will never turn up again; the black hole in time has swallowed it and won't give it back.

Then Robert says goodnight to his mother and gives her a kiss. He's looking forward to a bath, he's looking forward to his bed, and he's looking forward to seeing Ratibor. He'll call his friend tomorrow morning. Robert certainly appreciates being back in a world where there are telephones.

Only – what can he tell Ratibor? Should he ask if he can remember the old days in Alsace, and the raid on the mill? 'Hey, what does it feel like, being beheaded?' No, impossible!

Robert's last thought before he falls asleep is that no one,

not his mother, not even Ratibor, must ever know anything
about his adventures:

about the laundry room in Siberia where he almost froze
to death,
or his first love, Caroline, and the wonderful opal,
or his tiny little grandmother,
or the dead schoolmaster with the silvery eyes,
or the Princess who let him down,
or his career as a highway robber,
or how he painted himself back into the kitchen.

No. Robert will keep the secret of where he has been to
himself.

Choosing a brilliant book
can be a tricky business...
but not any more

www.puffin.co.uk

The best selection of books at your fingertips

So get clicking!

Searching the site is easy – you'll find
what you're looking for at the click of a mouse,
from great authors to brilliant books and more!

Read more in Puffin

For complete information about books available from Puffin – and Penguin – and how to order them, contact us at the appropriate address below. Please note that for copyright reasons the selection of books varies from country to country.

www.puffin.co.uk

In the United Kingdom: Please write to Dept EP, Penguin Books Ltd, Bath Road, Harmondsworth, West Drayton, Middlesex UB7 ODA

In the United States: Please write to Penguin Putnam Inc., P.O. Box 12289, Dept B, Newark, New Jersey 07101–5289 or call 1–800–788–6262

In Canada: Please write to Penguin Books Canada Ltd, 10 Alcorn Avenue, Suite 300, Toronto, Ontario M4V 3B2

In Australia: Please write to Penguin Books Australia Ltd, P.O. Box 257, Ringwood, Victoria 3134

In New Zealand: Please write to Penguin Books (NZ) Ltd, Private Bag 102902, North Shore Mail Centre, Auckland 10

In India: Please write to Penguin Books India Pvt Ltd, 11 Panscheel Shopping Centre, Panscheel Park, New Delhi 110 017

In the Netherlands: Please write to Penguin Books Netherlands bv, Postbus 3507, NL–1001 AH Amsterdam

In Germany: Please write to Penguin Books Deutschland GmbH, Metzlerstrasse 26, 60594 Frankfurt am Main

In Spain: Please write to Penguin Books S. A., Bravo Murillo 19, 1° B, 28015 Madrid

In Italy: Please write to Penguin Italia s.r.l., Via Felice Casati 20, I–20124 Milano

In France: Please write to Penguin France S. A., 17 rue Lejeune, F–31000 Toulouse

In Japan: Please write to Penguin Books Japan, Ishikiribashi Building, 2–5–4, Suido, Bunkyo-ku, Tokyo 112

In South Africa: Please write to Longman Penguin Southern Africa (Pty) Ltd, Private Bag X08, Bertsham 2013